Duke of Knight

Gentlemen of Knights

Book One

Elizabeth Johns

DRAGONBLADE PUBLISHING, INC.

Text by Elizabeth Johns
Cover by Dar Albert

Dragonblade Publishing, Inc. is an imprint of Kathryn Le Veque Novels, Inc.
P.O. Box 7968
La Verne CA 91750
ceo@dragonbladepublishing.com

Produced in the United States of America

First Edition February 2020
Print Edition

Dearest Reader;

Thank you for your support of a small press. At Dragonblade Publishing, we strive to bring you the highest quality Historical Romance from the some of the best authors in the business. Without your support, there is no 'us', so we sincerely hope you adore these stories and find some new favorite authors along the way.

Happy Reading!

CEO, Dragonblade Publishing

Additional Dragonblade books by Author Elizabeth Johns

Gentlemen of Knights Series
Duke of Knight (Book 1)

***** Please visit Dragonblade's website for a full list of books and authors. Sign up for Dragonblade's blog for sneak peeks, interviews, and more: *****
www.dragonbladepublishing.com

Chapter One

Rowley Knight, Duke of Knighton, stood at the window of his study, hands clasped behind his back and stared out at the vast parkland which was largely concealed by the rain blowing sideways and striking the panes. He did not particularly notice the weather, for his mind was consumed with his responsibilities. It was a deuced nuisance, having four siblings, but he loved them in his own way—even if it was not a particularly affectionate one.

Lord Heath, the second eldest, was probably now stumbling in from his night's revelries in London. Rowley shook his head. Soon, he might have to intervene there, but he still had hopes that Heath would have sown his last wild oats—if he did not kill himself first.

Lord Edmund was the third sibling, and Rowley worried about him for other reasons. He was entirely too pious and tender-hearted for his own good. One day, Rowley hoped to lure him away from trying to save his parishioners in the London slums to a safer parish where he himself owned the living.

Then, there was Felix, who served on Wellington's staff, and even though Rowley worried about him, he knew Wellington kept an eye out for his welfare. If only Napoleon would cooperate.

His most pressing concern for the nonce, however, was his young sister, Eugenia. At sixteen years of age, she was turning into a young woman, and Rowley was at a loss as how to deal with her and the violent emotions that overtook her with no warning. After long deliberation, he had come to the decision to hire a companion-governess for her. Rowley did not want a new person, especially a woman, added to his household, but he could think of no other way—and he had tried.

If his calculations were correct, he had about half an hour left before the woman's arrival. Miss Lancaster had been thoroughly investigated and selected from several hundred women by Cummins, his man of business. None of those available from the various agencies had satisfied Cummins or Rowley, so he had found her upon the recommendation of his Aunt Violet, which was his only reservation. The girl was young and inexperienced; however, she was well educated and came from a good family which had fallen on hard times thanks to her father's gaming habits. While not opposed to charitable works, it was not his primary concern. Edmund fulfilled that role for the Knighton Duchy. Row's only care was the lady's suitability for Eugenia—and for staying out of his way.

The rain eased a little, and Rowley thought he detected the sounds of hooves on the gravel drive. He checked his pocket watch and noted with approval that at least the woman was timely. He could not abide tardiness.

Watching as the party alighted from the carriage, it was difficult to obtain a satisfactory glimpse as the footmen efficiently ushered everyone into the house under umbrellas. Reluctantly, Rowley tried to prepare himself for this necessary intrusion upon his sanctum. If all went well, Eugenia's entrée into womanhood would be guided by someone of the female sex and thus some measure of peace would return to his daily routine.

The expected knock on the door came shortly afterwards.

"Your guests have arrived, Your Grace."

Rowley nodded and followed his butler, Banks, down the hall to the drawing room.

"Your Grace, may I present Lady Hambridge, Lady Sybil Mattingly, and Miss Lancaster."

Rowley withheld his groan. His aunt could never resist the chance to matchmake. He made polite bows to the guests, and kissed his aunt on the cheek.

"I trust your journey was comfortable?" Rowley asked, as he discreetly tried to see the new member of the household, but her bonnet was so large he could scarce see her face or her coloring, save one militant spark from her eyes.

He knew Lady Sybil's family and had little interest in the young girl just out of the schoolroom, who had not yet outgrown her spots or her childhood roundness.

"As comfortable as a long carriage ride can be," his aunt said as she sat down and waved the other two ladies to do the same. "It would help if you lived closer than Devon, but I suppose that cannot be helped."

Rowley did not bother to remark on the fact that the duchy and its holdings had been settled several hundred years before.

"Would you care for some refreshments before you are shown to your rooms?"

"Tea would be just the thing, Knighton."

Rowley glanced at Banks, who gave a nod and left the room. Rowley knew he would also direct the maids to prepare a room for the unexpected Lady Sybil, though truly, he did not know why he was surprised. This was not the first time his aunt had brought single ladies unannounced, in hopes of catching his attention. He refused to attend most events of the Season, so she brought ladies to him. It would make the business of arranging the post for Miss Lancaster more awkward, but so be it.

"If you do not object, Your Grace, I think I should like to refresh myself, first," Miss Lancaster pronounced as she stood up.

Rowley and his aunt exchanged glances. "Of course," Rowley said, also rising, "I will have Mrs. Haynes show you to your room."

"I think I will join her," Lady Sybil said shyly.

When the ladies had gone, Rowley sat back down and leaned his head against the chair.

"We have only been here five minutes, Knighton. Are you already bored of us?"

He cast an elevated eyebrow at his aunt, and otherwise ignored the rhetorical question. "Does she know why she is here?"

"Unless she is a widgeon, she does. I told her Lady Eugenia was in need of female guidance."

Rowley scoffed. "And she is in need of funds and a home, but does she realize she will not be chaperoned and be required to earn her keep?"

"She will know soon enough, if she does not yet."

"And dare I ask why Lady Sybil is here?"

"Sybil is also my goddaughter and they are friends from school. I thought it would be pleasant for them to spend a few more days together."

"Very well. As long as you do not attempt any tricks with a mind to matrimony."

"Hush! The ladies will return at any moment," his aunt chastised.

"Then I will have Eugenia sent for. The sooner I can establish if they will make shift together, the sooner I can attempt to return to my duties."

"Duty, duty, duty!" She threw up her hands. "When will you stop concerning yourself with everyone else and look to your own future?"

"I have all the future I need," he snapped coldly. "I do not wish to repeat an argument you will not win, Aunt."

"Oh, very well." She tossed her hand, wafting a handkerchief in exasperation. "Do not say I did not try!" She looked heavenward, clearly affronted.

"No one can fault your efforts," he drawled, wishing this interview were at an end. He had no patience for feminine dramatics or wiles, and he sensed a guilt-ridden lecture was bound to follow. Banks entered with the tea tray and Rowley sent for Eugenia, anxious to avoid his aunt's tirade and to have all settled. He refused to listen to one more lecture on why he needed a wife. He did not have to.

"WHY, SYBIL, WHY him, of all people?" Emma asked as she frantically paced the room, tearing at the ribbons of her bonnet and tossing it on the bed.

"Did Lady Hambridge not tell you who you would be working for?" Lady Sybil asked with a wrinkled brow. She removed her own bonnet, then tidied her locks in front of the glass.

Emma shook her head. "I did not think to ask, either. How could I have been so stupid?"

"You were rather preoccupied," Lady Sybil suggested. "Maybe it will not be so bad. You will be spending most of your time with his sister, not him."

"Did you see the scowl on his face? And... and... how large he was?" she asked, her eyes wide with dismay.

"He is just reserved—and he is not so very big. You came to his shoulders." Lady Sybil pointed to her own shoulder to indicate, as if it was the same thing.

"No, I cannot do this. He frightens me. His eyes..."

"I think him rather handsome; and he is a duke, which makes up for a great deal."

"You may have him!" Emma retorted. "Wait—you stay here with me and woo the duke, and I may hide in the schoolroom with his sister."

"I would if I could, dearest Emma. I will be remaining a few days, at any rate, so you may form a better opinion whilst his aunt and I are here. Besides, they gave you a lovely room, which means they intend to treat you better than a servant."

Emma bit her lower lip as she looked around at the beautiful white and pale blue room, decorated more finely than hers had been before the money was all gone. "I suppose so."

"Take a deep breath and let us go back down for tea. Everything is better after tea."

Emma allowed herself to be ushered back down to the drawing room. She did not know how she was going to bear this. Her nature was neither meek nor subservient, and she had witnessed the duke's dictatorial, haughty manner before. Would he remember her? It was improbable, but her feelings toward him were tainted; equally, it was unlikely she would find another post as lucrative as this. Swallowing her pride, she held her head high as she entered the drawing room. She would have to force herself to bite her tongue and avoid the duke as much as possible.

"Oh, you have returned," Lady Hambridge said as the duke rose to his feet.

"I trust everything was satisfactory with your chamber?" he asked, clearly assessing her.

Please do not let him remember me. Please do not let him remember me.

"Yes, Your Grace." She remembered to curtsy just in time.

"Excellent. May I present to you my sister, Lady Eugenia?"

"I am pleased to make your acquaintance, my lady." She curtsied.

"Miss Lancaster will be your new companion and governess, Genie."

"Oh! How exciting! I have never had a female companion before, except for Nurse, and she does not count since she is more than twice my age. Did you know I have four brothers and not one sister?" she asked Emma.

"I did not. I was blessed with a sister. It will be a pleasure to be your companion."

"Thank you, Rowley! What a wonderful surprise, to be sure!" the girl exclaimed.

Everyone sat down, and Emma could feel the duke's eyes upon her. It was all she could do not to squirm under his scrutiny and glare back at him. Instead, she focused her gaze on her new charge. Lady Eugenia was a gangly youth, just coming into her womanhood, with bright blue eyes and silky black curls. She was lively, and full of questions for Lady Hambridge and Lady Sybil. Emma used the opportunity to study and observe, but so did the duke. He said little and stared, and she could not ignore him, although she tried. His presence filled the room like a thick smoke that permeated all of a person's senses—suffocating them. Could he not leave and let her become acquainted with Eugenia?

"Miss Lancaster, may I have a few moments of your time?"

Emma looked up in surprise.

"To discuss the particulars?" he prompted.

"Yes, of course." Emma's heart began to race as she followed him into a study. What was there to discuss? She knew she would be paid two hundred pounds per annum, plus a clothing allowance for attending *ton* events when chaperoning Lady Eugenia.

The room was smaller and she felt confined. His presence was stronger in here, if that were possible, and she longed to escape or thrust her head out of the window for some fresh air.

"Do you think you will be content here?" he asked, disturbing her thoughts. He had not said happy, but content, she noticed.

"I shall try, Your Grace," she replied, endeavoring to avoid making eye contact with him. He saw too much. "Your sister seems a very pleasant girl. I think we shall deal quite well together."

"I am glad to hear it. Nothing is more important to me than my family."

Emma could not resist meeting his eyes, then. She knew all about how he dealt with people who crossed him and his beloved family. She looked away before he saw the hatred in her eyes and dismissed her on the spot.

"Of course, Your Grace," she muttered in a forced voice. She would have to control her emotions better than this. If only she had known and could have prepared herself.

"And the pay is satisfactory?"

"It is very generous, Your Grace."

An awkward silence followed before he finally spoke again. "Miss Lancaster, I am a man of few words and prefer my own company for the most part. However, if you ever need anything, do not hesitate to ask."

"Thank you, Your Grace." Emma stood to leave, assuming this uncomfortable interview was at an end.

"There is one more thing. Do I know you from somewhere?"

The duke stood also, towering over her. His chest was broad, his legs long but powerful in his fitted breeches. He was wrapped in a deceptive package of exquisite tailoring, but she could sense the danger barely contained within.

Emma halted mid-step. "I cannot imagine where from, Your Grace. We neither move in the same circles," she said, trying to keep the bitterness out of her voice, "nor do you frequent Shropshire, do you?"

He stared at her coolly for a moment before answering, his eyes black as night and unreadable. His face was the very model of an aristocrat with an arrogant bearing, accentuated by a crease between his arched brows. He had a presence that was difficult to ignore. "No. I cannot say I have had the pleasure of visiting Shropshire. I had thought perhaps London."

She did not answer and tried not to flinch under the heavy scrutiny. She did not wish to blatantly lie, but neither would she admit anything willingly. She kept her eyes averted until he dismissed her with the wave of his hand. She expected nothing more of him. She bobbed a curtsy and left the room, breathing a sigh of relief for now, but not fooling herself that she would be able to maintain anonymity for long. She would have to look for another situation while trying to make this one last as long as possible. People did not pay their governesses two hundred pounds. However, it did not seem enough for having to live under the roof with that man, and she intended to avoid him at all costs.

Chapter Two

He knew her from somewhere, that was certain. Yet, it was obvious Miss Lancaster did not wish to be recognized. Was that merely from embarrassment of her family's situation, or was it something more sinister? It would vex him until he knew. Hopefully there was nothing that would cause harm to Eugenia, but he would have to keep a closer eye on Miss Lancaster than he had intended, devil take it. He wanted nothing to do with any of this, which is why he had hired her in the first place!

Was it too much to ask for a meek and subservient woman to guide his sister in proper decorum? The venom and insolence with which she had treated him indicated she was no milk and water miss. Now she was here, and with Lady Hambridge who would be insulted if he dismissed her out of hand. Why did he feel as if he had lost control over the situation? It had hardly begun, and the Duke of Knighton did not lose control.

He walked to the window and stood with his hands crossed behind his back. It was where he did his best thinking. His household knew that if anyone found him thus, they interrupted at their own peril.

What was it about her? And what had Cummins missed, and his aunt neglected to mention? He would question her more closely. He would not be made a fool of in his own household.

He walked to the door and opened it to find Banks on the other side awaiting his every need. "Ask Lady Hambridge to call on me at her earliest convenience."

It took his aunt half an hour to await his pleasure. He suspected she was resting from the journey and he had disturbed her, but this was no light matter to be ignored.

Her thin, now wrinkled face was creased with sleep, and Rowley felt a slight twinge of guilt, but she was here. "Aunt, thank you for joining me."

"I am happy to spend time with you, of course. Was something the matter?" She took a seat flanking the fireplace and he handed her a blanket to cover her legs. She had aged considerably since last he saw her. Her once golden hair was now all white.

"Shall I send for tea?" It had only been two hours since their last, but it was habitual. He nodded to Banks, who had anticipated the duke's wishes, and the butler left quietly closing the door behind him.

Rowley sat in the chair opposite his aunt, crossed one leg over the other and steepled his fingers before him, his elbows resting on the arms of the chair. He did not rush his question, but he did not beat around the bush. "Tell me more about Miss Lancaster."

"We have gone over this already, Knighton. You cannot mean to tell me you did not have her investigated. Neither will I flatter myself that you took my word for her good character."

"Cummins looked into her background. Perhaps I should question him further." Rowley frowned. His aunt was not usually evasive. "She seems familiar to me, yet I cannot place her."

"Thirty is a bit young to be forgetting things," she said with a twinkle in her eye. "It happens to me all of the time. I cannot remember why I went to the next room by the time I get there most days," she chuckled.

Rowley shook his head. "I do not forget things. I will remember. She is too familiar to be a coincidence."

Banks entered with the tea tray and served them both before retreating.

"I would not let it bother you. She is a kind, intelligent girl who should have been having her own Season instead of going to work."

"Tell me about her family," he persisted in a calm voice.

"Her mother and I were neighbors in our youth. Her father was Lord Perth. Matilda married respectably enough and bore four children, Emma being the youngest."

"The others are suitably situated?"

"Are you wondering why they did not take her in?" she asked.

"Partially." Cummins did not delve as deeply as he thought.

"The eldest brother, John, married an American girl and lives there in Boston. The second boy, Matthew, is serving in the army, and the oldest daughter married a man of the cloth somewhere in northern Scotland. I suppose she could have gone to live with Ruth, but from what I gather they are burdened enough with their six children and a small rectory."

"And the mother died two years ago if I recall correctly?"

"Indeed. It was the downfall of Lancaster. He began drinking and betting, and lost his mind after her death."

Rowley felt the stirrings of anger grow within him. He had little patience for men who could not control themselves. Grief could do strange, inexplicable things to people, of course, but Lancaster still had a responsibility to his daughter who was not yet married or provided for. "Did Miss Lancaster apply to you to help her find a position? Or did you see the inevitable and recommend her when I asked for your help with Eugenia?"

His aunt hesitated before answering. She looked away into the fire, instead of meeting his gaze directly, as was her custom.

"I saw Lancaster in town a few months ago. I did not recognize him, I confess. He called out to me by name, and I was startled. He looked worn and haggard, his clothes heavily mended. I immediately inquired after my goddaughter, and he begged me to look after her."

"Did he confess his transgressions?" Rowley asked feeling his brows rise.

"Of course not. I discovered the whole later. He appealed to me as her godmother to sponsor her since her poor mother was not here to do so." At least he had some thought of her.

His aunt's face became distant as though she were in another place entirely. "There was a time when Matilda could have looked as high as she wished... even your father... but she loved Lancaster and appeared to be happy and content. She would be appalled by how he left poor Emma."

She paused to lift the delicate porcelain cup emblazoned with the Knighton crest to take a sip of her tea then continued. "Naturally I agreed to take her on. Emma was always a good girl with a comely face and so I told him to send her to me."

"In London?" he asked, growing deeply suspicious.

"Of course. Where else? I have use of the townhouse for life. I only go to Cynder Downs for holidays."

"So she came to you. Did she have a disappointing Season?"

His aunt shook her head. "It never came to that. She refused to be presented or attend any *ton* events. Regardless of my offer to stand the ready, she did not wish to be indebted to me."

"Even as your companion?"

"If another situation could not be found, of course I would have kept her with me. However I could not bear to see her wasted on the likes of me. At least with Eugenia, she will have the companionship of someone near to her own age and be able to attend some events. Perhaps she will catch some gentleman's eye. A country squire or someone who will not mind her... circumstances."

Rowley wondered to himself if Miss Lancaster had some other reason for refusing, but kept the thoughts to himself. "What of Mr. Lancaster?"

"He was found dead not two weeks after Emma came to me, God

rest his soul."

That explained the drab grey of her clothing, though it was a common enough costume for a governess or companion. "By his own hand?" Rowley asked, even though it was indiscreet to do so.

"If you consider drinking oneself to death by your own hand, then yes."

"And not a penny was left for Miss Lancaster," he stated.

"She has a very small competence from her mother, but her dowry was gone long ago. She insists on supporting herself, and I insisted she allow me to put her somewhere safe and respectable."

"And you can assure me there are no hidden scandals to taint my household?"

She looked offended as he had suspected would be the case. "Rowley Knight, how could you ask such a thing?"

"Forgive me, Aunt, but I must be certain. You are wont to forgive easily and help everyone. Perhaps you thought she could avoid recognition here in the country."

She blushed and Rowley knew he had made a hit.

"There was one situation with the eldest boy, John. But it was years ago and he left for America immediately. Emma is without hint of tarnish, Your Grace."

Rowley sighed. It was all he would get for now. Cummins had missed the detail of the other brother, but it must have been well covered up or it would have been discovered. It was unlikely to affect Eugenia now.

Rowley sat pondering his best course of action. The brother's incident would have to be looked into.

"What are you considering? Please do not tell me you mean to send her away!"

He eyed her sideways. "How long until you must leave?"

"Three days. Although if you take to Lady Sybil…"

He narrowed his gaze at her, not bothering to comment. "I intend to come to my own conclusion about Miss Lancaster before you depart."

"How can you determine so soon?"

"Unfortunately by involving myself." He could hear the resignation in his voice.

"Now, Knighton, give the girls a chance to become acquainted without interfering. Your hovering would be enough to make a lion turn and run with his tail between his legs."

"Have you ever seen me hover?" he asked with a quelling look which would have frozen the hottest flame.

"Don't you poker up on me. You know what I mean."

"Do I?"

"You are not exactly what one would call warm and inviting," she retorted.

"Since I am likely to scare the girl, as you so succinctly phrased it, please be so good as to inform Miss Lancaster that she will dine with us at eight." Giving up his solitude was no light matter, but it appeared to be necessary for a time.

"It would be my pleasure. I am happy to see her treated more as a companion than a servant, and I can keep my eye on you as well." She leaned forward in preparation to stand and he rose and helped her to her feet. She bussed him affectionately on the cheek and took his arm.

Rowley did not think Miss Lancaster was afraid of him at all. She was hiding something.

EMMA PARTED WITH Lady Sybil in the hall and went to her rooms. She took off her horrid bonnet that hid her hair and most of her face and sank into the cushioned window seat. Looking around at the luxurious room papered in a soft yellow with tiny pink roses, a coverlet to match and a thick carpet on the floor, she realized she had taken for granted such extravagance only a few years ago. It was ironic that the cause of her family's downfall was now the source of her luxury.

How had he recognized her? Certainly the name Lancaster was common enough, but was a family's destruction so commonplace to him that he did not remember? Clearly it was. As a companion, she should be grateful for everything she had. Looking out of the window at the view, over a vast wooded park and lake, she reflected that such a vista should not be afforded to someone in her current station, yet here she was. The options open to her now were few, and one she had tried had put her virtue in jeopardy.

In a rare moment of sobriety, when her father realized where the extra income was from, he had applied to Lady Hambridge to take Emma in. Despite her disguise, she feared being recognized in London. It was ridiculous, but here was the one person who could complete her ruin.

There was a knock on the door and Emma scrambled for her cap. Not that His Grace would lower himself to knock on her door.

"Enter," she said once she had the horrid head covering back in place.

It was Lady Hambridge. "There you are, dear," she said. "His Grace wanted to make sure you knew you were to dine with us."

Emma's heart sank to her toes. "I do not think it would be wise."

Lady Hambridge stepped inside the room and closed the door. "Now Emma," she began, "he specifically asked for you to be there. You cannot refuse. Besides, you are a lady and if you behave as such you will be treated as such. You will be expected to chaperone Lady Eugenia when she comes of age when necessary."

Emma had thought she had plenty of time to find excuses before that occurred. What could she do now?

"I can see your mind is working on an excuse. It will not do."

"I wish everyone would accept that I am now part of the working class."

"You still have a chance to make a match if you will make the most of the situation," she scolded. "Think of your dear mother."

Emma could not bear to. The thought was physically painful like a vice squeezing her chest.

"I will not force you into this position if you are not willing, but I gave Knighton my word. He knows your father lost his fortune through gaming; he need not know any more."

"I will try not to disappoint you, godmother."

"That's my girl." She smiled warmly at Emma, and Emma forced a smile back, feeling like the lowest scum of the earth. She could not disappoint her godmother, yet what would the duke do when he discovered where he knew her from?

Emma allowed herself to think back on those times after her mother's death, and what had led her to do what she did. Father had lost everything and she had received a note saying she had to leave school. He could no longer pay.

She arrived in London only to discover they were reduced to living in hired rooms in a less than respectable part of town near Covent Garden. There was no money for servants or food. Father rarely came home, but when he did, the smell of blue ruin was so strong she had to cover her nose, and he would lose consciousness for days. He was but a shell of the man he had been whilst she was growing up—while her mother had been alive. Emma mourned her, too, but was she, his daughter, not enough for him to want to live for?

Life as she knew it was over then. There was no chance for her to make any respectable match. What else could she do except find work? When the theatre manager had offered her a veritable fortune to take a part in one of his plays, she was hungry enough to agree—as long as her face was suitably disguised. However, it was not the stage from where the duke recognized her. That had come after.

Lady Sybil was the only one who knew of her disgrace, though Lady Hambridge knew enough. Her father had begged her godmother to take her in, or who knew where Emma would be now. At least he had thought of Emma in his final stupor.

John, Ruth and Matthew did not know the depths to which their father had sunk, or they would doubtless have tried to help, but it was too late when Emma realized Father would not get better.

Really, Emma had no choice. She would deal with the consequences when they came. She settled herself before the looking-glass and did her best to make herself unobtrusive. She pulled out her most covering cap and tucked every stray tendril under it. Not that she had remarkable color to her hair, it was a dark chocolate shade, but she did have a riot of curls that sometimes made her more noticeable, her mother had always said. Her gowns were old and had all been dyed for mourning for her mother; then there had been no money to buy new ones. She only owned one gown suitable for dinner, and it was a dull, black affair. Dull was precisely what she needed to be, which was a good thing since there was nothing else.

She stood ready to face Knighton. There was only one thing she could do—make herself indispensable to Lady Eugenia.

CHAPTER THREE

ROWLEY JUST REFRAINED from registering a mixture of shock and being appalled at Miss Lancaster's hideous appearance. He hated to see young women wearing caps, and he suspected it was another attempt to disguise herself. Her black, high-waisted gown was more fitted than the grey sack she had worn earlier, and with reluctance he noted her shapely figure, which had not been apparent before. Not that the gown was immodest, she was covered from neck to ankle, but it did not hide her womanly curves. Black was not a flattering color on her, he noted. It was obvious he would need to send for a modiste to attend to her wardrobe. Rowley could not abide even his servants to appear dowdy.

When the butler informed them dinner was ready, he greeted the ladies politely, and escorted his aunt into the dining room.

"Where is grandmother?" Eugenia asked.

"Her maid sent up a note that she would dine at home tonight. I will visit her first thing in the morning," Rowley assured her.

"Has the dowager been ill? I had planned on seeing her this evening, but I will also attend her in the morning," Lady Hambridge said with a frown.

"She has been in a decline for some time. The doctor says there is little to be done. I daresay you will be alarmed at her appearance since you see her less often."

"She is still a delight and as keen as ever," Eugenia added.

It did not escape his notice that Miss Lancaster was avoiding eye contact with him. Very well, he would observe her for now, but she would be unable to avoid him forever. It was the wrong move on her part, he now had to rise to the challenge of drawing her out.

After the footman had served the first course, Rowley selected a leg of lamb with broccoli and sweetmeats. He resigned himself to make polite conversation. "What would you ladies like to do during your visit?"

He directed the conversation to everyone since there were only the four of them.

"Perhaps we could ride and go into the village to do some shopping," Eugenia suggested.

"I love to shop," Lady Sybil said, and then her cheeks flushed as though she should not have said such a thing. Rowley did not know if someone had told her to act in a more mature manner in his presence or if she was simply very shy. Being in the company of youth was fatiguing. Miss Lancaster had said nothing thus far. He suspected she was holding her tongue, which normally he would have been grateful for.

"One afternoon, we could have a picnic on the coast if the weather is fine. There really is nothing like the cliffs and the view of the channels from here," Lady Hambridge suggested.

"Almost worth the trip to Devon," he murmured dryly, but Miss Lancaster heard him and cast what he would wager was an amused glance at him. He hoped he was mistaken; she was best left viewed as a mere servant, but Rowley felt the uncharacteristic urge to speak with the lady and draw her out.

"Do you ride, Miss Lancaster?"

Her head jerked up from the attention it was giving to her plate of cod, and then she immediately looked back down. For some reason he wanted those green eyes to focus on him and meet his gaze.

"I did ride, Your Grace, but I am afraid it has been some time."

"Eugenia is an avid rider and will need you to attend her on occasion."

"I do not have a habit."

"That will need to be rectified." He could hear the haughtiness in his own voice and almost winced.

"Yes, Your Grace," she said meekly.

What had changed since their meeting earlier? He had half-expected a defiant retort, though he could not say why.

"I am certain we may find something here that will do in the meantime. Mrs. Haynes can take your measurements."

"And Lady Sybil?" Rowley realized he should have posed the question to her first, but she visibly shrank when he looked at her and so he hoped in this setting he might be forgiven.

"I, I am afraid not, Your Grace. My mother is deathly afraid of horses and we could never ride in her presence."

"You need not do anything you are not comfortable with, my lady," he replied.

He cast a glance at his aunt, wondering what she could have been thinking to bring such a chit to his home, and she visibly sighed. At least there should be no more pressure from that corner. Eugenia and Miss Lancaster should be dining in the schoolroom without him. They would be more comfortable as well, he was certain.

"Is Devon very different from Shropshire, Miss Lancaster?" he asked.

"Quite," she replied and for a moment he thought she would not elaborate. "The climate is quite different and we have neither your rugged coast nor moors, but we share your beautiful hills and valleys. Alas, I have not been there since before my mother died. I was in school at the time and my father never returned."

Rowley felt irritation that somehow she was making him feel guilty for only trying to protect his sister. He would not apologize, but he did not prod further.

"Which school did you attend?" Eugenia asked. "I begged Rowley to send me to one but he would not hear of it."

He did not bother to comment.

"Miss Bell's school in Bath, it is where Lady Sybil and I met and discovered we shared a godmother." Miss Lancaster smiled at that lady.

Banks entered and whispered in his ear. "Lord Edmund has arrived, Your Grace, and awaits you in your study. He did not wish to interrupt dinner, since you have guests."

"We were just finishing. Please tell him I will join him directly." Edmund was here? And without warning? There must be something amiss.

The ladies finished their pudding and Lady Hambridge stood to direct them out.

"Please do not wait for tea. I have unexpected business to attend to." He could not imagine why his brother had not simply joined them in the dining room, so he did not feel it wise to share who the business was with. He would leave that up to Edmund to share if he so desired.

He watched as the ladies left the room, Miss Lancaster last. She kept her eyes averted and bobbed a curtsy, appearing to hurry after the other ladies as though he were some sort of threat to her. He shook his head and joined his brother in the study with relief.

"Rowley!" Edmund said as he stopped mid pacing.

"Edmund, to what do I owe the pleasure? Something tells me it is not a brotherly visit?"

"I need your help."

Of course he did. Rarely did Edmund leave his parish unless it was to assist one of his doves, as he called them.

"What, or should I say who, is it this time?" Edmund had a habit of stealing prostitutes away from their pimps and abbesses and hiding them out in the country. It was a thankless task, but occasionally he met with success.

"You know I will help as best I can, but you are likely to find more success appealing to Cummins for practical purposes."

"Normally, yes." Edmund had the grace to look sheepish.

Rowley leaned back against his desk and crossed his arms and one leg over the other simultaneously. He did not bother to speak.

"This particular person might be looked for. I was hoping there might be a place for her here at the Grange." His brother resembled him the most, but his temperament was more amiable and he smiled often. Rowley sometimes envied him his good nature.

"Doing what, precisely?" Rowley hated being the duke with his siblings, but when it came to charitable works, they were never-ending. Unfortunately, Edmund could not separate himself from these works and duties. They were one and the same to him. He was eminently suited to being a man of God.

"She is not afraid to work, Row, but she is deathly afraid of being found. I would not feel comfortable leaving her elsewhere, but I cannot keep her in London."

"Who, pray tell, is she running from? And will I be expected to provide a nursery in the next few months?" Rowley asked practically.

"Unless she has greatly deceived me, I believe I saved her before she was compromised."

"Good Lord, Edmund! You speak as though she is a lady."

"If I had it my way, all females would be treated as such. Simply look to how God protected Rahab in the book of Joshua, for example."

"Yes, yes." Rowley held up his hands. "I am certain there is somewhere we can hide your latest dove." *Soiled dove,* he thought to himself.

"Thank you, Row," Edmund said, and embraced him heartily.

"Where is the girl?"

"I left her in the kitchen with Cook. She was too afraid to go elsewhere."

"Will you stay awhile?"

"I think I will stay a few days to make certain Miss Thatcher is situated in her new position."

"Aunt Hambridge is here with the new companion I have engaged for Eugenia."

"Did you now? I still think she would have been better served to go to school."

"No." For all Rowley did not understand how females worked, he was not ready to part with his sister. She was still much too young to be completely thrown into the hands of some schoolmistress where he had little control.

"Find Mrs. Haynes and tell her to find a room for your girl. Once she has had some time to recover from her fright we can discuss what to do with her."

"You are the best of brothers, Row. I knew you would help." Edmund cast him a winning smile and left the study. Rowley eased down into one of the chairs and only wished he was half the man his brother thought him.

EMMA HAD NOT missed the look of disdain the duke had cast at her when she entered the drawing room before dinner last night. Nor had she missed his efforts to question her. Why could he not leave her to do her duties?

She dressed for the day and determined to do what she had been hired to do and serve Lady Eugenia. Putting on a dark gray carriage dress in lieu of a riding habit and another hideous bonnet with a wide brim, she decided it would have to do. Emma had been raised in the saddle, but she would not mention it since it would only bring more attention to how far she had fallen.

Lady Sybil had declined to ride with them this morning. She had instead chosen to stay with Lady Hambridge and visit the dowager. Emma could not say that she was surprised. Sybil had always been very afraid of horses at school.

Emma had wondered over and over how she had come to this point and why her father could not have waited to fall apart until she was satisfactorily settled. It was useless to dwell on such things, and while she had ever been pragmatic, she had been joyful until all of that had been stripped from her.

Lady Eugenia had gone ahead to the stables while Emma saw Sybil with her godmother. Emma felt a wave of nostalgia as she approached the red brick building that was separated from the main house by a series of arches covered in ivy. Horses had been her father's passion until they became his ruin. She had been brought up around riding and breeding; the smell of hay, horses and all that went with it was comforting to her.

Emma spied a gentleman she did not recognize, but he bore the same features as the duke and Lady Eugenia. Was he some cousin or relative? As she approached, the duke and Lady Eugenia joined the gentleman. Emma hesitated, wishing she could turn back. She had no desire to spend time with His Grace. However, he was dressed for riding and she very much doubted she would be given a reprieve.

Lady Eugenia saw her first and raised a hand in greeting. "Miss Lancaster, there you are. May I present my middle brother, Lord Edmund? He has joined us for a few days' visit."

Emma curtsied. Lord Edmund had a ready smile with laugh lines etched at the corners of his eyes. He seemed quite the opposite of the duke. She liked him instantly.

"Edmund, this is Miss Lancaster, my new companion and Aunt Hambridge's goddaughter."

"I am pleased to make your acquaintance, Miss Lancaster." He put his heels together and made her a bow.

The duke turned to greet her with a civil nod. The grooms were bringing out mounts for everyone, she noticed.

"What type of mount do you prefer, Miss Lancaster? We have a horse to suit every riding ability."

Emma bit her tongue to keep from retorting she could handle anything he dared to give her, but she did not quite quell a rejoinder. "I am comfortable in the saddle, Your Grace. Something that will keep up with your own mounts would be desirable."

He gave her the look which she was coming to associate with him. His face was etched into a perpetual scowl, with a deep line between his brows.

Knighton spoke to the groom, and soon a beautiful dappled grey mare was brought out for her. She was beautiful and lively, and was literally champing at the bit. Emma stepped forward to greet her ride and instantly fell in love.

"This is Helen, the twin of Cassandra, whom Eugenia will ride today."

"Shall we be on our way?" the duke asked.

Emma began to lead the horse, looking for the mounting block, but Lord Edmund was assisting Eugenia and His Grace came over to assist her into the saddle. She tried not to bristle at his touch when he placed a hand on her shoulder before interlacing his fingers to boost her up.

She studied him while he was mounting his own horse, a dark brown hunter who looked ready to lead a charge across a battlefield, not to go for a morning ride in the country. His Grace was lithe, his muscular thighs encased in tan riding breeches, tall brown top-boots on his feet, and a dark blue coat well fitted, and not masking his well-formed, athletic build. Clearly, he was no stranger to the saddle. He moved as one with his horse as they rode across a field. All three of them rode naturally, she noticed before quickly forgetting about her companions in the enjoyment of the feel of horseflesh's magnificence underneath her. She would be too sore to walk on the morrow, but for now she did not care. It was an unlooked-for pleasure to ride again—something she feared was lost to her forever.

They gave the horses their heads as they galloped across a large meadow, until they came to a hedge. She saw the duke glance at her for a second but she was already soaring over it without hesitation—or before thinking better of it. Riding neck-or-nothing hardly promoted the docile image she was trying to adopt.

They rounded the headland and immediately the coast was before them. Towering cliffs dropped suddenly into the wide expanse of the sea. Emma would have liked to have stopped to admire the view and inhale deeply of the wet, salty air—it was her first time to witness such a thing of beauty—but her companions only slowed the horses to a canter as they skirted the cliffs. *Such a vision must be commonplace to those who see it often,* she mused. The two brothers rode side by side, conversing, and Emma and Lady Eugenia pulled next to each other.

"You ride quite well, Miss Lancaster. I am relieved to know it for this is one of my favorite pastimes. Being raised with four brothers, it was the only way for me to keep up with them." She laughed.

"I had two brothers and one sister, so I did occasionally have someone with whom to play with dolls, though I prefer riding, myself."

"Rowley is forever scolding that I need to pursue more ladylike activities, but I see no harm in riding."

"Are there any things which you wish to accomplish?" Emma asked, thinking to make herself useful.

"I speak three languages, I am proficient in the pianoforte, I can paint, and have read every book in Rowley's library."

"Have you any areas at all in which to improve?" she teased.

"I cannot sew, but do not wish to." She laughed. Emma had learned by necessity more than any other reason. It was unlikely Lady Eugenia would suffer the same fate.

"Rowley has promised to engage a dancing instructor for me, but he taught me most of the dances himself."

That was surprising indeed, though dancing instructors were hardly commonplace in Devon.

"Have you attended any assemblies here?"

"Not yet," the girl said with obvious disappointment. "I am hoping now that you are here, I will be permitted more grown up activities."

Lady Eugenia was on her way to being a beauty, but had not quite grown into her height and was mostly arms and legs. She talked without thinking about the consequences of what she said, and her demeanor did not portray the bored ennui of the *ton*. Her bright blue eyes sparkled with expectations of happiness. Emma hoped Lady Eugenia maintained the joy and innocence as she matured as opposed to the cold hauteur of the duke.

Chapter Four

Rowley was more perplexed about Miss Lancaster than before, which only firmed his resolve to learn more.

"I know that look," Edmund said as they followed the ladies back to the house from the stables.

Rowley looked sideways at his brother but refrained from comment. So rarely did he see Edmund these days that he was determined not to be anything but pleasant with him, but he felt one of his sermons coming on.

"And what look is that?" he drawled.

"Something is on your mind and you will not rest until it is resolved. Do you care to talk about it?"

"In my study." They walked in silence the remainder of the way to the house, and Eugenia and Miss Lancaster excused themselves to go upstairs. Once he and Edmund were inside his study, he poured them both a drink and they sat before the fire.

"Your new governess is a bruising rider," Edmund observed. "She did not hesitate at any of the hedges or fences."

"No indeed. She looks born to the saddle."

"That is a wonderful thing for Genie. Although by the look on your face, you do not appear to be convinced."

"I do not know. She seems familiar to me, but Aunt assures me she comes from a respectable family in Shropshire. I gather her father gambled away their fortune and drank himself to death after her mother passed away from a broken heart."

"A sad tale."

"She could easily be one of your projects," Rowley mused.

"Yes. Now she is yours," Edmund said, a smile lurking in his eyes. "You did say she hailed from Shropshire? She would not, per chance, be the sister of John Lancaster, would she?"

John Lancaster. Rowley groaned. Of course! He had missed that connection yesterday, even though his aunt had said as much.

"I can see that she is, but she would not have been involved in the matter. Aunt must have not known or she would not have brought her here."

Rowley tried to think back to that fateful day, about two years ago, when Heath, his heir, had challenged Lancaster to a duel over some actress. Rowley had intervened just in time, and he had heard nothing more about it.

"Aunt said the eldest brother was in America." Rowley spoke in a soft voice.

"If I remember correctly, they had an excellent breeding stables but the father began making outlandish bets and lost the whole. The elder son had been the heart and soul of the enterprise, but there was nothing left for him to administer."

This explained much. It was also around the time of the mother's death, if he recalled correctly. Had the entire family lost their heads over the death of the mother?

Heath was forever getting into scrapes that he needed rescuing from. It had become a number amongst many, unfortunately. However, Rowley did not remember the girl. Did she know of the incident and somehow hold a grudge against their name?

"Perhaps I should speak to Miss Lancaster about it."

"She seemed to get on well with Eugenia. I would hold my tongue for now and address it if it becomes necessary," Edmund advised.

"Unfortunately, it will mean keeping a closer watch than I had intended." He had not planned to go riding with the group this morning, but Edmund's arrival had provided the perfect reason for him to do so. He had been intrigued by Miss Lancaster's riding ability, but if she hailed from the family of the famous Ellerton stables, he could see why. "I need to discover what else happened then."

"I do not recall, other than there was a big to-do at the theatre and Heath was left with a face so swollen he had to stay out of polite company for some time," Edmund recalled with exasperation.

"But the duel never happened. I need to speak with Cummins. Something does not make sense to me."

"Very likely, it is an unfortunate coincidence," Edmund predicted.

Rowley sent for Cummins, his secretary, a small, bookish man in his thirties, who hurried in with paper and pen to await the duke's commands.

"Sit down, please, Cummins. I only wish to ask some questions. There is a certain incident of which I need my memory refreshed."

"Yes, Your Grace."

"About two years ago Lord Heath got into a rather nasty brawl at the theatre over an actress and was challenged to a duel."

Rowley could see from the look on the secretary's face that he was trying to recall precisely which scrape he was referring to.

"I believe the man's name was John Lancaster," Rowley prompted.

Cummins appeared to be mentally reviewing the information and his eyes grew wide with recognition when it dawned on him the association he had missed.

"Quite. It is Miss Lancaster's older brother, we believe. I suppose this did not come up in your investigations?"

"No, Your Grace." The man looked like a chastised puppy.

"I would like you to see what information you can gather about that incident and the subsequent effect on the Lancaster family. I would also know precisely when Miss Lancaster left her school in Bath and where she went after that. She admitted she had not been back to Shropshire since school. I need to know precisely where she has been and what she has been doing."

"Yes, Your Grace. Forgive me for missing such an important detail."

Rowley waved his hand slightly. "Lancaster is a common enough name and my aunt recommended her. We were perhaps not as diligent because of this, but now I have need to know."

"The brother is in America, if I recall?"

"That is correct, and there may be nothing more to it, but I have a nagging feeling there is something we are missing."

The secretary was dismissed, and the brothers sat staring into the fire for a few moments.

"Do you think all of this is necessary? Eugenia likes her and she needs the position. I cannot imagine finding her another companion who will ride well enough to match our sister's ability."

"Perhaps not, but there is something she is hiding, I would wager an estate on it."

"Or you could forget about it and give me the estate," Edmund teased.

"Unfair, Edmund. You know I have offered you a living here with me, and all that goes with it. Besides, you would only turn it into a home for your doves."

Edmund laughed. "Speaking of which, I should see how Miss Thatcher is getting on."

Once alone, Rowley sat staring into the flames through his steepled fingers for some time. He did not have a good feeling about things turning out well. If he had been involved and the family had fallen apart afterwards, there could be some animosity and scandal ahead. It would be best to send Miss Lancaster on her way now. But Edmund was correct, it would be difficult to find someone who met his sister's horse-mad personality better. After all, he had tried already.

First, however, he needed to know what had really happened two years ago and if that was all Miss Lancaster was hiding.

EMMA WAS DELIGHTED when the ladies spent the afternoon alone without the scrutiny of the duke. First, she had been called to Lady Hambridge's sitting room in order to be measured for new clothing, despite her objections. Mrs. Crow, the housekeeper, had explained that all new members of the household were given new clothing. Emma had visions of a stiff, black uniform with a crisp, white apron, which she supposed would be no worse than what she already had. She submitted, though not happily.

"What do you do all day, out here in the country?" Lady Sybil asked Eugenia as they took their tea together and she selected a cake from the tray.

"I ride with Rowley in the mornings, then I practice the pianoforte and then I read or paint."

"Do you get lonely?"

She shrugged. "There are not many other people my age in the neighborhood."

"You have not had a governess before?"

"No, only a nurse. Rowley has hired a few tutors for lessons, but he has mostly taught me himself. He cannot abide most females."

"Extraordinary!" Lady Hambridge exclaimed. "I wonder what made him hire one now?"

"Oh, that is because he does not want to deal with my moods. I am constantly vexing him these days and I do not know why."

Emma chuckled. "Did these moods begin when your courses did?"

Lady Eugenia flushed. "I suppose they did."

"They are perfectly natural. I think your brother recognized you needed a female to discuss these matters with."

"I never told him when my courses started. My maid was the one who explained what it was to me. I thought I was dying!"

"Poor dear," Lady Hambridge said. "I should have realized you were of age and done better by you. Now you have Emma to help you, thank goodness. It will be good for both of you."

"I hope Rowley will let me attend the assemblies in the village now. I cannot wait to have a London Season," she said with a dreamy look in her eye. "Did you enjoy your Season, Lady Sybil?"

"I suppose so," she answered cautiously. "I confess I did not take very well."

"Did no one ask you to dance?" Eugenia asked in horror.

"It was not so bad as that," Lady Sybil answered, "but I do not enjoy dancing and talking to strangers."

"It will be better next year," Lady Hambridge assured her, patting Lady Sybil's hands. "You know some people now."

Lady Sybil did not look convinced. "I wish Emma would have come with us."

"You know I could not," Emma answered.

"I still have hopes of you finding a match, even if you are in the wilds of Devon," Lady Hambridge said.

"Rowley promised to take me to London when I can learn to control my moods," Eugenia beamed. "I know Miss Lancaster will teach me how to go on."

Emma tried not to show the horror on her face. She hoped never to see London again.

"Please tell me what I must do. I simply must go to London soon," Eugenia pleaded to Emma.

"You are still too young, my pet," Lady Hambridge answered. "Though Knighton might be persuaded to take you for a visit. This Season you would do well to be introduced to local society and prove to him how pretty your manners are."

Eugenia pouted, looking much like the sixteen-year-old she was,

Emma thought.

"There is no one here my age besides the Squire's son and he is oily and piggy and ogles me to make my stomach turn. Besides, he cannot sit a horse properly." She shuddered dramatically.

Lady Hambridge chuckled. "You are far too young to be thinking of a match and Rowley would never countenance a squire's son for you, never fear."

Emma's father had been the local squire before his downfall. It only confirmed how far beneath him the duke must think her. He had certainly not given a second thought to ruining her brother when he had a run-in with one of the Knight brothers. She prayed that brother never visited here. How was she to avoid him if he did?

"May we go shopping in the village now?" Eugenia was asking her aunt. "We may pick out new fabrics for Miss Lancaster's clothes and I can find something for my first assembly," she beamed.

"I think you should consult Knighton about that, first."

"Oh, pooh," she said. "He cares nothing about ladies' frippery. He will not even notice."

Lady Hambridge had little backbone, Emma knew. She had not been able to withstand Emma's objections to being presented to Society, and she was no more match for Lady Eugenia.

"Nevertheless, you will ask him. It demonstrates your maturity," Emma instructed.

Permission obtained, the carriage was called and the four ladies were on their way into the small village of Clovelly. Emma was less nervous than she had been before arriving and was able to look about her at the beautiful scenery.

They drove for half an hour through Knighton land before they even gained the main road into the village. Beyond the woodland, there were hills dotted with sheep grazing aimlessly and Emma envied them their lot in life. All her ambition now was to blend into the scenery and have a warm place to sleep and enough food to eat.

She was safe for now, but not many months ago, those basic necessities had been questionable.

"Look at the sea!" Lady Sybil exclaimed as they rode along the coast. It was a glorious view of a quaint village set into the steep cliffside. The houses and shops appeared stacked atop one another as though they would fall straight into the sea. The roads were too steep for the carriage, which slowed as they entered the village and stopped near an inn at the top for passers through. One's options were to ride on donkey or go on foot. People all stopped to watch the luxurious carriage and stared with open wonder at its occupants. They were probably used to the duke's family, but there were new people inside and that was always a novelty. Emma remembered when nobility had come to see Father's horses and she had never failed to be fascinated.

They walked to a shop on the high street, and the door to the linen draper's shop was immediately opened and the proprietor presented himself at their service. Apparently, he knew who buttered his bread and recognized valuable customers immediately.

"Lady Eugenia." The shopkeeper bowed low enough for royalty. "How may we be of service?"

"Good day, Mr. Hooper," the girl greeted genially. "We would like to look at your fabrics and fripperies," she answered, as though she had never before had such a treat.

Emma would need to speak with her about decorum, she supposed. There was no aristocratic hauteur about the girl whatsoever and Emma spitefully wondered how she had been raised to be so pleasant with only the duke for her companion.

Mr. Hooper was parading his finest silks before the ladies and Emma watched on, remembering when she had been full of hope and longing for her own London Season.

She did not feel envious, thankfully; she only felt sorrow for what was lost. Her dreams of a family and motherhood had changed to simply survival. Emma sorted through the small selection of fabrics, though there were more than she would have expected for such a small village. She picked a sturdy blue wool and a pale green cotton for her new dresses, trying to be practical.

"Miss Lancaster! This color would be divine on you, do you not agree, Lady Sybil?"

Lady Eugenia hurried toward Emma holding a bolt of green silk up to her face.

"Oh, I say! Your eyes look like emeralds."

"Her eyes are quite beautiful, as is her hair. She was the envy of every girl at school," Sybil remarked.

Emma wanted to shake Sybil.

"Why do you cover your hair? You are not an old matron or spinster," Eugenia asked with a gleam in her eyes that made Emma nervous.

"I would prefer not to draw attention to myself, my lady."

Lady Eugenia frowned. "I think the caps draw the wrong kind of attention, if you will pardon my saying so."

"It is Emma's choice, my dear. Now, which fabric would you want for your first ballgown? It does not hurt anything to look," Lady Hambridge said with a look at Emma as she drew the girl away. They had, with much roundaboutation, gone on and on about Emma wearing a cap before.

The bell on the door jingled, and an army officer entered the establishment.

A lieutenant, looking dashing in his bright red regimentals, removed his black tricorn hat, revealing thick, wavy brown locks. He was strikingly handsome, though young, and had a roguish smile that undoubtedly reduced many a young miss to sighs and swoons.

Emma could see that Lady Eugenia had already taken notice as well. In fact, she was openly staring. Emma had much work to do to shape her charge.

"Fresh from the boat, are you, Tom?"

"We docked in Plymouth yesterday. I am on my way to the house now. I would like to buy some ribbon for my sisters. I hear there is an assembly on Saturday next and I would like to take something to surprise them."

"A good brother, you are. The Misses Becker have grown so you will hardly recognize them!" Mr. Hooper said congenially as he cut two lengths of ribbon and wrapped them in paper.

"I have not a doubt of it." He turned and his eyes spied Lady Eugenia, who was still watching the officer, eyes wide with interest. Emma was too far away and would only make a scene if she said something. The Lieutenant inclined his head toward Eugenia, who smiled coyly back at him.

"How long are you home for, Tom?"

"Only two weeks. We came for supplies and must return to Spain."

"I hope that Bonaparte monster is routed soon. We need our men back home." Lady Hambridge had noticed the visitor and joined in the conversation.

Lieutenant Becker inclined his head and made her a bow. "I could not agree more, my lady."

"My nephew and Miss Lancaster's brother are both serving in the army."

The Lieutenant bowed to Emma, but had eyes only for Eugenia, who had made her way to the counter next to Lady Hambridge. Sybil was probably hiding behind a bolt of fabric. She was ever so shy around handsome gentlemen.

"I do hope I will see you at the assembly. I look forward to dancing with so many lovely ladies."

He bowed and left with one last look at Eugenia. To her credit, she waited until they were in the carriage before begging and pleading her aunt to speak to the duke on her behalf.

"I positively must dance with that Lieutenant! Was he not the most dashing fellow you have ever seen?" She looked dreamily out of the window, clearly to see if she could catch a glimpse of him.

"That would not be the way to convince the duke of your readiness for a come-out, I assure you," Emma warned.

"He thinks to keep me locked away in that house forever. It is not fair! What harm can come at our small assembly? Please, Aunt, speak to Rowley."

"I suppose he might be more inclined to allow it if I stay."

"Oh, would you please?" she asked hopefully, her eyes sparkling. "And you, too, Miss Lancaster? He cannot say no if both of you are for the scheme."

"I see no harm in trying," Emma conceded.

Lady Eugenia clapped her hands giddily, showing all of her youthful exuberance. Emma felt a veritable aged matron next to her charge.

Chapter Five

Rowley was sitting through his weekly at-home, the time when tenants and others could bring their problems and grievances to him. Unfortunately, he was having a hard time keeping his attention from wandering and found his secretary was answering more queries than he. His mind could not stop thinking about Miss Lancaster. The evening before, they had all gone into the drawing room together after dinner, and a spirited game of charades had begun. Miss Lancaster had not been able to hide her lively nature or, indeed, a certain talent for play-acting, although she seemed to try to stop herself when she caught him staring.

They had been on opposite teams, and the devilish twinkle in her eye added to the clever wit she displayed quite made him forget there were any other people in the room in that very moment. It was almost as if she lost herself in the game or act she was portraying. Next to such a timid one as Lady Sybil, she was a veritable Sarah Siddons.

How he had wanted to pull off that dreadful cap she wore! Her face and complexion were handsome, and with pretty hair and clothing, he dared say she might be stunning. Mrs. Haynes had taken her measurements and Lady Hambridge had seen to it that some fabrics were purchased yesterday without Miss Lancaster's knowledge. She had been very belligerent about his insisting on a new wardrobe, but he did not want to look at the drab sacks she considered gowns any longer.

"That is the last of them, Your Grace."

Rowley looked up, surprised, at his secretary.

"Is something amiss, Your Grace?"

"No, no. I have my mind on something else. Thank you for attending to the tenants."

"Is there anything else I can do for you?"

"That will be all for now, unless you have more information on the Lancaster situation."

"I sent off an enquiry but have not received an answer yet."

"Of course not, it is much too soon. Thank you, Cummins."

He must let this go. The dreaded woman was supposed to make his life less complicated, not more. Whatever had happened was over and done with, and she seemed to get on splendidly with his sister. Unless something damning came to light from London, he would ignore his suspicions and go back to his business.

There was a slight knock on the door.

"Enter," he called without looking up. He needed to go through the correspondence Cummins had deemed necessary for his eyes.

He sensed a person enter the room, but no one spoke as Banks or Cummins would have done. He looked up and was quite surprised to see Miss Lancaster there. He stood. "How may I help you, Miss Lancaster?"

"I would speak to you about your sister."

"So soon?" he questioned and indicated with a hand for her to sit in one of the seats in front of his desk. She sat down and resuming his own seat, he waited for her to speak.

"Your sister would like to attend the village assembly on Saturday evening."

"No. Will that be all?"

"That is it. It is not open for discussion?" Her green eyes flashed angrily at him and he bristled. No one ever questioned him.

She took his silence as license to plead her case. "She is only a year from being of an age to be presented. A few local assemblies will allow her to try her hand and become more confident."

"Miss Lancaster, since you have just arrived, I will overlook your impertinence, but I will make those decisions about my sister. She is not yet ready to be presented in any society, including one so small as ours. When my sister has learned proper behavior and a sense of her consequence, then I will consider allowing her out. It is to be hoped that she will learn to display more ladylike qualities after some lessons from her female companion. Do I make myself clear?"

"Perfectly, Your Grace," she said through a false smile. Rowley almost smiled at her brazenness, it was so fierce.

"You are a beast, Rowley!" Eugenia cried as she burst into the room.

Miss Lancaster stood up and reprimanded his sister before he had the chance.

"Lady Eugenia, this is not the way to convince your brother of your maturity. We discussed allowing me to approach him first. Now, kindly return to your lessons and I will attend you when my discussion with His Grace is finished." Her voice was calm but laced with steel. She was young to exhibit such mettle, he thought. How could that be?

Eugenia looked suitably chastised and hung her head. "I beg your pardon, Miss Lancaster... Rowley." She bobbed a curtsy and turned and left the room. Miss Lancaster watched her go, but did not turn back to him.

He clapped slowly three times and she spun about.

"There is no need to mock me, sir."

"There was no mocking intended. Had you not reprimanded her, she would be beating her fists on my chest. I can only hope she will continue to listen to you thus."

She inclined her head, accepting his compliment gracefully, but she did not resume her seat.

"Perhaps, Your Grace, we may consider a reward system for your sister? If she feels you are being tyrannical, her behavior toward you is unlikely to improve."

"Tyrannical?" he asked, feeling himself in the unusual situation of being scolded.

"I lived for several years amongst females, at school, and being one myself, I have undergone the change myself. Ladies have little control over their situations, Your Grace, and it is obvious to me she wants to please you, but having been isolated here with little society or female companionship, she feels you do not understand her situation."

"I live here myself."

"With all of the freedoms of a gentleman," she retorted.

He stared at her coldly. "Indeed. What would you have me do, Miss Lancaster? Allow her to attend the assemblies and witness an outburst such as the one she just displayed in front of the county?"

"I think that she knows her proper place in front of others. She feels safe with you and therefore able to express her frustration."

"Please inform my sister that there will be no assemblies local or otherwise until she can learn to behave with proper decorum around everyone, myself included. Is that understood?"

She stared at him. Apparently, when she was angry she forgot to be demure.

"Quite." She clicked her heels together and left the room with her chin held high—as proud as a duchess, he noted. He had not even dismissed her. He sagged back into his chair, feeling as though he now had two females against him.

He stared at the door after her. Was he a tyrant? No one else would have dared to suggest such a thing, so why would a governess? He frowned. Not since he was sixteen had he questioned himself, and he quickly decided her opinion was unworthy of further thought.

EMMA LEFT THE duke's study and hurried straight for her room. What had she done? He would surely dismiss her now without a reference. She must learn to curb her tongue! It had always been so when she perceived an injustice, and Eugenia had begged and pleaded at the unfairness of keeping her a prisoner in her own home. It was an exaggeration, of course, but Emma could see no harm in the local village assembly, having attended them in her own village by the age of fifteen.

She should have let Lady Hambridge argue for her niece, but Lady Eugenia had appealed to Emma, evidently knowing as well as she that Lady Hambridge would not make a good case.

Emma fretted and paced and worried herself to the point of a megrim. Therefore it was no falsehood when she sent word that she would not be dining with the family.

After dinner, there was a knock on her door that she barely heard through the fitful sleep with which she was trying to ward off the pain in her head.

"Miss Lancaster? Emma?"

It was Lady Sybil and Lady Eugenia.

"I think she is asleep," Sybil whispered. "We should let her rest."

"I need to make certain she is quite well. What if she needs the doctor?"

Emma propped herself up on her elbows and squinted at the faint light provided by the tapers the ladies were holding.

"It is only the headache," Emma assured them.

Lady Eugenia rushed toward her. "Oh, thank goodness! You must forgive me. I know this is my fault," she said repentantly.

"There is nothing to forgive, Lady Eugenia. I did speak out of turn with your brother and fretted myself into the headache. It is not your fault. Was he very angry?"

"He hardly said a word at dinner. It was most disconcerting! If Lady Sybil and Lady Hambridge were not here, I am certain he would not have spoken at all."

"Lord Edmund and Lady Hambridge did all of the talking," Sybil remarked.

"Would you like some tea? You missed dinner completely, did you not?" Lady Eugenia offered, surprising Emma by her kindness.

Emma thought a moment. Her head was feeling better and she was a little hungry. "Perhaps something small would be welcome," she admitted.

Lady Eugenia pulled the bell-pull and requested tea when the maid entered.

Emma sat up in the bed and patted either side of her. The two younger girls eagerly joined her on the bed.

"Emma was the one at school everyone would go to for comfort," Sybil said, arranging her skirts beneath her. "I was horribly depressed when she left."

Emma patted Sybil's hand. "I did not leave you because I wanted to."

"I know. I made do."

Lady Eugenia smiled as she settled at the end of the bed facing them. "I have always wanted to have a sister with whom to share moments like this."

"You could well have four, one day," Emma replied.

"I wish that would be the case, but Rowley says he will not marry. Heath is always in trouble and will never settle down. Edmund is too caught up in his works and Felix is in the army. I think you will be as near as I will get."

The poor girl was starved for a female friend. How lonely she must be.

"What would you like to do with a sister?" Emma asked.

"I would be content for now with an assembly. However, I cannot wait to see a play on the London stage."

Emma froze and cast a nervous glance at Sybil, who had a worried look on her face.

"Which play in particular would you like to see?"

"My favorite is *A Midsummer Night's Dream*, though I do think I would be pleased with any of them. Rowley allowed me to observe one the guests put on last year when we had a large house party here. There was a lady he was considering courting. She was mean and I am glad he did not marry her. I think that was when he renounced thoughts of marriage."

Emma could not imagine the cold, haughty duke doing anything so beneath him. There was no female on earth good enough for him, she was sure.

"Tell me what the Season is like," Eugenia begged. "Is it really routs and balls and garden parties and the theatre and rides in the park all day long?" she asked without taking a breath.

"It is. It is so very exhausting," Lady Sybil said, unable to mask her dislike of it.

"Were there no handsome gentleman or nice ladies?" Eugenia asked, looking disappointed.

"There were so very many," Sybil replied.

"Your father is an earl. I cannot imagine you not taking," Eugenia said, naively.

"There were some interested gentlemen." Emma intervened on Sybil's behalf. She gave her a knowing look.

"Not one who my father would deem suitable."

Eugenia rubbed her hands together with excitement. "Do you have a clandestine attachment?"

"I fear, my dear, that you have read too many novels," Emma chided without heat.

"No doubt," she agreed. "What else am I to do? The lending library is one place I am permitted without censorship from Rowley."

Emma laughed. "I enjoy novels myself, but you must be able to discern reality as well."

"I do not know why when I will never be permitted to do anything that is fun. I will be a thirty-year-old spinster before Rowley will let me go to an assembly."

"Do not give up hope. We will work on how I think he expects you to behave. You must trust me though and not be hurt if I correct you."

"I will not, I promise! Why did you not attend the Season, Miss Lancaster? Aunt told Rowley she tried to sponsor you, but you refused."

Why had she told him such a thing?

"Lady Hambridge is an optimist with a tender heart. It would only waste her money and time, for who wants a female with no connections or fortune to recommend her?"

"I do not think that would be the case, Emma. Before you donned your caps you were the envy of every girl at school, and gentlemen were always trying to gain an introduction when we walked about in Bath."

"Even if that were true, that was then and this is now."

"Did you ever have a suitor?"

Emma tried not to blush. What would Lady Eugenia say if she knew her brother, Lord Heath, had tried to court her to be his mistress? And that her brother John had almost dueled with him over it? At first, she had been flattered by his attentions and even thought perhaps they were of an honorable nature. How naïve she had been! Quickly, her illusions had been shattered and reality had come crashing down around her. Actresses did not receive honorable offers, and proper ladies did not work. John made it clear that their name was ruined, as were their stables, which were already failing after their father's risky bets had put them in heavy debt. One did not cross the Knight family and live to tell about it. He had left shortly afterwards to make his way in America. She had only had one letter from him since.

How she had hated the duke and his brother!

Her pride still chafed that it was him from whom she must now get her daily bread. Yet she liked Lady Eugenia a great deal. None of this was her fault, but Emma must start searching for another position soon.

"No, I have never had a proper suitor."

Eugenia looked at her with pity and a hint of mischief.

Thankfully, the maid entered with the tea tray, before the girl could think of something silly.

Emma helped herself to some sandwiches while the other two helped themselves to chocolate and biscuits. She was enjoying herself, she noted. It was similar to being back at school, with the camaraderie and understanding that only other ladies could have. She was optimistic for her charge. Lady Eugenia was perhaps a little spoiled, that was all.

"Lady Eugenia…"

"Please call me Eugenia. It seems silly to be formal when we will be spending so much time together."

"And you may call me Emma when we are alone. I do not think your brother would consider it suitable to use Christian names in public."

"Rowley is not always so stuffy," she remarked. Then she laughed. "Well, mostly he is, but sometimes he smiles."

"Let us make that our ambition, then. I will believe it when I see it."

"To make Rowley smile? Famous!" she said and went into a fit of the giggles.

It was impossible not to feel joy around the girl. Emma was already growing attached to her, and only hoped she would be gone before Eugenia found out what she really was.

Chapter Six

ROWLEY WAS EXHAUSTED and a long, hard ride was just what he needed to clear his head. He now had two troublesome females to contend with instead of one.

"There you are, Knighton. I have been wanting to have a word with you privately."

Make that three.

"How can I help you, Aunt?"

Aunt Hambridge came in and sat before the fire. He rose from behind his desk and stoked the fire before joining her in the chair opposite.

She frowned, then sighed. "I think perhaps I should extend my visit."

Rowley did not interrupt.

"I agree with Miss Lancaster that it is time to start allowing Eugenia out before she is thrown to the wolves in London, and I suspect that if I stay to chaperone her, you will be more agreeable to it."

"You think so?" he drawled.

"I do. Besides, the dowager is in decline and I should spend more time with her."

"By all means, you may stay as long as you wish, but do not be under any misconception that I will change my mind about the assembly this week. It is too soon."

"What are you afraid of? That she might talk too much? That she might dance with a groom or someone unsuitable?"

"Yes." *Amongst a long list of other things,* he thought dourly.

"Then allow me, as her chaperone, to guide her in making good choices. She is eager to please and perhaps a little boisterous, but she will soon learn how to go on. Eugenia is becoming a young lady, whether it fits your plans or not. I should have come sooner, but I did not realize I was needed."

"The fault is not yours, Aunt. If only you had seen Eugenia in one of her fits, you would not be so harsh toward me."

She placed a hand on her bosom. "I am not being harsh. I am only trying to alleviate some of the guilt you seem to feel. She will never be perfect, Knighton. You will have to allow her to make mistakes."

Rowley could not believe what he was hearing. Is this what she thought of him? He did not reply and she must have taken it for acquiescence. She began to rise, looking satisfied.

"I will consider what you have said," he proffered as he helped her to her feet.

For a moment, he thought she would argue more, but she smiled and nodded her head before leaving.

Rowley immediately strode toward the stables, not stopping to speak to anyone. When his anger was uncontrolled he found it best to be alone and find an appropriate outlet for his inner beast. The groom saw him coming and hurried off at a run to ready his hunter, Oscar. Rowley had been told he looked like Satan himself when he was incensed and he felt like raging at something. Soon, he was atop his horse, who seemed to sense his master needed to ride hard. The hunter never seemed to tire, and when Rowley finally pulled him back to a trot, the horse would have kept going. He looked around, having reached his favorite spot miles from the house. He was still frustrated with the women in his life conspiring against him, but at least he had vented much of his fury.

Gazing at the wide expanse of his estate, with the sharp cliffs and ocean to the south; hills, valleys and a river to the east, and the steep fishermen's village on the west, he remembered why all of it mattered.

He had a great responsibility to the people and the land. His father had brought him to this very place when he was a boy, to instill a sense of pride and responsibility in him. He had never forgotten. And when days like this intruded upon his ordered way of life, he always returned here as a reminder of why it mattered.

He stood there, atop Oscar, for some time, the horse gladly grazing away at the grass and clover. When he felt he had regained his composure, he directed his horse toward a stream and began to try to find a solution. After Miss Lancaster had dressed him down, he needed to step back and evaluate his sister's situation from an unbiased point of view. He had always prided himself on being fair, and perhaps he was trying too hard to shield Eugenia. Perhaps the locals were fond enough of her to forgive any childish lapses in decorum. She was becoming a young lady, much though he wished to deny it. It would also be an opportunity to observe Miss Lancaster's suitability as a companion. There had been no girls nearby for Eugenia to befriend. Rowley had been permitted to play with some of the local boys when he was younger, but it did not mean they were suited to overseeing his lessons in deportment and proper behavior amongst the *ton*.

Was he being overprotective of Eugenia? As the daughter and sister of a duke, she would not be held to the same standards as other ladies. While it was true much would be forgiven youthful innocence, a bad reputation once earned was nigh impossible to overcome.

"What would you advise a friend to do?" he asked out loud. Oscar was too engrossed in his snack to answer.

"Allow the girl a chance," Rowley conceded. He cursed to himself. He could not protect her forever and Aunt Hambridge had agreed to stay and help chaperone.

Rowley hated being in the wrong; it was not a sensation he had felt many times in the past. He hoped he was the one mistaken and that his sister succeeded. It would be nice to have all of his brothers here to aid in this monumental task, but Heath could not be relied upon, Felix was likely fighting for his life against the French at that very moment, and Edmund would help when he could.

He had exhausted himself to the point where he could laugh about the scolding he had received from the governess. *'If she feels you are being tyrannical…'* what courage and what stupidity all at the same time! He patted his horse's neck and spoke to him as though he were his closest confidant. "I think I will see exactly what she is made of, Oscar." The horse snorted in response.

"I am sure it is a bad idea. You can say 'I told you so' later."

Rowley had an idea and was doubtless playing with fire, but he would make a bargain with the governess. Feeling very pleased with himself, he let Oscar have his head again, galloping like the wind until they came upon the village.

He stopped at the posting inn at the top of the village and one of the grooms ran out to take Oscar, who deserved a rub down and a drink. He walked on down the steep slope to the linen draper's. Mr. Hooper was not expecting him, and was disconcerted when he realized it was the duke, not his secretary, who stood before him.

"Your Grace!" The man bowed deeply and Rowley resigned himself to being toadied to. "What brings you to my humble establishment?"

"I believe my aunt and sister were here recently?"

THE NEXT MORNING, Emma was excused from riding. Lord Edmund was to ride with Lady Eugenia, and Emma was to have a fitting for her new wardrobe. Lady Hambridge and Lady Sybil had gone to visit the dowager.

Emma did not look forward to wearing what the duke deemed appropriate for her. She had selected three modest patterns, but did not know if His Grace had approved them. Entering the sitting room she shared with Lady Eugenia, she halted when she saw the array of dresses laid out before her.

"Good morning," she said warily. "I trust some of these are for Lady Eugenia?"

Mrs. Haynes answered. "No, miss. These are for you."

Emma was furious… and speechless. "I, I…"

Mrs. Haynes mistook her fury for pleased astonishment.

"Now, miss, don't you be embarrassed. His Grace is very generous and wants you to look your best when you are with Lady Eugenia."

His Grace knew very well that a gentleman didn't dress a lady like this—unless she was his wife or his mistress. The gowns were fashionable enough for London drawing rooms.

Mrs. Haynes held out her hand, indicating a small woman standing to the side. "This is Mrs. Sharpe. She has made your gowns and will oversee your fitting. Then you may go and show His Grace your appreciation."

A poor turn of phrase, Emma thought, her hands shaking with anger. But it was not these ladies' fault that His Grace was a tyrant and liked to have his way. There were a dozen gowns that she tried on and became more livid with each one—none of them of the fabric she had selected, save the blue wool riding habit. She was not a débutante to be paraded before the *ton*!

The final gown was the green silk Lady Eugenia had held up to her at the shop the other day. Had Emma been the only one not to realize what was happening? The gown was trimmed with embroidery and sprinkled with spangles, and must cost more than her wages for a year!

Mrs. Haynes slipped the gown over Emma's head, knocking her cap askew and allowing her curls to escape their captivity. Both Mrs. Haynes and Mrs. Sharpe let out a gasp of shock. Emma tried to catch it, but it was too late.

"Oh, miss!" the seamstress exclaimed. "Why do you hide that beautiful hair? You look fit to be a princess in that gown." Emma turned to look at herself in the mirror and wanted to cry. Never before had she owned a gown so fine; it had been before her come out when they had still had money. She had dreamed of something like this, of course, and why now, of all times, did the duke insist on her having such finery? It made no sense when she was a hired companion. Perhaps this was a mistake.

She should return to London or see if Miss Bell would take her on at the school in Bath. No, she would never be demure enough to be a schoolmistress—she was eminently more suited to the stage—but she had no one to protect her now that John was gone to America. She refused to be anyone's mistress. Having spent a small amount of time amongst actresses, that was not a part of their profession she could join in willingly. Being a kept woman was not something she could bring herself to do. She was not yet that desperate.

Is that what the duke was expecting by dressing her like this? It must be, the blackguard! *Yet would he allow you to be near his sister if that was his intention*? A little voice nagged inside her head. And he had not shown any signs of attraction to her, had he? It was all so vexing. She wanted to march back to his office and give him a piece of her mind, but she had already risked too much when she had given her opinion about the assembly. Until she had another position, she would have to swallow her bile.

"What is the matter, miss? Do you not like the gown?"

"The gown is lovely," she reassured the seamstress. "I just do not think I will be needing any such finery now that I am a governess."

"Your godmother insisted. It was she who purchased the green silk for you," Mrs. Haynes confided.

Her godmother, bless her soul, truly did not understand the depths to which Emma had fallen. She shook her head.

"Miss Lancaster… oh." Lady Eugenia entered the room and halted, looking fresh and rosy from a ride, her eyes wide. "You are beautiful!" she exclaimed. Emma scrambled for her cap and pulled it back down over her head, stuffing her curls inside.

"Why must you wear those dreadful caps?" Lady Eugenia asked candidly.

"My lady," Mrs. Haynes scolded with the leniency of an old retainer. "I am sure it is none of our business if she chooses to hide her beauty. I am sure she has her reasons."

Emma looked at her gratefully.

"Oh, I see," Lady Eugenia said, as though she suddenly understood. "You do not wish to draw attention to yourself. You need not fear my brother, Miss Lancaster. I have never known him to look at any female with disrespect or philander with the servants."

"My lady!" Mrs. Haynes looked appalled.

"Why not speak the truth? I know of such things."

No, Emma doubted the duke would consider anyone worthy of his attentions. Besides, it was not this brother she was worried about.

"I am quite sure it is not proper to be speaking of such things," Emma gently reprimanded her charge.

"Why would you try to make yourself look ugly on purpose? As Aunt Hambridge said, you still have the chance to make a match. You will go to London with us and be in company with any number of eligible men."

"I know you mean well, Lady Eugenia, but you do not understand my situation. I am no longer eligible. Perhaps a country gentleman, but that is neither here nor there. Our job is to have you ready for your come out, not me." She turned and looked at the gowns that were here for her.

"Oh, my lady," Mrs. Haynes said. "You need to have your own gown fitted."

"My gown?" Lady Eugenia asked.

"His Grace ordered a gown made for you as well. Your aunt picked out an ivory silk for you. I hope you are pleased with it."

Eugenia's face lit up with excitement. She was growing into a great beauty, and Emma knew his Grace would have his hands full when she was presented to society at large.

Mrs. Haynes quickly divested Lady Eugenia of her riding habit and Mrs. Sharpe placed the silk gown over her head. The girl twirled about as though she was Cinderella receiving a most precious gift from a fairy.

"You look as pretty as a portrait!" Mrs. Haynes said fondly.

"Does this mean Rowley will allow me to attend an assembly?" she asked Emma.

"I have no notion." Emma was wondering the same thing. Had His Grace bent his iron will?

Lady Eugenia threw her arms around Emma. "You are the best of companions! I am so lucky Aunt Hambridge brought you to me. You are the best thing to ever happen to me!"

"I think it is premature to assume this is acquiescence on His Grace's part. Perhaps he only means to tempt you into proper behavior."

"That would be too cruel!" Lady Eugenia pouted.

"But we will soon discover what he means by it. Keep your chin up and do not let your emotions show. You must learn to mask your feelings in front of others."

"I know you are correct, Emma. I still think you are one of the best things to happen to me, however."

Emma was having a hard time practicing her own words, for she felt as though she would burst into tears at any moment. She gave Lady Eugenia a heartfelt smile and a kiss on the cheek before finding her way back to her own chamber to weep.

Chapter Seven

THE NEXT MORNING, Rowley called Miss Lancaster into his study as she and Eugenia returned from their morning ride.

She was looking invigorated, with her cheeks pink and a few stray tendrils of her hair escaping her bonnet. He felt as though he had been privy to a deep, dark secret—her hair was a dark chocolate color. He was even more convinced that his bargain with her would be a good idea. He was positively itching to stand up and tug her bonnet from her head.

"Yes, Your Grace?" Miss Lancaster asked as she came all the way into the room and Banks shut the door behind her. She raised an eyebrow—at the impropriety, he assumed—and then she seemed to remember she was demure. He almost smiled at her struggle to portray meek behavior.

"Please take a seat." He indicated the chair in front of his desk and he leaned back a little in his own chair, trying to appear relaxed. When had he ever cared what a servant thought of his appearance? There was something about Miss Lancaster which made him self-conscious, and he must consider that later, but for now, he was going to enjoy this conversation.

"I trust your ride was satisfactory?"

"Indeed, Your Grace. It would be hard not to take pleasure in such a fine piece of horseflesh."

"Oh, yes. You appreciate the finer points of cattle more than most ladies. I will remember to ask your opinion next time I am in the market for a mount."

Next time? What nonsense was he spouting?

"And how is your charge behaving?" he asked, reminding himself why she was here.

"Quite well, Your Grace. We have spent the past week becoming acquainted. I think we are getting on rather well."

She was behaving appropriately, and Rowley suddenly questioned whether his bargain was a good idea. He paused for a moment and then looked at her horrid bonnet and firmed his resolve.

"I am glad to hear it."

"Will that be all, Your Grace? I had planned to take Lady Eugenia on a walk to the cliffs, to try our hand at painting since it is a fine day."

"There is one thing. I have been considering your suggestion."

She leaned backward as though she expected reprimand.

"My aunt also feels as you do. I try to be reasonable, and therefore have decided to allow my sister to attend this week's assembly."

Miss Lancaster smiled with undisguised pleasure, causing something to stir deep within him—something he had not experienced before. She lit up the room when she smiled and it had been directed at him. He must not forget himself. There would be no duchess for him and he would not make her his mistress.

"Thank you, Your Grace. I do not think you will regret this."

"I trust you and my aunt will see to it that I do not. I consider myself a fair man, Miss Lancaster, and will be happy to admit that I am wrong if that indeed turns out to be the case."

"I confess I did not think you would even consider changing your mind once it was made."

It was his turn to raise his eyebrows and scowl. How could a woman go from being most charming one moment to a witch the next? She made him angry in a way very few people had ever done.

Anger was beneath a duke, he had always been told.

Perhaps one should not be so hasty in one's judgement, especially on such a short acquaintance—and especially not when one is paying their wages, he thought, immediately regretting doing so. He did not want his servants afraid of him. She was a lady, after all, and was clearly used to being able to speak her mind amongst her acquaintances. Did she consider him an acquaintance? No one besides his siblings spoke freely with him, and it was a novel sensation.

"I beg your pardon," she said, her eyes cast down. Rowley suspected she was annoyed by his reprimand, but he found he liked her better when she stood up to him.

"You have received your new clothing?" He knew very well that she had, but he was not ready to dismiss her… if she even waited for dismissal.

"Yes, Your Grace. As you can see." She indicated her dark blue riding habit. Unfortunately, the gesture drew his eye to the well-fitted garment over a well-formed figure.

"Did Mrs. Haynes fail to order you new bonnets? I clearly remember asking her to do so."

"You object to my bonnets?" She sat up a little straighter.

He should tread carefully, but it was not his nature and certainly not his way. "I will simply say I prefer to look at people when I speak to them. I can scarcely see your face."

She thrust her chin up into the air, causing the front of her bonnet to flop backwards. "Will that do, Your Grace?"

He did not answer, but stared. He was enjoying her anger entirely too much.

"If that will be all, I now have an assembly to prepare my charge for." She stood up quickly and he almost knocked over his chair in trying to stand up himself. It was almost undignified.

"That is not quite all. I have one condition in order for my sister to attend the assembly tonight."

"Beyond behaving as the perfect model of propriety?" He detected mockery in her voice.

"You will not wear one of your caps tonight, Miss Lancaster."

She clenched her jaw. He could see she wanted to claw his eyes out.

"May I ask what my head covering has to do with your sister attending the assembly?"

"It is my condition, Miss Lancaster, take it or leave it. You may inform my sister when you have made your choice."

He sat back down at his desk and looked at his correspondence, ignoring her. It was some minutes before she turned to leave. He was not reading a word on the page, of course. He was fully expecting her to pick up a vase from the mantel and hurl it at his head.

She did not. She did not even storm from the room but left with composure. Why had he done such a thing? He really did not care if she wore a bonnet. However, he did care if she was doing it to hide from him. He was having difficulty adhering to his own dictum of forgetting about her past. Why that was, he was not pleased to admit, even to himself. He was attracted to her, and she was hardly suitable. He did not consort with members of his household.

A knock sounded on the door and he groaned. He was too fatigued to deal with any more dramatics today.

Cummins entered and Rowley breathed a sigh of relief.

"What can I do for you, Cummins? I must go upstairs to prepare for the village assembly."

Cummins looked surprised. Rowley did not think he had attended an assembly since Cummins had been in his employ.

"I have received a response from London, Your Grace, but it can wait until tomorrow."

"No. I want to see it now."

Cummins handed him the reply he had received to his enquiry, from Rowley's man of business in London.

Mr. Cummins,

In response to your enquiry:

Indeed, there was a situation involving Lord Heath and a Mr. John Lancaster. They had a very public argument at Boodles over one Gemma Hamilton, actress. Lord Heath had made claim to said actress, but the lady did not wish to have Lord Heath as her protector. Mr. Lancaster defended the lady and Lord Heath threatened to ruin him in front of multiple witnesses at their club. Later that night, Lord Heath not only continued to pursue the actress, he challenged Mr. Lancaster to a duel and a large brawl ensued when Lancaster refused to meet him. I believe His Grace was privy to that event, since he instructed me to pay the gentleman's passage to America not long after the fact. Please let me know if I can be of further assistance.

Your servant,
T. Jamison

"THANK YOU, CUMMINS. Please inform the party to go on to the assembly. I will join them there shortly."

As the door closed behind his secretary, he leaned his head on his hands in a rare weak moment.

Lord Heath had been in part responsible for Lancaster's ruin, but had he, inadvertently, also been so himself? And why would Lancaster risk his reputation for this actress? Rowley did not recall Gemma Hamilton, he was quite sure, other than her reputation; if she had made fools of Heath and Lancaster, she must be something special indeed. Perhaps he would ask about her next time he was in London.

Begrudgingly, he went upstairs to change, quite certain he was going to regret this outing. He put the finishing knot on his Mathematical neckcloth and his valet helped him shrug into his tightly fitted black coat, which complemented his silver waistcoat and grey breeches. He loathed assemblies and public events where people treated him like a duke. He had been one since the age of fifteen, but he suspected people could not see beyond his title to the person beneath. The conversations were tedious, the ladies were overtly obvious in their attentions to him, and people expected him to do the pretty all evening. He did know how to behave as a gentleman, of course, it was part of his duty. It did not mean he enjoyed it.

EMMA WAS FEELING a little naughty but rather proud of herself as she surveyed her toilette for the assembly. The duke thought to be heavy-handed with her, did he? She almost laughed.

She could not wait to see his face when he saw the turban atop her head.

Unfortunately, it did not make her ugly as she had wished, but it nevertheless covered her hair. The green made her eyes look brilliant, even to her own, self-conscious opinion, and the turban made her look more mature and almost elegant. She had been dressed similarly to this when the duke had looked scathingly at her backstage at the theatre. The only difference then had been she had worn heavy cosmetics. Would he recognize her thus? What would she do if he did? Even though she had done nothing wrong, people would assume the worst. She had not even worn any costumes that would be considered improper. The theatre manager had teased her and called her the most prude actress ever to grace their stage.

Even though her behavior had been proper and demure, men had still sought her out. It was how she had encountered Lord Heath Knight for the first time. He was not accustomed to being told "no" and had been very persistent in his attentions.

Emma did not want to think about what had happened after that. She was looking forward to the assembly, even though she probably would not dance. She had been somewhat relieved of her duties as Lady Eugenia's chaperone since Lady Hambridge had stayed, but she did not know anyone except the duke and Lord Edmund and she could not imagine the duke asking her to dance. She laughed at the thought.

There were no jewels to adorn her neck and she did not even own any paste earrings, but she thought she would not disgrace herself, regardless. It was time to attend Lady Eugenia, whom she suspected would be beside herself with nervous excitement.

Stepping through the sitting room to that lady's apartment, she knocked lightly on the door and spied the girl positively glowing in her first bloom of youth.

"How pretty you look!" she said as she entered. "You will have a partner for every dance."

"Do you think so?" Eugenia turned and her eyes widened. "Emma!"

"Yes, 'tis I." She smiled with amusement.

"You look… splendid."

"Thank you," she answered, feeling uncomfortable with the praise. Her intention had been to avoid drawing attention to herself.

"Shall we see if Lady Sybil and Lady Hambridge are ready?"

"Yes, please!" Eugenia's maid clasped a fine string of pearls about her neck and she twirled around once before the mirror. Emma felt a slight pang of envy, if only for the exuberance and innocence that Lady Eugenia had. There were only a few years separating them, but she felt decades older, for all that. Lady Eugenia's gown was a cream confection, with pretty violet ribbon around the high waist and trimming her sleeves and hem. A matching ribbon was tied in her hair, holding the dark ringlets back from her face. The bright smile and roses in her cheeks would certainly draw all eyes to her.

They found Lady Sybil attending Lady Hambridge, and Emma thought Sybil was in very good looks herself. She wore a pale blue silk with silver trimmings and had dressed her hair in a simple chignon, which was eminently more suited to her than the silly ringlets her mother normally insisted upon.

"Oh, Emma!" Lady Hambridge exclaimed, having been told of the duke's dictum. "What am I to do with you?"

Although she tried, Emma was certain she could not keep a devilish gleam from her eyes. She could not fully contain the laughter that was bubbling up inside her, either. She had to bite her lower lip to contain her mirth.

"Do you think he will be very angry?" She almost hoped so.

"I think you are playing with fire, my dear."

"I am doing nothing of the sort. He merely said no *caps*."

"Did Rowley order you not to wear caps?" Eugenia asked with open astonishment.

"He did indeed."

Sybil let out a gasp and Eugenia clapped. "I cannot wait to see his face!" she exclaimed.

"What if he turns you off?" Sybil asked. *The poor girl would never do anything against the rules,* Emma thought.

"Then she will return home with me," Lady Hambridge said, shaking her own turbaned head.

"If he wanted your head uncovered completely, he should have been more specific," Eugenia said with her finger in the air. "He cannot let you go for that."

"He can do anything he likes," Emma said. "I should not have let my temper get the better of me, but we will be late if we do not hurry." As they made their way downstairs, she realized she was doing the very thing she was trying to teach Eugenia not to.

Lord Edmund was in the entrance hall, waiting for them, and looking quite handsome dressed in black from breaches to coat, save the white clerical collar.

"What a fortunate man I am to escort four beautiful ladies to the assembly! I will be the envy of every gentleman present. May I reserve one set with each of you?"

Lady Sybil and Eugenia both agreed, and Emma made known her intention not to dance.

"Where is Knighton?" Lady Hambridge asked.

"He has been detained by some urgent estate matters, but will join us when he can."

Eugenia pouted with disappointment.

Emma whispered in her ear. "He will be there soon to dance with you. He would not miss this for the world." Emma hoped what she said was true. It served to calm the girl for now. They were bundled into capes and muffs before being handed into the duke's coach, complete with footmen in formal livery and the ducal crest emblazoned on the side. It was darkening early this late in the year, but the sky was clear and the moon full, making the evening cool and crisp.

Eugenia could barely contain her excitement, and it was infectious. Emma hated to put a damper on the girl's elation, but felt she must remind her of the rules.

"Remember, you must be presented to any new acquaintances, and your chaperone must approve of your partners."

"We have been over this a thousand times," the girl whined.

"And you must never go anywhere alone," Emma added for good measure.

The assembly room was small. Even the village where Emma had been brought up boasted a larger hall for dances. The carriage stopped before a posting inn and on alighting, they were escorted upstairs to a general purpose room. The walls were lined with chairs and there were a few tables covered with refreshments. The windows had been opened for some air to circulate, and a small group of musicians, on a dais at the far end of the room, were tuning their instruments and warming up for the evening. A crowd had already gathered and gasped with delight as their party entered.

Chapter Eight

ROWLEY PLANNED TO slip unobtrusively into the assembly. It seemed as though everyone in the village was packed into the room, and there was a dull roar as the crowd greeted each other and the musicians prepared to play. He should have known there was no such thing as unobtrusive in his life. Immediately, one of his old friends found him.

"Knighton! Has Hell frozen over?" A familiar voice accosted him as he approached.

"Tinsley. I did not realize you were home. Still in the diplomatic corps?" he asked his tall, blond friend whose pale blue eyes still sparkled with humor, but he was no longer the lanky youth he had been when they had haunted the Devon countryside.

"Returned from Vienna for good, it seems. My father's health is failing and he wanted time to pass the torch to me."

"I am sorry to hear that. I had not heard. I might be forced to socialize again, then, with you home."

"What has brought you out from your self-imposed hermitage?"

"Eugenia." Rowley inclined his head toward the group of ladies who were surrounded by army officers in their bright red regimentals.

"That is Eugenia? The little elf who shadowed us everywhere? She is becoming a beauty, Knighton. You are to be pitied, my friend."

"I know it. This is her very first assembly." He watched as his sister was being flirted with, and he debated how much to permit. So far she was smiling and looking very pretty, so he would allow her chaperones to guide her—for now.

"Who is the dasher in green?" Tinsley asked with a gleam in his eye.

She had her back to Rowley, so he had not noticed. Miss Lancaster turned and Rowley's blood turned to ice in his veins. How dare she defy him!

"That… is Eugenia's new governess." His voice sounded calm, but he was angry.

Tinsley let out a low whistle. "Where did you find her?"

"She is my aunt Hambridge's goddaughter. The father lost their fortune and Eugenia needed female companionship, so she asked if I would take her in."

"If she does not work out, old chap, please let me know. Caroline is only twelve, but are you ever too young for a governess?"

Rowley was growing irritated by his childhood friend, and he knew it was unreasonable. Why should he care if another gentleman admired Miss Lancaster's beauty? Because she was a beauty, even though not in the classical English sense—despite the turban, which she had worn just to spite him. It did nothing to hide her stunning good looks, as all the horrid bonnets and mob-caps had. The green silk which his aunt had had made for her was simple and unadorned, save a few spangles, and only drew more attention to her natural beauty. He was seething, and his begrudging attraction to her only angered him further.

"Introduce me, Knighton. I will ask Eugenia to dance too, of course."

They walked toward the group of ladies, and Rowley tried to think of how to handle the defiant chit. It would serve her right if he dismissed her on the spot, but he had to admit she was full of pluck to have done such a thing. Perhaps he would ignore it.

"Good evening, ladies," he said with a bow when they reached them.

"Rowley! You got here before the dancing started."

"As you see. You remember Mr. Tinsley, Eugenia?"

"Of course I do, silly!"

Miss Lancaster made a slight gesture of warning to his sister, while he raised his eyebrows. Eugenia glared back before turning and smiling at their childhood playmate and offering her hand. She had always come along or chased after them and Tinsley had treated her no differently then than he would have done his own sister. Tinsley engaged Eugenia for a dance.

"You remember our aunt, Lady Hambridge? And this is her goddaughter, Lady Sybil Moreland."

"A pleasure, my lady. I am acquainted with your father. Do you have an open set for me?"

The poor girl curtsied and accepted a country dance, but her face turned beet red, which did not enhance her looks.

"I would be delighted, thank you, sir." She shrank back behind his aunt.

"Are all your sets spoken for, ma'am?" Tinsley teased Aunt Hambridge.

She smacked him with her fan, although she was pleased. "Save yourself for the young ladies. I fully intend to prop up the wall and watch."

"If you change your mind..." he said flirtatiously.

Knighton envied his friend his easy manners. People did not toady to Tinsley, despite him being heir to a prosperous viscountcy, but genuinely enjoyed his company. That friend was now elbowing him discreetly.

Rowley sprang to attention. "Mr. Tinsley, may I present Miss Lancaster of Shropshire? Mr. Tinsley grew up on the neighboring estate."

She curtsied, then held out her hand to Tinsley. "I am pleased to make your acquaintance, sir."

"May I beg the honor of a dance this evening?" He smiled charmingly at her. Rowley clenched his fists.

"I am a chaperone, sir. I am not going to dance. It is more important for the young ladies to be partnered."

"Balderdash! This is not your doing, is it Knighton?" His friend pretended to be horrified.

"I am no tyrant to forbid her to dance," he said, daring her to contradict him.

"See there? Knighton does not mind, so unless you object to sharing a dance with me...?" Tinsley asked, allowing the question to hang between them.

"No, of course not. I would be delighted to dance with you, sir." What else could she have said? Rowley caught the slight scowl she cast in his direction.

Two of the army officers, who had been lingering nearby, began to object and ask for her to partner them. She smiled quickly and accepted them.

"Do you have any openings for your eldest brother?" he asked Eugenia.

"I am sorry, Rowley. We did not know when you would arrive and I am already engaged for every set!" She beamed at him, looking lovely and happy. Edmund winked at her and led her out for the first set.

Lady Sybil was led off by one of the army men, and Aunt Hambridge began making her way to a chair. Miss Lancaster watched her charge with obvious pride and then turned to follow his aunt to the perimeter. Some stroke of madness prompted him to step forward.

"Are you not engaged for the set, Miss Lancaster?"

She stopped and hesitated before returning to him. "I am not. I had intended to observe Lady Eugenia first."

"How better to observe than right next to her? Will you dance with me?" He held out his hand. She looked at it for a moment before placing her hand in his. She could not, of course, refuse.

They did not speak at first. He found his heart was beating rapidly and he suddenly seemed aware of every breath he took. Her scent, which he could not place, filled his senses and he felt like a tongue-tied youth, not prepared for the sensation of touching her.

Rowley hated that she made him doubtful.

Yet he could not ignore her.

"Is this to be my punishment, then?" she broke the silence by asking.

"Is that what I am to you?" he retorted, somehow scorched by her words.

"I was referring to your lack of speech."

"I did not think you would wish to speak of trivial matters such as the weather, but if you wish to play the game, we can."

"No, you are quite right. I was expecting you to scold me and I suppose I was waiting for it," she answered candidly.

"Yet it has not come."

They were forced by the pattern of the dance to take another partner and his mind raced while he watched her take a graceful turn with Tinsley, who was openly admiring her.

"Will the scold come? Or are you too proper to do it in so public a place?" she demanded in an under voice when they faced each other again.

He watched her for a moment, debating how to answer. "I could dismiss you for insubordination."

"Covering my head offends you so much?" Her wide eyes evidenced her astonishment.

"Is covering your head worth risking your position? Or is it satisfying enough to thwart me that you do not care?"

"I should think, as long as I am a proper chaperone, it would be of little concern to you." Her eyes flashed at him and her lips were thinned into a tight line.

"I will confess you look very becoming in a turban, even though it should make you look old and matronly. It does not have that effect on you."

"I suppose that was a compliment." One brow arched at him suspiciously.

He did not respond, thankfully saved by the movements of the dance. Any other *ton* female would be swooning at a compliment from him. They were so rarely given. What was it about her that disconcerted him so? He must discover it in order to rid himself of this unwanted and unlooked-for attraction.

Since he was a small child, Rowley remembered being taught to be decisive and deal with problems as quickly as possible before they grew out of control. Is that what he was doing? Drawn to this problem by some sense of duty? It did not feel like any problem he had encountered before.

"Why are you scowling, sir? Have I done something else to offend you?"

Rowley jerked his attention back to Miss Lancaster. He had been ignoring his partner.

Everything about this woman seemed to make a mockery of him and his duties. He had forgotten his manners as a gentleman several times with her in a few short days.

"You look very formidable when you scowl," she remarked, with a twinkle in her eye. She was toying with him!

"You forget yourself, Miss Lancaster."

"Never that," she snapped.

He was unused to being taken to task and now he had insulted her again, devil take it. He did know how to be a gentleman, but she was bringing out the worst in him. There was a reason he stayed away from such gatherings. The music drew to a close and he offered her his arm to lead her from the floor. He owed her an apology, though how he had been made to be in the wrong, he could not quite say. He had not cut up stiff over her turban and had even told her she looked well. Why did he suddenly feel like a piece of horse dung?

"This is my dance, I believe?" Tinsley walked up to her with a smile on his face and she suddenly brightened again. He watched them leave, then went into the corner to brood.

EMMA COULD NOT believe His Grace had condescended to dance with her, but her elation had not lasted long. How silly of her to think it was a compliment! Instead, he had found ways to insult her. Although, when she had expected a scolding for wearing a turban, he had said she looked pretty…or words to that effect. Why had she been looking for good in this man? He had ruined her family and nothing could change that. He had insulted her again tonight, and she vowed she would not let him know it. Her smile would be the biggest in the room and she would dance every dance and enjoy herself. The gentlemen here were treating her like a lady. It was as close as she would ever likely get again. Mr. Tinsley was a flirt, but seemed harmless nevertheless. She danced with Lieutenant Becker, whom they had met at the linen draper's, and a Captain Morgan, who knew her brother Matthew from the same regiment but a different battalion. He was to be so kind as to deliver a letter for her, personally, into the hands of her brother when he returned to the Peninsula from his leave.

Emma had quite forgotten what it was like to be doted upon for herself and not for her favors. Gentlemen were bringing her punch and she had a partner for every dance. It would not be like this in London, of course, amongst the vipers of the *haute ton*, but she was going to take this night and enjoy it.

Life over the past two years had taught her that tomorrow was not a guarantee, and you must enjoy things when presented with the opportunity.

She could not stop thinking about the dance with the duke. She almost felt sorry for him. Almost. For all the airs of a gentleman, he had seemed uneasy while trying to converse with her. It had been difficult not to shrink from his touch, when she recalled those same dark eyes that had looked upon her scornfully in the past, judging and condemning without any facts. Whatever had possessed him to ask her to dance? There had been no need. She had made it clear that she would watch Lady Eugenia from the side and he had insisted. He did not seem to care for her any more than she did him, so was this another test?

It could not happen again, that was certain.

Thankfully, she was dancing a country dance, which required little thought on her part or conversing with her partner. It was difficult to attend with so much on her mind. Truly, she should be watching her charge, but hopefully Lady Hambridge was fulfilling that role. When the set ended, it was time for tea. They were not having a large supper at this small assembly. Emma looked about to find Eugenia and see how she was enjoying her first dance, but she was nowhere to be found. First, she looked to the red uniforms, which had been the most solicitous of her hand for dancing. Next, she looked for Mr. Tinsley, then Lord Edmund and then the duke.

The latter three were heavily involved in a discussion, no doubt of horses or politics. Her gaze continued around the room, but Eugenia was nowhere to be seen. Emma hurried over to Lady Hambridge and had to wait for her to finish a heated discussion on the merits of Olympic Dew versus Denmark Lotion for the complexion with another matron.

"What is it, my dear?" she asked with concern on her face.

"Would you excuse us a moment?" she asked the ladies nearby and escorted her godmother away from listening ears.

"Have you seen Eugenia? She was last dancing with Lieutenant Becker."

"Now I think on it, she did not come back to me at the end of the dance, as is proper." The lady frowned and scanned the room. "I assume you have not asked Knighton?"

"Of course not!" That was the last person she wanted to tell unless she had exhausted all other options.

"I will search the retiring room. You look outside. Perhaps she needed fresh air. If she is not in either place then we shall have to tell him."

Emma nodded and began to fan herself as though she needed air herself, so people would not think much of her going out of the door.

It was quite chilly, and Emma wished she had sought her cape before she had ventured out here, but that would have defeated the purpose and she needed to be quick.

At first, she saw nothing, but she stood breathing in the aroma of chimney smoke and looking at the stars for a moment when she heard something that distinctly resembled a giggle.

At first she was relieved she had found her, but then she was unbelievably cross. "You stupid, stupid girl!" she muttered to herself. She marched straight over to the tree beyond the courtyard and forcefully took Lady Eugenia's arm.

"If you will excuse us, sir, her chaperone is concerned for her whereabouts."

"Emma! We were just taking some air," Eugenia said, seemingly oblivious to her mistake.

"Let me escort you back inside," the lieutenant offered unrepentantly.

"No, thank you," Emma snapped. "You would do best to either leave or use a different entrance."

"Will you call on me tomorrow?" Eugenia called as Emma pulled her back to the door.

"Hush. You do not want to draw attention to the fact that you were out here unchaperoned. If your brother gets wind of this, you will be locked in the dungeon until you are of age, and I will be on the streets begging for my bread."

"Just so."

Emma had been so busy scolding Lady Eugenia that she had not seen the duke standing at the door, watching them, his arms folded across his chest and looking like the devil himself. She jumped with fright.

"May I suggest you each take my arm and smile as we walk back inside together? We will discuss the appropriate recourse for your behavior once we are at home and in private. Understood?" He pushed away from the wall and held out both arms.

Emma could see Lady Eugenia was biting back an argument, so she stepped in.

"Very good, Your Grace. Shall we claim fatigue and make our goodbyes?"

"I believe Eugenia was promised for the remaining sets. It would be best for her to keep her engagements and not give cause for speculation."

Eugenia was eyeing her brother with distrust, but he had diffused her outburst for now. As they entered the ballroom, Mr. Tinsley came forward to claim Eugenia's hand.

"I was beginning to think I had been abandoned for a more handsome beau," he teased as he led her to the floor.

Emma was left standing alone with the duke.

The silence was deafening, standing next to him, despite the swell of music and gay voices filling the assembly hall. Yet, it did not seem proper to walk away.

"Thank you, Miss Lancaster," he said, breaking the awkward moment.

She turned to look at him, for she could not believe her ears. "I beg your pardon? What would there be to thank me for?"

"It seems you saved us from embarrassment and possibly worse."

"You should be pouring recriminations upon my head for abandoning my responsibilities. I should not have taken my eye from her."

"Neither should I have done, nor my aunt, for that matter. You were given leave to dance, yet you found her before the lieutenant was able to do any harm and before anyone noticed her absence."

"Let us hope so. I do not think she was seen, nor do I think he meant any harm. They were only talking."

He cast a look of disbelief at her. "Nevertheless, I think it proves she needs more bronze before facing the *ton*. Eugenia is yet too young to understand everyone's intentions are not well-meaning. Her fortune and title are enough to lure anyone into thinking they are in love with her."

Yet that had not been the case with him; she held back the words on the tip of her tongue. It was a very unkind thought, and she did not know his history. Perhaps he had been thwarted in love.

"I will do my best to see that she understands, your Grace."

"May I escort you to Lady Hambridge?"

"Yes, thank you." She accepted his arm, expecting to be repulsed by his touch, but found it made her feel warm inside. She must not allow herself to become complacent and soften to this man. She could not forget that he could turn on her in an instant if he knew the truth.

Chapter Nine

"I MUST BE away to London," Edmund said as he strolled into the study where Rowley was reviewing papers. It seemed a never-ending task.

"So soon?"

"Miss Thatcher is doing well under Cook's wing. She seems to feel safe there. I always have more work than I have time for, and Lady Hambridge has offered to take me in her carriage."

"It sounds fortuitous," Rowley answered. His brother could have his own carriage if he wished, but he found little use for it in Town.

"I thought Eugenia did rather well last night," Edmund remarked as he helped himself to the coffee that Rowley had on his table. "Miss Lancaster was rather a success as well. Aunt Hambridge means to find her a match, so do not get too attached to her for Eugenia."

"As with any member of my household, she is free to leave whenever she wishes."

"But it is rare that anyone does." He sipped his coffee.

Rowley inclined his head. He did his best to make this estate a home for the hundreds of people required to make it run well.

"I have enjoyed being home again, Row. It would be nice if all of us could gather for the festive season."

"This is your home as well, Edmund. You are welcome any time."

"I know that, but would you consider coming to London? It is one of my busiest times and difficult to get away. Perhaps even Heath would stay sober long enough for Christmas dinner with us."

Rowley did not even bother to comment. Heath's peccadilloes were still reaping consequences on the entire family years after they took place.

Rowley hated London, but he went when duty required it. Heath had not been heard of in some months, and perhaps he should go and see how he did, even though Jamison, his London man of business kept an eye on him.

"I will think on it and let you know. First, I wish to see how Miss Lancaster and Eugenia get on once the company leaves."

"I do not think you will have much to worry about there. She seems a great companion for our sister." He drained his cup and stood up. "I must gather my things and bid Miss Thatcher *adieu*."

Rowley stood to see his brother out, and Edmund wrapped his arms around him. Ever the one with tender sensibilities, was Edmund. Rowley hugged him back and found he did not wish to let him go. As they walked out into the entrance hall, they surprised the servants bustling about preparing for the ladies' departure.

He stood watching, hoping, with something akin to desperation, that this would mean he could have his quiet, placid life back.

And then he heard the ladies in the hall upstairs.

"I wish you did not have to leave," Miss Lancaster said.

"Do not worry, my dear. We shall see you soon. I have no doubt that Knighton will bring Eugenia to London for next Season now he has seen how prettily she can behave."

Rowley wished he could see Miss Lancaster's face. "We shall see. I would not mind some time here in the country, first."

His aunt sighed. "If it will help to convince you that you are making a mistake, then I am all for it. There are plenty of gentleman who would be willing to have you despite your circumstances, Emma."

"I think we should worry about Lady Eugenia and Lady Sybil,

first."

"You know I will never stop worrying about you, until I see you settled."

"You have been so, so good to me."

Rowley could sense tears coming on, yet he did not move from where he stood, eavesdropping. This was a side of Miss Lancaster she would likely never show him.

"You are like the daughter I never had. If only you would let me treat you as such."

"You have. I assure you, you have. Now, be on your way before we both become watering pots."

He realized they were coming down the stairs and moved so that his prying would not be obvious. Moving in front of the stairs, he went to his aunt, who was being escorted by Miss Lancaster.

She was wearing a pale green muslin, and looked as fresh as spring, but to his astonishment, no cap adorned her head.

He found he could not speak. What a dolt he was!

It was only pulled back in a simple knot, but a few waves of hair had escaped and were surrounding her face like a halo. He supposed there was nothing spectacular about the color of her hair in particular, but when blended with her eyes and her skin it was the perfection of an artist's. Instead of satisfying his curiosity, it only whet his appetite. Her eyes met his, looking vastly amused and he at once snapped out of his musings.

His aunt was speaking, and he struggled to listen and comprehend. "Edmund said we are having a Christmas gathering in London. What a marvelous idea!"

"Is it true?" Eugenia asked, hurrying down the stairs beaming with excitement. "May we see a play while we are there?"

Rowley opened his mouth to protest, but something about the look on Miss Lancaster's face stopped him. Did she not want to go to London for some reason?

"I told Edmund I would *consider* it. You still have several weeks to behave yourself, young lady."

Eugenia threw her arms around him. "You are the best of brothers!" He tolerated the unladylike show of affection as best he could, but these extremes of temperament were precisely what he was concerned about. She was not ready to be a wife or a mother, and he did not want to take away her innocence, but she was not ready for the *ton*. Perhaps a few small gatherings would begin to prepare her.

Edmund strolled into the entrance hall where they were still gathered. "Are we ready to depart?"

"I do not believe I will ever be ready for the long trip back to London. Knighton, you should consider moving closer," declared his aunt.

"I will take it into consideration." He smiled and kissed her on the cheek as they walked outside to the waiting carriages.

Rowley, Eugenia, and Miss Lancaster stood on the steps and waved them on their way. The three of them. Suddenly the estate seemed too small. *Do not be ridiculous*, a small voice inside him said. *She is only a woman and she is here for your sister.*

He had too much work to be distracted by a little slip of a woman. They would go about their business and he would go about his. It would restore a much-needed sense of peace and harmony to his life again. He need not see them if he was careful, which would be for the best until he could quell this ridiculous attraction he felt—and it was nothing more than attraction. There was hardly anyone more unsuitable for him than Miss Lancaster, not that there was scandal precisely attached to the name, but she was now dependent on him and a duke did not consort with an employee.

"We are going to go riding, Rowley. Would you like to join us?" his sister asked.

"No, you go on ahead. I have enough work to keep me in my study for weeks."

"You poor duke," she remarked. "Very well, Emma and I will have fun without you."

EMMA HAD KNOWN their departure was coming, but she felt as though her last well-wishers in the world were leaving as she watched her godmother and long-time friend roll away in the carriage. Lady Eugenia was a happy enough companion, but still seemed so very young. She could not confide all of her secrets. At least, not yet.

However, she need not have worried. It seemed the duke no longer felt the need to attend them without Lady Hambridge and Lady Sybil present, for he was nowhere to be seen once the two ladies had left.

"Where shall we ride to today, my charge?" Emma asked, trying to hide her blue-devils.

"I think I should like to go into the village and then to tea with Grandmama. The horses will be fresh, therefore it might be better to exercise them first rather than begin there."

"We should send a footman to warn her cook," Emma said, and the butler nodded his head in acknowledgement that he would attend to it. Emma still had not accustomed herself to her every wish being taken care of before she could blink.

"Miss Lancaster," the butler addressed her. "I do apologize, but I could not help but overhear your plans to go to the village. Cook was intending to send Thomas, but if you would not mind collecting an item for her, I know it would be appreciated since some of the staff have fallen ill with colds."

"Of course; we would be delighted. If you will have our horses made ready, I will go and visit Cook."

Soon they were on their way, riding Helen and Cassandra to the village and leaving them at the posting inn at the top of the hill. They began to traverse the steep road, and Emma had more time to notice that the village was more than a cleft in the cliffs. It was fascinating to see how the houses were built. It truly looked as though they might tumble into the sea.

"It is so lovely to be able to come to the village whenever we wish!" Eugenia said, looking sprightly and smart in a brown wool riding habit.

"Have you not come here often?" Emma asked, thinking it odd since the girl had been brought up here.

"Not particularly. Rowley has been my only companion for years and he does not enjoy shopping. He would not let me come alone with the servants."

"Not even with your maid or nurse?" Emma was astonished.

Eugenia thought for a moment. "I cannot say I recall them ever shopping, though they must have done."

"What did Cook need?" Eugenia asked as they reached the village and began to walk down the high street.

"She asked for some sugar. Perhaps we should place our order now and collect it on our return."

As they made their way to the grocer's shop, Emma felt nostalgic for her own small village. There, she had known everyone and had felt a part of a community. London had been crowded with people, yet she had not had any true friends, only fellow actors who were trying to survive, as she was.

"Do you never visit the tenants?" Emma asked. She had not noticed any neglect, but it did not mean it did not exist.

"I have, yet not often. Rowley and his steward take care of everything."

"And the ladies of the neighborhood?"

"Well, there is a charitable association at the church. I assume the vicar and his wife oversee those sorts of things."

"Yes, I would imagine so." Since there was no duchess to do it, Emma mused. They walked on in silence and she felt less charitable with the duke for being so selfish as to neglect his duty.

"There is Lieutenant Becker! Halloo!" Eugenia called loudly and she waved to the dashing officer before Emma knew what she was about. She must stop brooding about the pompous duke, she silently chastised herself.

Before she could protest, Eugenia led her over to the Lieutenant, who had a young lady on his arm. At least he had the grace to flush a little when his eyes met Emma's.

"How do you do, ma'am, my lady?" He removed his hat and made an elegant leg to them. "May I present my sister, Miss Charlotte Becker?"

His sister was a pretty brunette and they all curtsied to each other.

Emma stood back as the three chatted, feeling very old even though she was not yet three and twenty! She had experience enough to age her before her time, and she would not wish that on these girls.

Emma looked around at the quaint village as they talked, and saw the usual shops. Besides the baker, there was a butcher, the smithy, the linen draper's attached to the grocer's shop, and a potter. The last was not typical in every village. Nor was the silk maker, which explained the fine selection they had here. Emma had assumed the goods were smuggled, the village being on the coast. The larger towns of Tavistock and Bideford were where most goods had to be purchased.

Emma was desirous to be on their way. She turned her gaze back to her charge, who appeared to be conspiring with Miss Becker.

"I should like it above all things!" Eugenia exclaimed.

Emma raised her brows and stepped closer. "We must be on our way if we are to reach the dowager's house in time for tea."

"I had lost track of time!" Eugenia exclaimed.

"I shall see you soon, then." Miss Becker curtsied and her brother bowed. Having taken their leave of the brother and sister, Emma inquired, when they were out of earshot, "Do you care to tell me what you were scheming about?"

"I suppose I must," the girl answered, somewhat warily. "Miss Becker has invited me to a rout party at their home. It is to say farewell to Lieutenant Becker."

"And did you accept?"

Eugenia looked guilty.

"You know your brother will not give his approval, especially after Lieutenant Becker's behavior at the assembly."

"But there can be no question of the propriety. It will be at the squire's house, with his parents hosting!"

"And when is this event to take place?"

"Saturday afternoon. It is even in the daytime! I was hoping you would escort me without Rowley being any the wiser."

Emma felt torn. She knew the duke would not approve, yet she did think he was overbearing. A rout party would have other young adults of age on the guest list; it would not be a formal evening gala.

"We must seek his permission," Emma said at last, knowing she must.

Eugenia at once flew into a temper, there in the center of the village. "How could you? I thought you were better than him!"

"That is most unfair," Emma said in a low voice trying not to draw every eye to Lady Eugenia's tantrum. "Lieutenant Becker showed a wont of conduct in leading you outside alone the other night. Your attendance would most certainly reach his ears whether I told him or not. You know I cannot defy him or I must certainly lose my position."

"I forget I am only a charge to you!"

She stormed away as Emma watched. Deciding she would not reprimand her charge in public and make the situation worse, Emma instead went into the shop. After making a quick purchase of some fabrics for some elementary sewing projects for Eugenia, she then walked back up the hill to collect the sugar Cook had requested, hoping that Eugenia was waiting for her at the stables. Emma could only imagine the extent of the duke's fury if she were to ride home by herself.

Thankfully, when she exited the grocer's shop, Eugenia was sitting on a bench looking repentant. As she walked toward the girl, they heard a child scream.

They both looked around, curious to see where the noise had come from. The scream turned into wails, and together they followed the noise. It seemed to be coming from an alley between two cottages, and without a second thought, Emma hastened into the fray to see if the child was harmed. Moments later, they reached the source of the noise, in a cobbled yard behind an alehouse, where a crowd had gathered. When Emma hurried forward, Eugenia close behind her, the onlookers began to part and drift away.

"Is something amiss?" Emma asked, spying the child. About five years old, with large tears streaming down her face, the girl was being held down by a crone while a younger female looked on.

"Nothing to concern yourself with," the old, wrinkled woman snapped. In her hand she held a small knife, about to cut into the wound.

"You forget yourself, Meggie! Forgive her, my lady, she is just concerned for our Daisy, here," the younger woman, presumably the child's mother, said as she dipped a rough curtsy.

"Is Daisy harmed?"

"She burnt 'erself a few days ago, grabbin' a hot pot from t'stove. Now it's gone putrid. Meggie is the village healer."

"May I see?" Emma was always wary of healers since she blamed one for her own mother's death.

Meggie scowled at Emma as Eugenia watched with curiosity.

Emma crouched down to eye level with the small child. "Release her, please."

The mother gave a nod and the child sat up, looking wary but grateful. "Daisy, I am Emma. May I look at your hand?" The child turned her hand over to reveal an angry-looking suppuration which covered most of her palm. Emma tried not to show how her stomach curled at the sight and smell. Many of the crowd turned away, their revulsion evident. "What has been done for this?" Emma asked the mother.

"I been using the salve that Meggie prepared."

"And cleansing?"

The mother looked anxiously at Meggie.

"May I try a poultice? It is not a guarantee, but it has always worked well for my family."

"I'd be grateful, m'lady."

"I will be back shortly. While I am gone, I want you to soak the hand in saltwater." She turned to Daisy. "It will hurt at first, but I know you are very brave. What I put on will not hurt so much."

The little girl sobbed, but nodded her head.

Emma and Eugenia left to go to the stable at the inn and hoped they would have something.

"Are you a healer, Emma?" Eugenia asked.

"No, but anything I do will be better than Meggie's efforts. It was apparent the burn had not been cleaned, and she put lard on it, which makes burns worse."

"Where did you learn that?" Eugenia seemed awestruck by such a basic fact.

"I suppose I was not so sheltered as you. I spent a fair amount of time with my father in his breeding stables and with my mother, who took pride in personally managing the household and, in particular, the still-room."

At the stable, she supplicated the head ostler and was given some of the ingredients for one of the poultices her father had used, including barley and elder flower, and returned to apply it to the girl's hand.

The girl immediately calmed when the paste and bandage were applied. Emma left the recipe for the mother, and all of the ingredients she had purloined from the ostler at the posting inn.

"I do not know how to thank 'ee, miss!" Daisy's mother exclaimed.

"She is not well, yet, I am afraid. I hope this will be just the thing. It must be kept clean and the paste reapplied morning and night."

"Yes, m'lady."

Emma did not bother to correct her. "Send word to the Grange if you have need of me. I will try to come again as soon as I may."

Returning once more to the inn, Emma and Eugenia mounted as soon as their horses were brought out, and made their way back to the Grange. By the time they arrived at the Dower House, however, the housekeeper informed them the dowager had taken her tea and was now resting. "Most disappointed, she was," the woman confided, "not that she would admit as much, of course, if you will forgive my being so bold, my lady."

"Poor Grandmama!" Eugenia moaned.

Chapter Ten

The next morning was cold and dreary, with the wind rattling the windows and rafters hard enough for Rowley to worry the roof would blow off, which was, of course, unlikely. There was no question of going for his customary ride that day. He had lived on this volatile coast his whole life, and made certain that his tenants were well protected from the elements, yet it never ceased to disturb his peace… just like knowing Emma Lancaster was under his roof.

Banks knocked, then stepped inside. "Your Grace, Miss Lancaster has requested an audience with you. Shall I tell her to consult with your secretary?"

Rowley hated to jump at her whim, but since he was not occupied at the moment, he decided he might as well speak with her now.

"Do you know where she is?"

"In the conservatory, Your Grace. She seems to spend most of her spare time there," he added.

Rowley nodded as the butler left. Stopping to check his appearance in the glass, he checked, deeply annoyed with himself for doing so. He was not one to preen or give another thought to his appearance once he had completed his toilet for the day. He shook his head and went to find Miss Lancaster. He could not blame her for choosing to spend a good deal of time in the conservatory. A room with three walls of glass that looked out onto the sea in the distance, it was a place one could almost forget one was in the midst of winter. Luscious green plants and flowers were kept alive by warm fires and humidity, causing a pleasant sensation of a tropical garden.

She did not hear him enter, which gave him the advantage of watching her in repose. She was sewing, but clearly thinking or daydreaming, as she would occasionally pause and gaze out of the window with a wistful look.

Rowley thought the image would make a beautiful portrait and then quickly told himself he must stop thinking of her that way. She *worked* for him.

He cleared his throat, announcing his presence. Hastily, she sat up straight and then rose to her feet.

"You wished to see me, Miss Lancaster?"

"Yes, Your Grace. Forgive me, I did not expect your immediate attention."

He cleared his throat. "It happened that I had time now. I presume this is not a social call?"

"No, indeed." That made her bristle a little, bringing that militant spark he so dearly loved into her eyes. She sat back down and he took a seat across from her, crossing his legs.

"Has my sister done something to trouble you?" he asked.

Her face registered surprise—or was it guilt? "I do not know if you would call it trouble. She has accepted an invitation to an afternoon party at Squire Becker's house, to bid his son farewell as he is to return to the Continent."

Rowley mulled this over. His initial inclination was to forbid it, but that is what she would expect of him. "And what is your considered opinion about this?"

She hesitated. "I believe she should have sought your approval before accepting."

"But?" he prompted.

"I also think it would be harmless for her to meet with other young people her age."

"One of those being the young lieutenant who attempted to lead her astray at the assembly."

"Well, yes." She flushed.

"Are we to come to cuffs over this?" he asked, enjoying himself.

"If you wish."

He did wish. Very much. She tilted her chin up defiantly, and Rowley felt hopelessly attracted, yet it did not seem Miss Lancaster returned his regard in the slightest. Was that why he could not put her from his mind?

"This is absurd." She surprised him by laughing and drawing him further into her net. "I find I quite agree with you that Becker—and Eugenia—did not behave as they should, but what harm would there be in an afternoon of silly infants dancing under the watchful eye of old matrons?"

"An afternoon of silly infants dancing," he quipped, and felt a reluctant smile forming.

"Since I should be the one to suffer, I cannot think why it should cause you so much as a second thought!" she retorted, looking daggers at him.

"I assure you, knowing my sister far longer than you, if she wishes to get into mischief, it will matter not if the sun is shining. There were an abundance of matrons' watchful eyes, as well as mine and yours at the assembly, if you recall."

"Yes, and I quite blame myself! Apparently, my instructions had not been specific enough."

Rowley raised his brows in enquiry.

"I merely told her not to go anywhere alone, or so she informed me."

"Ah, yes, so she made you feel it was quite your fault she almost found herself compromised at the wise old age of sixteen!" he answered with unaccustomed heat.

"Not exactly."

"But close enough to gain your sympathy for my tyranny. I am a beast, if you recall," he added sardonically.

"A very ferocious one," she agreed with a twinkle in her eye.

"Were you at least subjected to a bout of tears and a discourse about my unjust rules?"

"Not this time."

"No?"

"No."

"I am all astonishment. However, I still think she deserves to send her regrets and remain at home."

"Now I do think you a beast!" she said hotly. A moment later, she changed her manner, seeming to recall her position. "There are so few people her age in the neighborhood—so few opportunities to have friends."

"So you opine I should reward her behavior at the assembly and thereby encourage her to repeat it?"

She shook her head, more in exasperation than agreement, he thought. "You must do what you think best, Your Grace."

"Had she not gone outside alone with the lieutenant, I would have gladly let her attend the rout. Perhaps she will then reconsider when next time a handsome face makes her an unsuitable offer."

"Yes, Your Grace."

Gone was the militant spark in her eye. She was back to being agreeable and meek. He had disappointed her, and consequently himself, but he knew better than anyone how Eugenia could manipulate a rock if she thought it suited her purpose. It was for the best, anyway. He had no business trying to charm sparks out of his sister's governess, even if it did make him feel more alive than he had felt in an age.

For the next month, Lady Eugenia and Emma settled into an almost dream-like routine of riding every morning, painting or reading in the afternoons, while practicing their French and Italian, and then, horror of horrors, she even taught Eugenia how to sew a little to make some clothing for some of the poor in the village after asking the vicar how she might be of service. Mr. Tinsley joined them for their morning rides on many days and the only time she was subjected to the duke's presence was at church on Sunday mornings. It was a far cry from her life in London and all she could have hoped for. Lady Eugenia showed no more of her outbursts and seemed to be more receptive to the lessons in how to behave. It was ironic Emma was the one to be teaching a duke's daughter, when she had never had the opportunity to use her own lessons. But life was full of ironies, such as the fact the person to ruin her family was now the one she was working for. He still seemed to have no idea of the connection, and she was grateful. She could live here a long time under the current conditions, but feared it was too good to be true.

Lady Eugenia came down with a cold, and Emma found she had several days to herself. Eugenia was tended by her old nurse and was not particularly pleasant when she was awake. It suited Emma very well.

One morning, Emma went to exercise the horses, looking forward to some time alone. Not that Eugenia wasn't pleasant or was what one could call work, but there was nothing quite like time alone. She was longing to explore a path Eugenia had told her about, but had not yet shown her. Apparently the Knighton estate carried all the way to the far reach of the River Torridge.

"Good morning, Samuels. Can you saddle one of the twins for me? I intend to exercise them both this morning since Lady Eugenia is under the weather."

"Why don't I follow along behind you on one of them, miss? His Grace would not be pleased to have you go alone."

"I have been in the saddle since I could walk. I am not a young child to need a chaperone."

She could see the groom was uncertain. He was about of an age with her.

"His Grace said Lady Eugenia was never to go alone. I cannot think he would feel any differently about you." The groom was blushing. It was clear he did not relish having this conversation with her.

"I am hardly her ladyship. I am a paid servant, like you. If His Grace asks, you may tell him I insisted and his complaint is with me. Now, kindly help me into the saddle."

The groom did as he was told and Emma regretted being heavy-handed with him, but she did not wish to have a shadow today.

Once free from the house, gardens and fences, she was free to gallop and roam. It was pure joy. It was a pleasant day for November and she intended to take full advantage. Helen seemed equally pleased. They crossed meadows and valleys which were yellow and brown in their dormancy, but there was still beauty in knowing they would soon have new life again. They reached the cliff path to where the river poured into the sea and began climbing upwards to the overlook point, which Eugenia had assured Emma was the prettiest place in all of England.

Even as they climbed more slowly, Emma knew what Eugenia said was true. She had never seen anything like it. The view went for miles and miles from the small village to the grounds of the Grange and beyond to the open hills of the tenant farms.

"What must it be like to own all of this?" she asked out loud to her horse.

"Only think of how much good you could do with so much." She was being harsh again, she chastised herself. Perhaps the duke did some good; his brother Edmund certainly did. Having met Miss Thatcher and befriended the girl, she knew the girl was one of many who he helped find a better life.

Having been at Knighton Grange for a month now, she had never heard a cross word spoken about the duke or the way he ran his estate. Would anyone say anything to her, knowing she worked for him? Who could say?

The wind was whipping them fiercely at the top, blowing her skirts and hat, so they continued on until they met the river again and were sheltered by a copse of trees. She had not known this peace since she was a girl in Shropshire. Emma allowed Helen to rest for a while, grazing away at the grass, and then she walked her over to the stream for a drink. If she thought she could mount again, she would get down and sit for a while.

Recollecting she was to exercise Cassandra as well, she turned to head back when she saw a rider coming toward her. It was probably Mr. Tinsley, looking for his usual riding companions, although they never rode this far. As he drew closer, she knew at once it was the duke. No one had quite the same presence as a duke, did they? It was too late to hide, so she waited.

He looked splendid, she had to admit, and at one with his horse. Of course he did, she thought spitefully.

As he pulled up near her, he was on his hunter and the horses greeted each other. "Good day, Miss Lancaster. I see you have found my favorite spot."

"I beg your pardon," she said hastily, trying not to bristle at feeling like an interloper.

"I did not mean you are not welcome here. I have never encountered anyone else, that is all."

"Your sister recommended it to me. She gave me leave to exercise the horses."

"I am glad you did. I wish you had let Samuels accompany you, however." She looked up and he was watching her. Not with scorn, but perhaps concern?

"I hope you did not exert yourself unnecessarily on my behalf?"

"No, I did not know where you had gone, and this is where I come to think."

"Then I shall not disturb you any longer." She began to turn the horse to leave.

"May I accompany you back?"

She could hardly say no, it was his land and his horse. "It is not necessary, Your Grace. I understand how welcome time alone to ride must be for you."

"Indeed, but I have ridden all the way here alone." He appeared disappointed.

"Very well, then. Thank you."

They cantered along beside the river and Emma did not wish to speak, but he kept his horse abreast of hers.

"Are you finding Knighton Grange satisfactory?" he asked, surprising her.

"Yes, Your Grace. It is more pleasant than I could have imagined."

"And your pupil?"

"Also very pleasant. I am enjoying my time with her very well. It almost does not seem fair to be paid to spend time with her." Emma smiled, forgetting her companion for a moment.

He seemed very pleased by her remark. "Do you think she is ready for a few weeks in Town? I would not allow her anywhere but small engagements, but perhaps I would allow her to see a play."

"She will do very well, Your Grace. There have been no more... incidents."

He nodded and remained silent for a while. "How about yourself, Miss Lancaster? Would you enjoy going to Town?"

"I will go wherever you wish me to, your Grace."

"But that is not what I asked you, Miss Lancaster."

She debated how to answer and decided to be honest.

He must have sensed her hesitation for he pulled up his horse and looked at her. She reined in her own mare and met his gaze. She was surprised by the sincerity she saw there. Did he truly care what she thought? Emma relaxed her hands on the reins and turned to face the duke.

He was waiting for her answer. "I confess the country suits me better."

He seemed to relax at her response. "I confess I prefer it here myself, but my brother has asked me to come—has asked us all to come. Would you be averse to accompanying Eugenia for a few weeks? As you suggested, give her a small reward for good behavior?"

He was trying to be a good brother, Emma could see. How could she deny her charge such a treat? "I know Lady Eugenia will be delighted. I would be happy to accompany her to Town." And all the while she would be praying that her good fortune would not come crashing down around her.

As she pondered this, they rode into a narrow belt of woodland. It was dark after the sunlight and surprisingly quiet, even the birds stilled by the duke's presence. It made the ensuing rustling more startling. The horses stopped, their heads up and ears flickering. Suddenly, a pair of deer leaped out across their path. Alarmed, Helen shied and took off through the trees, catching Emma off guard. The reins slipped out of her grasp and she was left with only the mane to hold on to. Taking a track Emma could barely discern, the mare galloped faster than she had ever gone on a horse, made worse by the downward slope of the path. Emma could not remember the last time she had been afraid on a horse. Clutching desperately at the mane and using her voice in soothing, low tones, she tried to convince the horse to slow down.

Somewhere behind her, over the noise of her own horse's hooves and breathing, she thought she could hear the duke coming after them. The path was too narrow between the trees for him to overtake her and a silvery gleam of the river lay ahead. It was hard to maintain her seat and she was out of control, the mare frantic and oblivious to commands. Dodging overhanging branches, Emma leaned forward over Helen's back as far as she dared without endangering their balance. Eventually she would tire and slow her pace—if she did not bring herself down with a foot through the reins or drown them both in the river.

If the track had not taken a sharp turn, Emma might have been successful, but the horse skidded on the bend. The laws of nature were such that Emma could not hang on, and was thrown from Helen's back into the ice-cold river.

Chapter Eleven

ROWLEY SAW THE disaster coming long before it happened. He knew all the woodland paths like the back of his hand, and although this one had become overgrown from lack of use, he caught up to Miss Lancaster with relative ease. It was of little consequence, however, for there was not room for him to overtake her. She was an excellent rider but was powerless to stop the accident that befell. He watched in horror as the horse, normally so well mannered, took flight in a frenzied gallop down the slope. Reaching the sharp turn in the path ahead of her, the mare skidded, almost lost her hindquarters and careered around the tight bend, barely saving herself from going into the river.

Unfortunately, Miss Lancaster was not so lucky. Pulling his own horse to an abrupt stop, he leaped from the saddle and slid down the bank into the knee-deep water, trying not to panic as he waded toward Miss Lancaster. She appeared lifeless, not moving as the water forged a path around her. She had been thrown hard, but face up, fortunately. A pulse still beat at her neck, but she was unconscious. As soon as he reached her, he lifted her into his arms; her immobile form was weighed down by her heavy skirts. He placed her up onto the bank, and having climbed up after her, took her in his arms, willing her to live. In a moment of weakness, he held her close, whispering a prayer of desperation. He must get her back to the house and out of the wet clothing.

When he pulled back, green eyes were watching him.

"Miss Lancaster?" he whispered, unable to hide his relief.

She blinked a few times and began to shiver. "W-what happened?"

"Helen shied and took flight. You were thrown off her back into the river when she lost her footing around a sharp bend."

"Is, is, s, s, she hurt?" she asked through chattering teeth.

"I do not believe so. Hopefully she will return home on her own."

He pulled off his cape and placed it carefully around her. "Are you injured anywhere? My cursory inspection did not reveal any broken bones."

She shook her head. "I believe only the breath was knocked out of me and I am quite cold."

He nodded. "Oscar, come." The horse obeyed and lowered his head to his master, nudging him gently. Rowley gathered Miss Lancaster in his arms and carefully rose to his feet.

"Gracious, I can stand!" she insisted, putting her feet down.

"Then I lose my opportunity to show off my chivalry."

"I imagine you are permitted any number of opportunities in London," she said wryly, as he carried her to the horse.

Ignoring her remark, he lifted her into the saddle; when she tried to put her foot into the stirrup and take her seat, she slipped sidewards. His hand caught her bottom as he strove to catch her and a jolt of desire pulsed through him. Chagrined, he immediately thrust her back up as he would a hot coal and she landed aboard his horse with an "oof".

"I beg your pardon," he muttered.

She began to laugh as she half-sat, half-lay across the top of Oscar, who side-stepped at the violation of his dignity.

Miss Lancaster's body shook with hilarity—and cold, he imagined—and Rowley found that it was quite contagious. He found himself laughing with her and was quite helpless to move her from his vantage point. He could not remember when he had last laughed uncontrollably and when she finally calmed down, their eyes met and Rowley felt a strong urge to kiss her. If she had been beautiful before, then there was not an adequate word to describe her now. Her hair had come loose from its pins and was cascading around her in an array of damp curls. He leaned forward and almost brushed his lips across hers... and saw her eyes widen in fright. Idiot! He barely caught himself in time, and it took every ounce of restraint he possessed not to draw her down to him. She would freeze to death if they remained out in the elements much longer, and he was lost in thoughts of passion!

He broke their gaze, but at least a little flush had returned to her cheeks. "Can you sit up?"

"I believe so. I cannot quite feel my hands and feet."

He took her hands and placed them on the low pommel of his hunting saddle, then tried to hold her steady as she propped herself into a sitting position. He placed his own foot in the stirrup and managed to mount without embarrassing himself further, which was no small feat on a large hunter already bearing a passenger.

He reached around to take the reins and enclosed her body within his arms.

She stiffened immediately.

He thought he had moved beyond primitive, base urges long ago, but this did nothing to quell his growing attraction to her. If he ever doubted God had a sense of humor, this was more proof than necessary.

She was trying so very hard to sit properly and keep her distance, but he could not see a thing beyond her lovely, dark curls. Should he apologize for almost kissing her? Although he had not done so, the look on her face had only just stopped him in time.

"I am sincerely sorry you are forced to be in such close proximity to me, ma'am, but I do think it would be easier on us both if you relaxed. Oscar is sure-footed and well used to this ride, but I still prefer to see where I am going."

"Oh! I did not realize… I was trying not to… how would you like me to sit? I do not think I have shared a horse since I was ten years old on my father's lap."

He was definitely not her father.

"If you could lean back against my shoulder? I promise not to bite."

Gingerly, she put her head back against him and though he could see ahead, it was infinitely worse having her so near. He tried to imagine it was Eugenia he held in his arms, yet the scent of her, mixed with river water and weeds, was somehow intoxicating. He let out a little laugh.

"What is so humorous, Your Grace? My having to eat humble pie and accept your help? I am certain most ladies would give a limb to be in my position at this moment."

"Freezing to death?" he asked evasively, knowing very well what she meant.

"Can you tell me women have not been casting lures at you since you took the title?"

"I could have five chins and spittle with each word I speak, and I suppose I would be thought a good catch because of my wealth and title," he admitted. Yet she wanted nothing to do with him.

She laughed. "How I would hate that! Not knowing whether someone liked me for myself. Now I understand you a little better, I think."

"Do you?" He was annoyed by her presumption.

"I did not mean to be judgmental, but do you disagree that you hide away in your castle?"

Rowley was furious at her audacity, but why should he be surprised? She had always dared to speak her mind with him where very few would. They had arrived back in the home wood and the clearing to the house would soon come into view. He slowed the horse subconsciously.

She turned to look at him. "Have I offended you?" Her green eyes bored into him. He was unused to being examined so closely. He had always prided himself on honesty, but the things she asked were not things he wished to reflect on.

"You have not offended me. That would require me to be concerned by what people think."

"I am properly set down, then. I beg your pardon." She turned and sat straight again, refusing to lean back.

Fool! Why did he always say the wrong thing when with her? Oscar knew the way by now, anyway. Rowley was relieved to be back. They reached the front of the house and Samuels came running out to meet them.

"Thank goodness you were unharmed, miss. Helen returned without you and I was right concerned."

"His Grace has found me, thank you, Samuels."

Before Rowley thought better of it, he slid from the horse and pulled Miss Lancaster off into his arms, carrying her up the front steps. She let out a squeak of protest, but the door opened and he began to bark orders to send a hot bath, blankets, and warm drinks to Miss Lancaster's apartments.

After Mrs. Crow had taken over, he went back to his own chambers and removed his wet boots and clothing. He spent a long time staring into the fire, wondering what he should do about Miss Lancaster.

EMMA SAT IN front of the fire, letting her hair dry and wondering what had just happened. She had seen a side of the duke that she doubted he showed to many people. She hated to admit that perhaps he was not as detestable as she had thought him, and not near the villain she had painted him. It had been easier to hate him than to like him, and when his lips had hovered near hers, she had wanted him to kiss her. What did that say about her?

It was not as though they could ever have a proper courtship. It was obvious, when she asked him personal questions, that he at once became guarded. His cold, curt demeanor had returned in an instant, and Emma had wanted to scream. She had not been fishing for a position as a duchess—hardly—but he seemed to need friends. Although, when he had let down his guard and laughed, she had found him dangerously attractive. Shame on her for being a weakling!

A knock on the door jolted her out of her musings and Eugenia looked in. Her nose was red and swollen and she spoke as though her head were trapped in a bottle.

"Rowley told me what happened, you poor dear! You have come to no harm?"

"Only to my pride," Emma said, smiling in self-deprecation.

"Helen does not usually become disturbed so easily. I cannot think what came over her," Eugenia said apologetically, then blew her nose like a foghorn into her handkerchief.

"Are you feeling better?" Emma asked.

"I am, thank you. The fevers have gone, but I am left with this dreadful dripping red nose. I should be normal in another day or two. Will you come down for dinner? I think I will venture out of my apartments tonight or I will go mad," she remarked. "Mr. Tinsley will be joining us and he will not mind my red nose." She laughed. "He has seen me in much worse states! He and Rowley were the best of friends when we were younger. The boys all used to play horrid tricks on me, and I did my best to return the favor." She smiled wistfully.

"I suppose I will," Emma said, though she had been looking forward to a quiet dinner alone in her room. Mr. Tinsley was a pleasant gentleman and would hopefully keep the presence of the duke from feeling too awkward. She felt a little guilty for berating his lone existence, when he did have at least one friend here. A more unlikely pair of friends she could not imagine, but perhaps the duke had not always been so arrogant and unyielding.

Eugenia left to dress, and Emma forced herself to rise from her comfortable position in front of the fire. She winced with pain from the bruising she had sustained to her hip and back, and though her limbs were now pink, she did not know if she would ever feel warm again.

She selected one of the gowns the duke had given her, a violet-colored gown with intricate pleating of the skirts that caused it to swirl beautifully when she walked. The bodice was simple with a few pearls sewn into the embroidery, and it suited her coloring quite nicely. She was tempted to put on one of her caps again, after the duke had rebuffed her this afternoon, but instead she styled her hair simply with a riband around the top of her head, allowing her curls to fall down and, hopefully, hide some of her dark bruises. It would never do in London, but she wanted to torment the duke a little, if she were being honest. She knew enough to know that he desired her, and it made her want to look her best. Even though she knew nothing could ever come of it.

Emma went downstairs to join the others in the drawing room. It was strange and somehow intimate for just the four of them to be dining together.

"Miss Lancaster!" Mr. Tinsley exclaimed as he bowed, then strode toward her with his hands out. "What a breath of fresh air you are."

"Miss Lancaster." The duke inclined his head, though she noticed his expression of admiration before he mastered it and averted his gaze. "I do not believe you have met my grandmother, the Dowager Duchess of Knighton." His hand indicated an elderly, fragile-looking woman sitting in a chair by the fire. Emma had not noticed her at all.

She walked over to the lady and dropped into a deep curtsy. Her head came up and her eyes met a very shrewd gaze.

"Who are you?"

"This is my new companion, grandmother," Eugenia said, coming up to take Emma's arm as if they were old bosom bows.

"Lancaster..." The woman tried the name on her lips as though trying to remember. "Do I know that name?"

"My father was a country gentleman, but you may have known my mother, Mary Hamilton."

"Perth's daughter?"

"Yes, Your Grace."

"Is dinner ready yet? Has your cook forgotten we are in the country, not town?" she demanded, seemingly forgetting or not caring any more about Emma.

The duke came over to help his grandmother up out of the chair while Mr. Tinsley took the other arm, charming the lady.

"I am not an invalid to need both of you!" she scolded.

"Of course not," he soothed, "but why should Knighton get all of the beauty merely because he is the duke?"

"Excellent point," she said with a wink to Tinsley.

Emma could not help but smile. She hoped if she lived to be that age that she would still have some sense of humor.

"What is wrong with your nose, girl?" she asked Eugenia once they were seated, completely without tact in the way of the very old. "It looks as if a tomato is growing there."

"I have had a cold, Grandmother."

"Then stay away from me. A cold could kill me, you know."

The servants placed bowls of turtle soup before them and then laid out several more dishes *à la française*, and Emma was grateful for the distraction. She found herself seated next to the duke, and Mr. Tinsley had taken it upon himself to charm Lady Eugenia and the dowager.

"I am pleased to see you at dinner. I confess I did not expect it. Are you sure you are quite well?" the duke asked.

"I am rather sore and bruised, but I do think I will live to see another day."

"I am glad to hear it," he said dryly.

She cast him a sideways glance while taking a sip of her soup. Realizing her lapse, she set her spoon down hastily.

"Forgive me, Your Grace, I owe you a debt of gratitude for saving my life."

"I would hardly go as far as that. You might have awakened and saved yourself, but I am glad I was there to assist you."

"What has happened to you?" the dowager asked loudly across the table.

Emma was perplexed. Could the old woman overhear their muted exchange, or could she tell, just by looking at her, that Emma had fallen from a horse and been deeply chilled?

"You have a bruise on your face and your arm." The dowager pointed with her knife.

Subconsciously, Emma reached up to her cheek and felt the tender spot thinking it had been disguised.

"I fell from a horse this afternoon. I had the breath knocked out of me and His Grace fished me out of the river."

"You should ask Knighton to teach you how to ride better," she said in a loud, conspiratorial whisper.

Emma's gaze reluctantly flew toward the duke, who was also watching her. His brows raised at her with a twinkle in his eye and she looked away with a mixture of irritation and pleasure.

"I would be happy to assist you if Knighton is too occupied with estate matters," Tinsley teased.

"That reminds me of the time you had the breath knocked out of you," the duke surprised Emma by saying to Mr. Tinsley.

"For the love of God, please not that story!" Tinsley laughed.

Knighton's face took on a devilish gleam and he set his fork down. "You can imagine, Miss Lancaster, how many scrapes five boys got into."

"And a girl," Eugenia protested.

"And, on occasion, a girl. However, you were not yet born for this one." He took a sip of his wine and smiled at Tinsley. "We were playing a game of rounders, and Tinsley decided to see how hard he could hit the ball, and drove it straight into my nose. You might have noticed the little bump. I was not born with it." The duke tapped gently with his forefinger on the little bit of his nose that was crooked. It was the only noticeable imperfection Emma had found, yet in her opinion it made him more handsome.

"That is courtesy of our Mr. Tinsley here."

Emma turned to look at Tinsley, who was smiling hugely. "Just wait, it becomes more flattering to me, if you can imagine."

The dowager appeared to be paying them no mind, attacking her stuffed quail with deep concentration.

"I was a little angry." Tinsley cleared his throat loudly.

"And hurt," the duke added, giving his friend a look of recrimination. "So I decided I would hit one harder, except I missed his nose and hit him in the chest. It knocked him over and I thought I had killed him."

"He knocked the air out of me and I passed out," Tinsley explained.

"Trying to be helpful, my brothers and I began to beat on his chest, and poor Edmund pushed on his stomach so hard that Tinsley relieved himself."

The duke and Tinsley began to laugh so hard that they were shaking with mirth.

Emma looked at Eugenia, who was also laughing but looked perplexed.

When they had quieted somewhat, she said, "I thought we were not supposed to speak of such things, Rowley."

Emma had the urge to tell her to hush, that she rather enjoyed seeing the duke smile, but Eugenia was correct. Besides, seeing the Duke smile did not help her resolution to dislike him.

The duke and Tinsley tried to bite back their smiles. "Of course, we would not do so in Society, but this is a family dinner," he answered.

"I have a better story than that," the dowager chimed in, astonishing Emma.

"Grandmother, no."

"I forget how old he was, but he was still in short trousers. We were having a house party, which we used to do often in those days," she said with a knowing glance at the duke. "He was of a height to come to most people's waists. We were having a garden party that afternoon, and the poor boy felt neglected."

"It seems I am to have no dignity left at all this night," he muttered.

"What did he do?" Eugenia asked eagerly.

The old dowager cast a glance at the duke, and then looked back to Eugenia. "He bit the Countess of Sutherland on the behind." She hit her hand on the table and cackled.

"You did not!"

The duke had a slight flush across his cheeks, but smiled. "I did, and I do not regret it. She is still a shrew. However, I could not sit down for a week after that."

They all laughed and settled into the final course with good humor while they ate their pudding.

"Take me into the drawing room, boy," the dowager said to Tinsley at length. "You can have your port in there."

"It would be my pleasure," Tinsley said and jumped to assist her from her chair. Eugenia was on her other side before the duke or Emma could help.

Emma bumped into the duke as they were all hurrying to assist the dowager and fell against his chest. She was very conscious of his hard body and his hands on her, and what it did to her breathing. Before she thought better of it, she looked up and saw it was having a similar effect on him. His pupils had darkened and he was looking at her as if he would feast on her next.

She noticed a speck of food on his chin and felt the strange desire to lick it off. She then had to fight back the urge to giggle at the image.

His hands tightened on her instead of releasing her. "What is it?"

She reached up and wiped off the offending piece of cream, and held out her finger to show him.

For a moment, they both stood there, and she thought he might kiss her. The longer he waited, the more she wanted him to do so, but they could not stay in there forever, and it would be a monumental mistake.

"You missed a spot," she whispered impishly.

To her great surprise, he bent over to her finger and licked it off—and then raised his brows seductively.

"So I did."

Releasing her, he held out his arm to escort her to the drawing room, leaving her wits muddled and her insides wishing for more.

Chapter Twelve

Eugenia was improved, but did not wish to attend church with a red, swollen nose. No one would hear the sermon over her nose trumpeting, she said. That left Rowley alone in the carriage with Miss Lancaster. He had bungled avoiding her, and had not been able to stop thinking about her since he had held her in his arms. The groom had come to tell him she had gone out alone and he had felt the need to make sure she was not harmed. What if he had not been there? He could not bring himself to think on it. Then he had done the unthinkable last night and flirted in the most regrettable lapse of decorum. He had been unable to sleep with thoughts of her. He should not desire his sister's governess. He knew he should apologize, but felt vexed with her all the same.

Wearing her new clothing today, a fitted, dark brown wool walking outfit, she looked every bit the lady, especially now that she had set aside those horrid caps. A jaunty brown chapeau de crêpe with two blue feathers sat at an angle atop her head, with a few curls hanging down to hide her bruises.

"Good morning, Your Grace," she said bobbing him a curtsy.

He bowed in return. "I trust my sister is well?" He had already been to see her, in fact, but he could think of little else to say since Eugenia was the link between them. "And you are suffering no ill effects from yesterday?"

"Other than feeling as though I was thrown from my horse, I am quite well, thank you."

Thankfully, the church was just beyond the gates of the Grange, for the carriage felt too small with both of them in it. Silence had never bothered him before, so why did it with her? He was conscious of her scent, which he still could not identify. It was not something he could just ask her. It must be something exotic because he would have recognized one of the more usual fragrances like roses or violets or lilies.

"Are you feeling quite well, Your Grace?" Miss Lancaster asked.

"I believe so," he answered, somewhat befuddled.

"You were snuffling as though you needed to sneeze," she explained.

If he were younger he would have blushed. How undignified! "Forgive me, I was trying to place your scent. It eludes me."

"Jasmine with a hint of something else I am afraid I cannot name. I apologize if it is too strong. I will take more care next time." She looked chagrined.

"Not at all. I find it quite pleasant." Dear God, let them be at the church soon. He was making a fool of himself.

When they arrived and he handed her down, he realized there was no Eugenia to sit between them. He was again tortured by her nearness and her sweet soprano voice which kept him from concentrating on the vicar's words. He found himself nervously tapping his hand and then his foot, and he was growing furious with himself. He really must convince Edmund to take the living here, for Vicar Richards was rambling and had been speaking for half an hour with no sign of reprieve.

"Are you certain you are feeling quite the thing, Your Grace?" Miss Lancaster leaned over and whispered in his ear, sending shivers down his spine. He was going to Hell, he was certain. Were he not a duke, he would be running down the nave and out of the door faster than his hunter could take him. This would never do.

He turned and forced a smile at her. "Yes, I am quite well, I assure you." Her mossy eyes were looking into his, searching to see if he told the truth. She must be some kind of witch, for they felt as though they were searing a path through his head.

At last, the keys on the organ bellowed out a hymn and he stood and held out his hand to assist her. Heat bored through his hand and he squeezed hers harder than he intended.

"I beg your pardon," he said, then looked at the figure of Christ at the top of the church for help. He roared out the hymn to drown out his wayward thoughts.

When the service had at last finished, he offered Miss Lancaster his arm as he would have done to Eugenia. He did not know why. It only served to make the situation more awkward. They greeted all of the tenants and villagers as they walked down the aisle, and she played her part without batting an eyelid. In fact, she seemed to know many of these people. He tried to listen to her with one ear while carrying on his own conversations.

She let go of his arm and knelt down to speak with a little girl. She was holding up her hand for Miss Lancaster's perusal.

"It looks much better, Miss Daisy!" she exclaimed.

The child's mother smiled shyly. "We cannot thank you enough, Miss Lancaster. She didn't cry or complain after that poultice you made her. I was afraid she would lose her hand, how poorly it were looking afore you helped us."

"I am delighted it worked. My father always swore by it with his horses."

They moved on out of the church and another family, with a new baby in the mother's arms, came to show her their offspring.

She cooed and admired the baby and even took it in her arms for a few minutes. A strange image of her with his babe in her arms flashed before his vision and he had to shake his head. Perhaps he was coming down with something.

She handed the infant back to its mother.

"Thank you for the beautiful gown and blanket. I will never forget it," the young mother said, smiling at Miss Lancaster as though she were the queen herself.

He stood still, waiting for her. Had she and Eugenia been visiting the tenants unbeknownst to him? They must have done.

"Your Grace, I am convinced something is wrong. I shall send for the doctor when we reach the house." Miss Lancaster was frowning her concern for him.

She raised her hand as if to feel his forehead, but she stopped herself. No one had done such a thing since his nurse when he was in short coats. He bit back a smile and handed her into the waiting carriage.

"That will not be necessary. I have a lot on my mind today. Perhaps I should have stayed at home."

She looked unconvinced but said no more.

"Do you miss your family, Miss Lancaster?"

For a moment, he thought she would not answer.

"I have Lady Eugenia for company, but nothing has been the same since my mother died. I am sensible, sir. I must learn to be content wherever I am. And I am grateful for the home I have."

"Do you ever long for more?" Why had he asked that? It was irrelevant. He almost hoped she would not answer.

"I once had dreams, but they died with my mother. There is no point in dwelling on it. We do not all get a storybook ending."

"If there is something I can do to make your time here more pleasant, please let me know. Aunt Hambridge still harbors hope for your marriage prospects, you know."

She smiled as though she had forgotten she was with him, and she really was beautiful. She was wearing a bonnet, but now that he could picture the whole of her, it did not bother him.

"You and I both know that cannot happen now," she answered, looking down at her gloved hands.

"I know nothing of the sort."

Her eyes flashed at him but she quickly looked out of the window.

"What of yourself?" she asked boldly. "I would suppose you would be very sought after on the marriage mart."

He was irritated by the question, but it was only fair. He had pried into her personal business.

"I have three heirs, Miss Lancaster, and I do not find marriage a tenable prospect. Contrary to my class' propensity for mercenary unions, I do not relish being united to someone for life without some measure of affection. I see I have surprised you." She had cast one of those suspicious glances at him. Those emerald eyes spoke volumes without a word uttered.

"A little," she confessed.

"It is difficult to find true love matches for one in my position. I had thought, perhaps once, when I was younger…" He did not finish the statement. What was it about her that made him reveal his thoughts to her? He never did such a thing with anyone except, perhaps, on occasion, Edmund.

She looked over to him. "What happened?"

"I was mistaken."

She nodded her head as though she understood. Perhaps she did. Perhaps she had also lost a love when her family's fortunes were lost.

They drove back to the Grange in silence; she stared out of the window and he stared at her.

It had been weeks since he had wondered at her familiarity and she seemed to have settled in here nicely. Yet now, looking at her, he was struck with the familiar feeling again. Did it matter?

"It seems there is a rider at the front door."

Rowley strained to look and indeed there was a horse and a messenger waiting at his door. Something must be wrong. The only other times he could recall such an occurrence was when there was an emergency. One did not send a message post on a Sunday otherwise.

Rowley jumped from the carriage before it stopped moving and the messenger met him halfway down the steps.

"Has no one invited you in?" he asked the young man.

"Your Grace?" the rider asked, ignoring his question.

"Yes, it is I."

He handed him a letter. "I was instructed to see it in your hands personally."

"Now you have done. Please take a meal and rest your horse in my stables. My man will see you paid before you leave."

"Thank you, Your Grace." The messenger bowed and took his horse around the back of the house.

Miss Lancaster was standing off to the side. He glanced up at her before opening the seal. It was Edmund's handwriting.

Heath has been shot. Situation is dire. Come at once.

Edmund

He looked up to see Miss Lancaster was now standing before him. "Sir, is there something I can do?"

"My brother has been shot. I must go to London at once. Will you take care of Eugenia?"

"Of course. Is there anything I can do for you?"

Rowley could not remember the last time anyone had asked him that.

"No, I thank you." He gave her one long, assessing look before hurrying into the house, with a sinking feeling, to prepare to leave. What had Heath done now?

EMMA WATCHED HIM ride away within the hour and began to pace about the room.

She felt so very conflicted. She would have wished herself anywhere other than in a tête-à-tête with the duke, because he had become human and she had felt her hatred abate toward him. Was that a good thing? She could not say. There was really little benefit to holding on to her anger, but she did not want to like him. To make that even more difficult, when he had received news of his brother, she had seen the raw pain on his face before he masked it.

Take care of Eugenia, he had asked. What was she to do? *Lord Heath had got what he deserved*, she thought spitefully.

She made her way upstairs to break the news to her charge. She wished she had thought to ask the duke what his wishes were.

Emma heard crying when she approached Eugenia's door. She knocked lightly but opened the door and peered inside. The girl was weeping, and was frantically directing her maid to pack a portmanteau. Emma supposed that answered the question.

"Emma! Have you heard?"

She gave a slight nod. It would be best for Eugenia to tell her herself. It did not take long.

"Heath has been shot in another one of those dreadful duels, I gather!"

"I gather your brother informed you before he left?"

"Yes, and we must follow post haste! I have ordered the carriage to be ready in an hour. You will come with me, will you not?"

"The duke approves of our going? He said nothing to me."

"He did not argue when I said we would follow."

Emma had suspected Lady Eugenia would wish to run to her brother's side. The duke had not expressly forbidden it, and it was not very long until the Christmas holiday. Would they help or be a hindrance? She wished she knew. It would be a great risk, going there, but perhaps she could stay out of the way and wear her cap. If it were her brother who had been shot, she would want to be there. If only the duke had made his wishes clear on the matter before he left!

"If it is your wish. I would not keep you from your brother."

"I knew you would say yes!" She threw her arms around Emma, and began to sob. Emma hugged the girl back, knowing how much human touch—kind human touch—had meant to her when her mother had died, although there had been precious little of it. If nothing else, she would try to provide that for this girl.

Perhaps it would be best if they stayed with Lady Hambridge and visited each day. If Lord Heath were indeed dying, it would be no place for Eugenia. They could only go to London and see how things stood. He might not survive until they arrived.

"Thank you, Emma. I cannot tell you the last time anyone held me like that."

The girl cried a while longer and Emma held her and stroked the hair from her face.

"I must see to my own packing if we are to be off within the hour," Emma said as Eugenia's tears eased.

"I have already asked Sadie to do it for you," Eugenia said coyly. "I knew you would not fail me."

Emma shook her head in disbelief. "Then I will ask Cook to pack a hamper for our journey. The less we have to stop, the sooner we will be there." Nevertheless, Emma had to go to her room and compose herself. She wanted to retch. Not only was she going back to London, but to the house of the person who had caused so much of her grief. Her trunk was packed, but she opened her drawers to find her caps still there.

"That will never do." She stuffed them, and a few other items, into the trunk as the footmen arrived to carry them downstairs.

She hurried down to Cook who had already anticipated their needs. It seemed there was nothing left but to get inside the carriage. She began to tremble with fear, which was ridiculous. If the worst happened and Lord Heath lived to recognize her, she would simply have to find another position. She was not destitute, with her small competence from her mother, but it was not enough with which to live on her own. It would not do to dwell on it any longer.

She made her way outside to let the cold brisk air calm her. However, she had no sooner entered the shrubbery than a wave of queasiness assailed her, and she had to rush to be sick in one of the hedges and pray no one had seen her foolishness. Why could her heart always overrule her head in these matters?

Once inside the carriage, Emma settled into the corner for a long, weary ride, even though the plush blue velvet curtains and warm bricks at her feet now felt nice. Sunday travel was frowned upon, but in such an emergency, allowances had to be made. It also meant the roads would be free of traffic and they would hopefully make good time.

"This is not how I had hoped to go to London," Eugenia said softly. Emma could barely hear her over the rattling of the carriage, despite the fact that this was the nicest, most well-sprung conveyance she had ever been inside.

"I know, my dear. It may not be the festive season everyone had wished for, but at least you will be there together."

"Tell me about your family," she said. "We have a very long trip and you have never spoken of them."

"There is not much to say. My mother died and, with her, my entire family."

"They all died?" The girl's eyes were wide with pity.

"Forgive me, I spoke poorly. When my mother died, my family fell apart. My father did not wish to live without her and made some poor financial choices." *To say the least.* "My oldest brother was unable to recover the losses and was forced to leave for America to try his hand there."

"Is he doing well? I would miss him horribly!"

"I do miss him." She blamed herself, as much as her father, for

John leaving. If it had not been for defending her honor, he might have been able to recover the good name of their stables. "He is doing well. I had a letter from him; he married a wealthy merchant's daughter and is running a shipping business with his father-in-law."

"I hope he will be able to visit you. Perhaps he will arrive one day on one of his ships," Eugenia said with her youthful idealism.

"I should like to visit America one day." Very soon it might be her only option.

"So you have no family here in England?"

"No. My sister is in northern Scotland, and my other brother is fighting in the peninsular wars, but I do not know when, or if, I shall see him either."

"Felix is also there. I shall write to him about your brother."

Emma had to smile. There was once a time when she had thought she could fix everything, but that was before she had tried and failed.

"I hope we arrive and find Heath is recovered and it was not serious. I should be a little sad not to see anything of London whilst we are there. That is a horrid thing for me to say. Of course I would not think such things if he were to..." She swallowed hard, unable to say the word.

"Let us not think of it. You should rest. You are still recovering from your cold."

And Emma did not wish to think about Lord Heath. If she did, her thoughts would not be kind when she should be praying for his soul.

Eugenia was asleep within minutes. Emma envied her, for she did not think sleep would be within her grasp until they left London again.

Chapter Thirteen

ROWLEY WAS BEYOND weary when he arrived in London. He had only stopped to change horses and grab quick meals. The wind had been in his face for most of the way, intermixed with sleeting rain. It felt like a foreboding of things to come. His mood was sour and he needed to sleep for at least a day, but he knew he must be strong for the family, now more than ever. A groom ran out to take his horse, and Quincy opened the door for him. He climbed the steps to the grand, grey stone house his grandfather had had built over fifty years before. The house was not shrouded in black, at least, he noted.

"Welcome, Your Grace. There is a fire in the study. Shall I send for some tea or food?"

"Something warm would be very welcome, Quincy." He walked into the study and began to thaw his hands before the fire. When the butler returned with a steaming bowl of stew and some fresh bread, he asked how his brother did.

"What can you tell me about Lord Heath?

The butler hesitated for a long time.

"I wish to hear it all. Do not keep anything from me."

"Yes, Your Grace. There was a duel, as you know. Lord Heath deloped into the air, but his opponent did no such gentlemanly thing. He hit him in the shoulder. Who knows where his aim was? He claims he meant to wing him only."

"And how is he?"

The butler hesitated again and then spoke. "He is burning with fever, Your Grace. Lord Edmund has not left his side and the doctor has been here as much as he can."

Rowley sighed. When would Heath ever learn? *He may not have the chance.* He dismissed Quincy and made his way up to the chambers when he had finished eating.

Edmund was by Heath's side, sleeping in a chair. If Rowley thought he was weary, his brother looked haggard with his hair disheveled and his open shirt wrinkled. The room reeked of the sick bed. If he'd had any question of how ill his brother was, there was no mistaking it now. The always vital Heath was unrecognizable. His skin was pale and clammy, and he shook with fever as he gasped for ragged breaths. Wet cloths were on his forehead and his neck; his arm and chest were wrapped in bandages that were soaked through with some putrid substance. Rowley had to fight back a wave of nausea at the smell.

Guilt overwhelmed him, as it always did when something went wrong with one of his siblings. He had been the parental figure for them all since their parents had died, but Heath had been old enough that he had never allowed Rowley to advise or correct him. Heath had suffered most when they lost their parents. Rowley did not know what else he could have done. He had not coddled him—how could he? Heath had his own income from their mother's legacy and he did as he pleased. If only he'd had some direction, perhaps he would not have fallen into this debauched lifestyle that was literally killing him. If he lived, something would have to be done.

"Rowley, is that you?" Edmund asked through a yawn.

"Yes, I am here."

Edmund sat up and stretched.

"You may sleep in your own bed tonight. You look as though you have slept here for days. How long has it been?"

"A week? I have lost all sense of time."

"And what does Dr. Evans think?"

Edmund's face fell. He shook his head. "It all depends on the fever. The bullet hit the lung and the doctor thinks part of it has collapsed. He will never be the same again, even if he recovers."

"When was the last time the bandage was changed?" Rowley asked, eyeing the offending object with distaste.

"Two hours ago when Dr. Evans was here. They soak through again almost immediately."

"We need someone here with the knowledge to do this. I will ask him if he knows of a nurse who can stay with him. You will exhaust yourself if you have not already."

"Mrs. Potts has been helping. I cannot claim pure martyrdom here." Edmund smiled wearily.

"I hope she was worth it," Rowley said caustically to his unconscious brother.

"I do not know the details, only rumors. I thought he was making an effort to reform himself. He was the one who alerted me to Miss Thatcher's plight." Edmund shook his head.

Rowley raised his brows in surprise. "What are the rumors? Who is responsible for this?"

"Lord Emerson. It was he who thought to misuse Miss Thatcher."

"And Heath saved her?"

"And was shot for his good deeds. For all our brother's faults, I have never known him to consort with innocents. He said it made him think of our little sister."

Rowley closed his eyes. This was why he wanted to keep Eugenia safe at the Grange. London was full of rakes and cutthroats who thought nothing of hurting those less powerful than them.

"Has Emerson fled?"

"I do not know for certain. I would think he would be in hiding, waiting to see the outcome. He is a very nasty fellow, Rowley. I do not know what Heath was thinking of, to become involved with him. For he must have been, to know of Miss Thatcher."

Rowley looked at his brother fighting for his life.

"I have my suspicions about Lord Emerson. It is not the first time his name has been mentioned in my dealings with the doves. I strongly suspect he is behind several of the more infamous brothels where the girls are treated violently." Edmund shuddered.

Rowley felt sick thinking about it, but he had no illusions that such things did not take place. But how involved was Heath?

"Have you heard his name associated with any of these places?" Rowley looked searchingly at Edmund for any sign of prevarication. If anything was to be done, he must know the whole of it.

Edmund hesitated and let out a heavy sigh. "Not directly, but indirectly, yes. I think it had gone too far for him and he was trying to stop it."

"So Emerson intended to send him a message or permanently end Heath's interference?"

"Quite possibly."

"Help me change this bandage and then you will go and sleep. I will wake you if anything changes." Edmund did not argue but nodded.

They lifted Heath in order to unwind the bandage. Rowley had never felt a person so hot. It did not look good for Heath. The best thing he had in his favor was his stubbornness, and Rowley could only hope that would see him through.

He was not prepared for the sight of the wound. Copious amounts of yellow, putrid pus was oozing out of a gaping hole in his brother's chest. He had to fight back the urge to retch.

"It is very bad." Edmund stated the obvious. "It was why I sent for you. Frankly, I am surprised he has survived this long. It defies logic."

"Which sums up our brother's existence." Rowley looked for some cloths with which to clean away the infection. He and Edmund worked to wipe it away but it seemed to multiply as they did so.

"Is there no ointment or basilicum to put over the wound? My knowledge is very limited, but I at least know something must be done to fight the infection."

"I have no idea what the doctor is using," Edmund admitted.

Rowley frowned and thought of Miss Lancaster's poultice. Would such a thing work on a wound so severe? He had seen them used on horses, but he had no idea what went in them. He felt like an incompetent fool.

The head groom at the Grange would know, but he did not know if one of the grooms here would. He pulled on the cord and rang for Mrs. Potts. If nothing else, basilicum would have to do for now.

Mrs. Potts fetched the basilicum powder and Edmund and Rowley did their poor yet best imitation of a proper bandage. Edmund left to get some much-needed sleep, and Rowley lowered his weary bones into the chair next to the bed. He leaned his forearms over the edge and watched his brother struggle for life. It was such a waste of a beautiful human being. Rowley could do little to help him at this point. A duke was not used to feeling helpless. Rarely did he feel the need to beg the Almighty for an intervention, but that seemed to be his last hope.

Again his thoughts turned to Miss Lancaster and he wished she were here. Why did thoughts of her pervade even in such a dreadful moment? He secretly hoped she agreed to bring Eugenia, even though he had left it to her discretion. She was full of good sense and it comforted him to know Eugenia was in her hands. Could she help Heath? Rowley did not know, and he was very much afraid for the first time he could remember since he learned of his father's death. He leaned his head down on his hands and wept.

THEY TRAVELED FOR long days and nights since they had a favorable moon and good traveling conditions, but Emma had never been so glad to arrive at a destination, even if it was London. Immediately she felt exposed, though no one could possibly recognize her or expect her to be at the Knighton townhouse. She planned to keep it that way and stay as far away from Lord Heath as possible. The duke had not recognized her, yet Lord Heath might.

When they entered the house, the duke came immediately to greet them and seemed genuinely pleased they were there.

"How is he?" Eugenia asked with proper concern.

The duke led them into a small, but cozy study off the entrance hall, where a fire was roaring in the grate.

"He is not well, I am afraid. His wound is infected and he has been raging with fever since before I arrived. If the infection is not controlled soon, I fear we will lose him."

"No!" Eugenia shouted, to then immediately place her hands over her mouth.

"It is why I wish to tell you now, so you may be prepared when you see him. You must be able to remain calm in his presence. Do you understand?"

Emma felt like an intruder. She suddenly regretted the ill-will she bore the duke. She would retire to her quarters and remain out of sight unless they called for her.

"Miss Lancaster, could I trouble you greatly?" the duke asked, his eyes pleading. He looked so vulnerable, Emma found her heart softening toward him. It was much harder to see someone as a villain when they were not a real person to you.

"How may I help you, Your Grace?" she asked, though she was afraid of his answer. Though she had known him but a short time, she knew he would not ask a favor of her lightly.

"Would you please look at my brother's wound?"

She was not certain she had heard correctly. Surely he could not be asking for her to look upon Lord Heath in a medical capacity? He, who had access to the best physicians money could buy? She could not help staring in astonishment.

"Dr. Evans does not know what else he can do for my brother. He thinks ill humors must be cleansed from the inside, outwards. I remember, at church last week, you had applied a poultice to a little girl's wound. I was hoping you could try the same for Heath. Please, Miss Lancaster. I am desperate."

She shook her head. "I do not know what to say. I have no medical training and a burn on a hand is a different proposition from a gunshot wound, your Grace."

"Would you please try? I do not think any harm can be done to him at this juncture, if that is what you fear."

She could not tell him what she was truly afraid of, but if Lord Heath was as ill as it sounded, his last concern would be an actress who had refused to be his mistress.

She let out a deep breath. "If it is your wish I will try."

The look of relief on his face was palpable. Emma could not fathom how there was no one else in his stables who could make a poultice.

"Let me take you to see it. I must warn you, his situation is very dire."

"I understand."

They walked up a curved mahogany staircase, a plush, puce-colored carpet underfoot. A chill draught wafted through the hall from the entrance below, sending chills up her spine. A strong sense of foreboding took hold, which did not cease when she entered the sickroom. She had nursed her mother, and to some extent her father, but she was ill-prepared for such a sight.

The stench of disease assailed her as she crossed the threshold. His long limbs were twisted in the bed sheets, evidence of the raging fever he had been fighting. His skin was pale and covered in a sheen of sweat. His eyes had rolled back into an unconscious stupor and his mouth hung open, trying to capture the elusive deep breath he was gasping for. The scene made her feel close to suffocating.

Could this be the same person who had accosted her in the green room of the theatre? The very same gentleman who had been so vital and robust? She had felt small and fragile next to his overwhelming masculinity.

Emma forced her gaze away, past the body, beyond the tables littered with tisanes, tinctures and bandages, to Mrs. Potts, whom the duke was addressing.

"Mrs. Potts, this is Miss Lancaster. She is Lady Hambridge's god-daughter and has been so gracious as to help Eugenia prepare for her come out."

Mrs. Potts bobbed a curtsy. "I am pleased to meet you, miss."

Emma found it interesting, the way the duke had introduced her. He had not named her as governess or companion, which would have marked her immediately as a paid servant, but neither did she have a chaperone herself, a circumstance that would confuse the housekeeper. Emma smiled at her, and returned the woman's curtsy.

"I have asked Miss Lancaster to look in on Lord Heath. She has some experience with wounds. Would you help me remove his bandage so she may examine it?"

"Of course, Your Grace. We have been changing it every two hours."

The stench got worse when the bandage came off, which Emma had not thought possible. She had to breathe through her mouth to control her revulsion. Lord Heath groaned a little at the movement, which meant he was not fully unconscious as she had thought. The wound immediately began draining pus, and Emma knew the situation was dire. How long had it been like this?

"What do you think, Miss Lancaster?" the duke asked gravely.

"I have never seen anything suppurate so badly," she answered candidly. "Have you any Epsom salt? My father used it to draw out infection when applied with heat. I can try to make a poultice similar to the one I used with the little girl. Would you show me to your still-room?" she asked the housekeeper.

Mrs. Potts nodded and bobbed a curtsy to the duke. Emma cast a glance at him and wished she had not. The look of gratefulness he gave her made him seem human and it was best if he remained the cold, unfeeling man she had thought him.

She turned and followed the housekeeper down into the room where herbs were stored, next to the kitchens, thinking the whole time that she hoped the duke's faith in her was not grossly misplaced, as she feared it was.

Mrs. Potts secured some Epsom salt from one of the grooms. The stable was where Emma had learned to use the commodity, and she begin sorting through the herbs, in the hopes that somehow she could find something with which to perform a miracle. She selected ginger, mustard powder, flower of sulfur and garlic, then ground them into a paste with some honey. She really thought her success with the little girl had been from cleaning the wound and little else. This was far beyond her healing powers, but she would try nevertheless.

CHAPTER FOURTEEN

MISS LANCASTER BEGAN taking turns sitting with Heath and helping to nurse him. She also prepared poultices of Epsom salts, alternating them with herbs.

They smelled almost as bad as the wound itself, and Rowley had to open the window for some fresh, cold air. He was helpless to do anything for Heath save menial labor, so that was what he did. He took shifts with Miss Lancaster, Mrs. Potts and Edmund. Eugenia flew into hysterics at the sight of Heath.

The first day after Miss Lancaster's poultices were applied was the most wretched. The wound seemed to worsen, and Heath continued to burn with fever and suffer violent convulsions. All of them hovered nearby, as if waiting for death to finally take him, but no one wanted to stop. They changed dressings, gave ice baths, and kept busy as though it would make a difference. Rowley was not certain any of it was helping.

He decided to stay with Heath that night and wondered if he somehow sensed it would be his brother's last. He sent everyone else to bed, then sat in the chair beside Heath and watched him, although he did not really see him. The world stood still. Nothing else mattered except for Heath and saving him. Trying to envision life without his brother… it was impossible not to dwell on what he should have done better as a parental figure. Rowley did not think Heath envied his own position as duke—who, in their right mind, would? Yet, there had always been some underlying tension and resentment, Rowley could not deny. None of that mattered now. If he could give his own life to save his brother, he would.

"Your Grace, Dr. Evans is here," Quincy said, causing Rowley to jump from his awkward position and flinched at his wrenched neck. It was light; he had obviously fallen asleep.

"Thank you, Quincy. Please show him upstairs." Rowley stood and stretched and went over to the basin to splash his face with cold water before the doctor entered the room.

"Good morning, Dr. Evans. I am anxious to see how you think he is doing."

"The fact that he is still alive after a week is encouraging. Most people would not have been strong enough to fight for so long." Dr. Evans entered the room and placed his bag on the bed next to Heath. He was frowning as he removed the bandage.

"He is also very, very stubborn," Rowley remarked as he watched the doctor closely.

"What is this? Some kind of stable medicine?"

Rowley noticed that, to his amateur eye, the wound looked improved and Heath's breathing was less labored.

"I asked a friend with some knowledge of treating wounds to try a poultice."

"I trained at the Edinburgh School of Medicine, Your Grace."

"Nothing that was done interfered with the medicines you prescribed. In fact, I would dare to say my brother has improved since the poultices were applied."

The doctor scowled, but refrained from comment. To argue with Rowley could be professional suicide. He placed his stethoscope over Heath's lungs and performed a cursory examination.

"I agree he has improved a little. I will not redress the wound since your *friend* appears to be in charge of that. I will call again in the morning, unless you no longer desire my services?" How much bile had the doctor had to swallow to admit his brother to be improved? The man was clearly offended, but Rowley had no patience with Dr. Evan's tender feelings.

"Heath is far from well, sir. We will see you when next you call."

The doctor bowed. "I will show myself out."

Miss Lancaster and Eugenia had slipped into the room. Rowley did not know how much the former had heard.

"He thinks much of his consequence," he remarked with a small smile as his eyes met Miss Lancaster's.

"Was he very angry?" Miss Lancaster asked. She walked to Heath's bedside and looked at the wound.

"He was not pleased," he remarked. "Whether from our interference or from your providing superior care, I could not venture to say."

Eugenia had pulled the handkerchief from her sleeve and was covering her nose. "What is that smell? Please make it stop."

"It is his wound," Rowley snapped. "You had better leave, Eugenia. The sick room is no place for hysterics."

She ran from the room and he shared a look of commiseration with Miss Lancaster.

"What is your opinion, Miss Lancaster?" he asked, noticing she was surveying Heath's wound.

"To my untrained eye, sir, it appears to be improving." She moved her hand to feel his brother's forehead and hesitated before placing the back of her hand against it. "He feels cooler, although not completely normal. What would you like me to do, Your Grace?"

"Continue, please." They were standing across the bed from one another, but he still felt her presence surrounding him. "If he lives, it will be thanks to you."

She nodded before biting her lower lip and looking down.

Before thinking better of it, he reached across the bed and placed his hand on hers. Immediately, he felt warmth radiate up his arm from where he touched her, and was surprised by the sensation at a time like this. He felt very drawn to this woman. Perhaps it was a product of the situation and his vulnerable emotional state.

"My family is indebted to you, Miss Lancaster."

She shook her head and pulled her arm away. "I have done very little. He is far from safe yet, Your Grace. I will continue plying the poultices, and I believe we should also continue with the saline draughts Dr. Evans prescribed."

"Of course."

She busied herself with the paste of herbs she had brought with her, and set about rinsing and cleaning the wound before applying the poultice. She seemed to be avoiding eye contact with him; he had the distinct feeling she wished him elsewhere. That grated on his nerves. Never before had he concerned himself with whether anyone liked him or not, but she was part of his household and he was giving her a home.

"Does my presence disturb you, Miss Lancaster?" he blurted out, though he knew it was not a wise choice. Being wise would have been taking more time to observe and get to know her better. Instead, he had avoided her because of his attraction to her.

She looked at him with those wide, green eyes. Her hair had been pulled back into a severe knot, he noticed, but at least she was not wearing a hideous cap. She was not going to answer him, and he felt all of the awkwardness of a teenage boy, but his training and age had taught him to endure such circumstances. He watched her and waited.

"It does not disturb me, Your Grace," she said quietly.

"But you wish I were not here?" He could not let it pass.

She busied herself in finishing the bandage and he lifted Heath up so she could wrap it around his shoulders and back. She placed another cool cloth on his brother's brow and pulled the covers up and tucked him in.

"May we speak more in my study?" he asked, and then wished he had not. The look of panic that crossed her face was not his intention at all. He stepped outside and directed one of the footmen to stay with Heath until he could send Lord Edmund or Mrs. Potts to relieve him.

He waited for Miss Lancaster to proceed him and followed her down the stairs into his study. Her back was ramrod straight, and her chin was high. How was he to extricate himself from this mess? He had only meant to reassure her and perhaps become better acquainted.

As he followed her inside, he signaled for Quincy to send for coffee. Perhaps that would show her he meant no harm.

He closed the door and held out a hand for her to sit down, then clasped his hands behind his back and walked back and forth in front of the fire.

"Miss Lancaster, I wish all members of my household to be comfortable."

"I am not uncomfortable here, Your Grace."

He raised his eyebrows in disbelief.

"Well, perhaps a little, but the situation is unusual, you must admit."

"I will allow that," he said, feeling a small smile intrude upon the gravity of the situation. He was normally more reserved. "I have informed my Aunt Hambridge that we are in Town. She does not think it appropriate for you to be here unchaperoned."

"The arrangements are no different from in the country," Miss Lancaster argued. "I am now a servant; she must be made to understand that."

"On this, she will not be moved. She very much thinks it her duty to see you married. Perhaps it is the presence of Heath that worries her. I cannot say that is not a concern without merit; however, he is in no condition to harass you at present."

Something in her face changed. Had it been the mention of Heath? It must have been.

"Would you be more comfortable at your godmother's house? I do not know how long he will be here."

"For now, I am in no danger, as you say. I appreciate your consideration, Your Grace."

He inclined his head as there was a knock on the door.

"Enter," he called, and Quincy opened the door and informed him that some of Heath's friends had called.

Rowley had not imagined it. Miss Lancaster's spine stiffened and her face was pale. What was she afraid of?

"You may show them in once Miss Lancaster has gone, Quincy."

"Yes, Your Grace."

He nodded his dismissal to Miss Lancaster and she left the room with her head down. Rowley watched her go and more than ever wanted to solve the puzzle that was her. For despite her position, he was intrigued and wanted to know everything about her.

AS SOON AS Emma left the room, head down, she heard Quincy show the guests to the duke's study. She waited nearby in an alcove, because she needed to know if they had seen her. Perhaps she did need to remove to Lady Hambridge's house, but that would give her godmother false hope.

She should be safe until Lord Heath awakened—if he awakened—and then she would make a decision. She remained in the alcove on the other side of the study and listened.

"Lord Perth, Sir Martin, and Mr. Petersham, Your Grace."

"Perth?" Emma's heart skipped a beat. Her cousin was here? She had not seen him since her mother died. Would he recognize her? She did not wish for him to know she was working here. It had not been a good relationship between her mother's family and her father.

"May I offer you gentlemen anything?" she heard the duke ask.

"No, no, we wanted to see how Lord Heath was recovering. We

have heard many rumors but no real news. We assume he is alive or we would have heard something," one of the men said.

"He is still fighting to live," the duke replied.

"That is good news indeed," a different, higher voice said.

"What can you tell me of Lord Emerson?" the duke asked. "I assume you were there."

"Emerson is keeping out of sight but has not fled, the last I heard."

"I also heard his business is suffering from the negative publicity surrounding the duel," Perth added.

"If you happen to hear where he is hiding, I would like to be apprised," the duke said in his quiet, steely voice.

"Of course, Your Grace. Would you send word once Heath is well enough for visitors?"

"If that occurs, I will let you know," he answered. "Thank you for asking after him."

Emma breathed a sigh of relief. No mention of her had been made. The door opened and she hid back into the shadows of the alcove. She had almost been caught.

"One more thing, Your Grace," her cousin's voice said. "The woman who was in here when we arrived. She looks familiar."

Emma could not breathe. Her heart was beating so hard against her chest, she thought it would surely stop. This was it, then.

"That is my aunt's goddaughter. She is here as companion to my sister. I cannot imagine you would be acquainted, since she is from the north part of the country."

"I must have been mistaken," he said. "Good day, Your Grace."

Emma heard the men's boots echo across the hallway and out of the front door. She slumped with relief against the wall.

"Miss Lancaster, are you well?"

"Lord Edmund!" She jumped with fright. "I did not see you there!"

"I have good news! I have just come to tell Rowley. Heath seems to have broken his fever," he said with great excitement.

"I am relieved to hear it," she said with a smile, turning to retreat to her chamber. Whatever had she been thinking to remain here? Perhaps she had done some good for Lord Heath, and somehow, that would make up for any deception she had unknowingly perpetrated on His Grace. Yet it was too dangerous for her to remain here, she could see that now. She would pack her belongings and return to her godmother's while she searched for another situation. It would probably be best if she told Lady Hambridge the truth so she would face reality. *Poor Eugenia,* she thought, as she pulled out her trunk and began to fold away her new gowns. She took them reluctantly, only because His Grace had ordered her old ones destroyed or given away. Her possessions were still meager and it only took a few minutes to complete her task. She would tell Eugenia first. No, perhaps it would be best to tell the duke first. If he was angry and forbid her to see Eugenia, she would send a note through her godmother.

Emma rang for a footman to carry her trunk down. She would arrange a hack after speaking with His Grace. However, he was not in his study. The room was empty, and she took a moment to acknowledge that he had been good to her and even friendly. He had been concerned for her comfort and well-being while under his roof. From her first impression of him, she would not have credited him with such compassion. Perhaps she had even wronged him to some degree. There was no doubt that his word had caused her family to suffer, but he had been trying to protect his family. She could forgive him that, a little. She took one deep breath before leaving the study.

The scent of bergamot and musk would remind her of him for the rest of her life. Why did he have to be Lord Heath's brother? She could even admit to finding him handsome if she could have found a way to erase his perpetual scowl, she thought with an ironic laugh. He was still very, very attractive—dangerously so—and she thought he felt some attraction, too. That was why it was best to leave now, while she still had some dignity.

"Quincy, do you know where His Grace went?" she asked as she went back into the entrance hall. The butler was standing at his post near the door.

"He went with the Lord Edmund to Lord Heath's room, miss."

"Thank you, Quincy." She smiled at him.

"Will you be leaving us, miss?" he asked with concern. "Shall I have your trunk delivered somewhere?"

"Lady Hambridge's if you please, thank you."

"Yes, miss. It is only two streets away."

Emma had not realized it was so close, but if she could walk, that would save her the fare for a hackney.

She climbed the stairs reluctantly, but at least it would be the last time. The door was open, and the duke spied her before she could retreat once she understood the situation.

"Emma!" Eugenia called.

All three siblings were standing around the bed, looking with joy upon their brother who was awake. Emma wanted to die or be swallowed whole by the floor below. She would have preferred almost anything but be in the situation she was in—and to think she had been only a few minutes away from freedom. So many things crossed her mind in those few moments of speechlessness. She could have stayed in the country; she could have left the duke's employ with her aunt that first day—could have, should have. It was too late. She could only hope that Lord Heath would not recognize her, or keep it to himself.

He turned his head and their eyes met. Those dark eyes bored into her and though he scarcely looked like the same man, with two weeks' growth of beard and a thinness born of putrid fever, there was no doubt that this was the same man and that he recognized her. She willed him to hold his tongue.

"Miss Hamilton, did you change your mind about my offer?" he drawled, surprisingly well for a man who had been unconscious for days.

Emma turned and ran.

CHAPTER FIFTEEN

ROWLEY REMEMBERED WITH startling clarity. Lancaster had proclaimed to the end that Gemma Hamilton was not his doxy, but a childhood friend he was protecting. She was his sister, by God!

"Not another word, Heath."

"I am glad to see you, too, Row."

"You know her?" Eugenia asked. "Why did you call her Miss Hamilton?"

"Our brother has not recovered from his fever and is confused. Why do you not give him a kiss and then leave us alone for a while?" Rowley suggested in a voice that brooked no argument.

Eugenia gave Heath a look of pity, but kissed him on the cheek and hugged him, carefully avoiding the bandage, at which she made a face of disgust.

Once she was gone, Rowley considered Heath, who though looking tired, was smirking. "I suppose someone will explain to me what that was about?"

"I had hoped to have more pleasant conversations to begin with and express my thankfulness that you are alive," Rowley drawled. "I suppose it would be too much to hope that you left your unrepentant, profligate manners behind at the duel."

Edmund was looking quite perplexed, as though he had not put the puzzle pieces in their places yet. Rowley felt stupid for not having realized sooner, yet was angry for being duped, nonetheless.

"Would you care to tell me why there is an actress in your house, Row? Did she accept your offer where she rejected me? I never would have thought you had it in you, old man," he said, though he gasped harshly for air between words.

"I would dearly love to draw your cork, Heath. If you only knew what your escapades had put your family through. Miss Lancaster is not my mistress, and if you thought I would bring such a person into my household with our sister living here, your fever has addled your brain."

"Miss Lancaster?" he asked, looking astonished.

"Oh, dear Lord," Edmund said as he finally drew the correct conclusions. "John Lancaster's sister, I presume?"

"The very one. Now you may understand why she refused to be your doxy, he defended her, and lost his livelihood." Rowley put the pieces together as he spoke.

"Lancaster ruined himself when he refused to behave as a gentleman. I cannot be held to blame for his refusing my challenge. You do not expect me to marry her now, do you? I never touched her! Not that I did not try," he added ruefully.

Rowley wanted to strangle his brother. Heath never did want to take responsibility for his actions.

"I doubt she would have you," Rowley retorted. "And she saved your life."

"The poor girl!" Edmund said, distraught.

Edmund would defend her, of course, Rowley thought dryly.

"I still do not understand why a *lady* would be upon the stage. It was natural for me to assume she would be like the others," Heath defended himself weakly. He was looking fatigued.

"I think, perhaps, she had no other choice," Rowley answered, trying to justify her actions. He needed to know. For some reason, he felt very hurt by her deception.

"And you did not wish to take no for an answer," Edmund retorted.

"Heath needs to rest. He has just awakened from a life-threatening fever. I wish this had not occurred at this time." Rowley needed to think carefully before any more was said. He began to lead Edmund out of the room.

"Would you send my valet to me? I would dearly like a shave."

"I will send for him. I sent him away, for he was fretting worse than Eugenia." Rowley turned to leave as Heath barked a laugh, which set off a coughing spell. Edmund and Rowley rushed to lift him and get him a drink of water.

"That hurt like the devil," he said, fading into sleep with his eyes closed. "Do I have a big hole? Emerson hit me all to nothing, I will give him that."

"Yes, Heath, you have a horrid hole in your chest."

However, he was already asleep and did not hear the answer.

Edmund followed Rowley to his study. He did not wish to speak to anyone, even Edmund, for he had a way of knowing the truth. Quincy was there in the entrance hall, apparently waiting for him and looking distraught.

"What is it, Quincy?"

"Miss Lancaster, Your Grace. She has left."

"Do you know where she went?"

"She had us send her trunks to Lady Hambridge's house before she went to find you in Lord Heath's room. Then she ran out of the front door and would not answer my pleas to have her taken."

"We must be grateful my aunt lives close by. You did quite right, Quincy, thank you."

Rowley went into his study, feeling even more unsettled. She had intended to leave before he recognized her, then. Why?

"What a pickle!" Edmund exclaimed. "Poor Miss Lancaster."

"I do not think I wish to speak on it, Edmund."

"You do not know what I was going to say." He was offended.

"You are correct. I was fearing you wanted me to continue as though nothing had occurred with Miss Lancaster, as you would with one of your doves."

"Well, now that you mention it, perhaps that is the best solution. I do not know all the details, but if she was the unfortunate recipient of Heath's unwanted attentions, then perhaps we need to ensure she is provided for in some capacity. She is a lady, and our aunt's goddaughter."

"Yet she willingly took to the stage," Rowley argued.

"Willingly? What lady of gentle birth would expose herself to ruination willingly? Did you not say her father had ruined them? Perhaps she had little alternative to fend off starvation."

"But if the *ton* knew or recognized her, it would be disastrous."

"Need they know? She does not have to remain in London. I do not have the perfect solution, but perhaps you need to speak with her. Did Cummins not say that Lancaster had to leave for America after the fight with Heath?"

"He did. Lancaster refused quite publicly to meet Heath in a duel and his reputation suffered." Rowley turned to the window with his hands crossed behind his back. If only he knew the truth of the situation!

"I must leave now, though I am truly delighted our brother has awakened. I only pray his brush with death will help him see the error of his ways."

Rowley would not hold his breath, he thought. Heath's behavior would have to be addressed, of course, but he could not think about that now. His thoughts were all for Miss Lancaster and how she had played them false. In her situation, he would have likely done the same thing, but why did she not simply choose another position when she discovered who she would be working for? How must she have felt when she realized? He laughed bitterly. How she must hate him! How he wanted to hate her, too.

Would she tell Lady Hambridge what she had done, or hope somehow to keep her secret? At least he had discovered the truth before he had done something stupid and embarrassed them both. No wonder she did not want to take off her caps. She was afraid of being recognized!

His conscience pricked at him when he considered Edmund's words. How desperate had she been to have taken to the stage? Why did she not simply go to her godmother? She had, at some point. Had she thought she could work in secret as an actress and not be accosted as Heath had done? Was she still an innocent? Rowley was furious and had more questions than he had answers. At least they had escaped scandal before having her go into Society with Eugenia! Perhaps it was for the best that she had escaped to Lady Hambridge's... but should he warn his aunt? Or should he leave that to Miss Lancaster?

It was still early yet, he decided, to go riding and try to clear his head. He hoped after that he would know what to do. Nonetheless, hard riding to Richmond and back did little to rid his mind of the problem of Miss Lancaster. Why could he not let her go and not think of her again? It was certainly for the best, but something nagged at him that much of this was his family's fault and he should therefore make it right.

OH, GOD! WHAT would happen to her now? It was only two streets that she ran to her godmother's, but her sides were aching with pain and her chest was heaving. She stopped at the park across the street and leaned against a tree in order to catch her breath. How foolish she had been! To think she had been moments away from avoiding discovery... and why did it matter so much? She should be able to move to another position and never see the duke or his family again, but she was mortified that her secret had been discovered and in such a way! She did not know why it mattered so much for them to have a good opinion of her. For she was good; there was nothing at all wrong with acting itself and the stage had been an act of desperation. It was unfortunate the associations people made based upon little knowledge. Unless a person had been in a position to know what it was like to go days without food, to have debt collectors beating down your door and threatening you with prison, or feeling as if you would freeze to death in the cold, damp winter because you had sold all of your good clothing in order to eat... no, she would not be judged and found criminal or ruined. She had done what had been necessary to survive. Anger began to replace mortification as she remembered why she had done what she had in order to survive. Perhaps there had been a better way. Perhaps she should have called on her godmother sooner, but pride cometh before a fall. If her brother had not saved her that night, she would be ruined and making her living on the streets because she had no alternative.

Emma was tired of hiding. Her best option would be to go in and confess to Lady Hambridge. It would be much better for that kind lady to find out from herself than from the duke. She was certain he knew by now, if he had not realized at the time. To think pride had kept her from telling anyone to begin with, and now pride also demanded that she confess to her godmother before anyone else could. The consequences could hardly be worse than anything she had suffered before, although now there would no longer be any hope of recovering her reputation or finding a good marriage.

Her breathing had returned to normal, though she was certain her cheeks were rosy from running in the brisk winter air. Surely her trunks had proceeded her, so she should be expected. She lifted the knocker on the door and Wallingford, one of her favorite people, opened it for her.

"Welcome back, Miss Lancaster, we have been expecting you," the butler said with a kind smile. He was one of those plump, older gentleman who had a genial demeanor and a ready smile for everyone.

"I suspected you might be. Is my godmother at home?"

"She is in the morning room, miss."

"Thank you, Wallingford. It is good to see you again."

Having made up her mind to confess the whole, she was ready and wondered why she had waited so long.

"Emma!" Lady Hambridge exclaimed. "Wallingford informed me your trunk had been delivered, but whatever has happened? Come, sit down and have a cup of tea and tell me everything." She patted the chair beside her.

Emma managed a small smile at her godmother's eagerness to see her. Would she feel the same in half an hour?

She took off her bonnet and pelisse and laid them over one of the tables by the door. Then she sat in one of the comfortable, worn green chairs that her godmother reserved for her special room.

"I have left the duke's house," she said quietly.

Lady Hambridge looked up from her tea but said nothing.

"You will be delighted to know that your nephew awakened from his unconsciousness this morning. The fever broke some time during the night."

"Thank the Lord!" Lady Hambridge said, looking upward with closed eyes as though she were uttering a prayer. Emma gave her a moment. Lord Heath had always been a favorite of hers, and Emma dreaded telling her story.

"Now, I know you did not send your trunks home just to tell me that Heath was recovering. What has happened to you, girl?" She reached over and squeezed her hand.

"You may not want to see me again when I tell you everything, but I must."

"There is nothing—nothing—that would lessen you in my eyes, dear Emma."

"Please hear me out before making judgments." She swallowed hard before beginning. "Two years ago, after mother died, my father began behaving erratically. A few months later, I received a note at school that I could no longer continue there and must return home, but home was no longer in Shropshire. I must come to London. Imagine my confusion!" Emma said with a slight laugh.

Lady Hambridge looked concerned, but did not interrupt.

"When I arrived here, Father was living in rooms with John, but of course I could not stay there so we took separate rooms—in Covent Garden."

Lady Hambridge gasped. "Why did you not come to me then, dear child?"

Emma's eyes filled with tears, but she shook her head to recover her composure. She needed to finish her tale.

"Father was drinking heavily, and it got worse. He had been betting heavily against our horses and had lost our home, and then our stables. John had some stud horses of his own, and was making an effort to recover enough to start again for himself. There was not enough to keep both Father and I as well."

"The little money we had left, he spent on spirits. I began selling everything but it was not enough. There was no food and there was no coal to keep us warm."

Emma saw Lady Hambridge wipe away a tear from her eye, but Emma kept staring into the fire. She had to tell her the whole.

"One afternoon, when I was returning to our rooms from looking for work, I was desolate. No one would hire me with no skills or references. I was in tears and was not watching where I was going. I am pretty sure I no longer cared. I had not eaten in days and I was so very cold." She was lost in the memory and shuddered at the recollection.

"I bumped into a man and he must have sensed my desperation. He took me into the nearest tea-room and bought me a meal. Once I had staved off the pangs of hunger, he asked about what had happened to me. He knew I was a lady."

"Of course he did! Anyone with eyes would know that," Lady Hambridge protested.

Emma shook her head. "No. I was hardly recognizable, but my speech was unchanged. He offered me a position at the theatre. He is the manager there."

Lady Hambridge gasped.

"You do not know the worst of it, I am afraid. He offered me a very handsome sum to act, and I agreed as long as I could remain disguised beyond recognition. I still had my reputation to protect, after all," she said bitterly.

"What about your competence from your mother?"

"It is not so very much money. It went quickly on the rent and Father's drink."

"Did he know what you were doing?"

"Neither he nor John did at first, but in a moment of rare sobriety, Father realized there was suddenly more food and coal. I even had a new coat."

"I do not see why you are berating yourself. You did what you had to do, even though I am hurt that you did not come to me. If you were disguised, no one is the wiser."

"That is only part of the story, I am afraid. You know that people assume, if you are an actress, you are open to propositions."

"Emma." Her godmother began to sob. "It could have been prevented if you had just come to me!"

"I wish I had known before I agreed to act. It is not exactly what you think, and I am ever so grateful you took me in when you did or who knows what would have happened. John found out what I was doing and came to be my protector. He took me to the theater and waited for me afterwards and escorted me home. He hated everything about it, but he also understood why I had to do it. No one would hire me elsewhere. Having John to protect me was very effective for several months, until one night, when one gentleman would not accept no as an answer. He became more and more persistent in his attentions toward me—and according to John—bets were being placed at the clubs. I did not think, in my disguise, anyone would pay me any mind, and very likely they would not have done if it had not been for this man. John made the mistake of admitting he was not my protector in the usual sense. He told someone I was a childhood friend and word spread."

"Oh, dear."

"The gentleman continued with his efforts, becoming more and more persistent. One evening, John was late to escort me home and I found the man in my dressing room."

Her godmother's hand was on her chest and she was holding her breath.

"If John had not arrived when he did, I am quite certain I would have been ravished. The man had me up against a wall and was being forceful with his kisses and hands. I was no match for his raw strength."

"You tell me who it is. I shall see to it that he never has the ability to ravish anyone again!"

Emma had never even known her sweet godmother to raise her voice. She could not have loved her more in that moment. She did believe the lady would castrate the gentleman if she could—until she found out who he was, that is.

"John took care of me that evening, but then things got worse. The man challenged John to a duel, but John refused to meet him. He said he was not worthy of the name of a gentleman. The man continued making threats and boasting of John's cowardice around the clubs, and that was more painful than anything. John was ruined."

"The next time the gentleman came to my dressing room, the other players tried to protect me, but he is a very powerful man. He challenged John again, in front of a room full of spectators. When John refused again, a fight broke out."

Tears streamed down Emma's face as she relived the entire scene. "Someone arrived to break it up. John left for America the next day and I have not seen him again. Father saw you soon after that; my acting career was over and so I came to live with you."

"Thank God you did! I am sorry you had to go through such a dreadful ordeal and that John was ruined, but this is not something we cannot overcome, my dear. You are still an innocent and a lady. Any man worth his salt would understand what you had to do, and if you were disguised as you say, who would recognize you?"

"The gentleman who accosted me. He saw me, as did his brother."

"Well, you had better tell me who it was, my dear."

"Lord Heath. The duke was the one who broke up the fight."

Chapter Sixteen

ROWLEY SAT DOWN at his desk to work, which had been neglected for more than a week, but could no more read a word on the page than ignore his obsession.

He gave up and went to his aunt's house.

"His Grace, the Duke of Knighton has called, my lady," Wallingford announced.

"Show him in."

Rowley heard the opposite door to the room close as he entered. Was she avoiding him or had it merely been a servant? He walked over and took his aunt's hand and kissed the back of it.

"How are you, aunt?"

She dabbed at her eyes with her handkerchief. "I have been better, Knighton. What can I do for you? I presume this is not a social call?"

"I came to see if Miss Lancaster arrived safely, and to ask if she might speak with me."

His aunt sighed. "She is quite upset. I do not think she wishes to entertain visitors yet." She glanced toward the door which had closed upon his entrance.

Rowley could feel his eyebrows lift. "I am a visitor?"

"She is living with me again, so yes."

"She has neither given me notice nor informed me of her decision. I would assume, at the very least she would wish for references and her salary."

"Do not behave like a duke now, Nephew. I know what happened, and Emma is very upset. Give her a little time."

Rowley felt himself deflate and he sat down in the chair next to his aunt. It was still warm. It must have been where Miss Lancaster was sitting moments before.

"You are not upset with her?"

"The only thing I am upset about is that she did not come to me for help sooner. If you knew what that poor child had been reduced to, you would not judge her so harshly."

"Have I said anything to condemn her? I am most angered by the deception."

"She could hardly have come to you and said she had spent eight months on the stage and been welcomed into your home, now could she, Knighton?"

"Yet you did not see fit to do so either?" he asked, incredulous.

"I did not know the whole of it until a few moments ago, but it does not change my opinion of her."

"She told you of Heath's attentions toward her and of the brawl that took place in her dressing room?"

"Heath may wish he was never born when I have finished with him! Something must be done about his behavior. It has never been so personal to me, I will admit, but he is eight-and-twenty and it is time he grew up."

"I have some ideas on that matter, I assure you, but I will deal with him when he is fully recovered," Rowley said quietly.

"I want you to help me find another position for poor Emma. I cannot believe she did not say something to me when she realized where she would be working."

"I assume she did not think she would be recognized."

"She says her disguise was very, very good and that only you and Heath had seen her."

"I did not realize until this morning, I will admit, but do you know who she was on stage?"

She shook her head. "I am not an avid theatre-goer."

"Gemma Hamilton."

"Emma. Gemma. Hamilton was her mother's surname. Oh, good heavens!"

"I am told she made quite a name for herself."

"Something must be done, Knighton."

"Even if I forced Heath to marry her, I would not wish that on Miss Lancaster."

"No, I suppose not, although she could be the making of him."

Rowley cast her an incredulous look.

"What of Eugenia? You may send her to me. She should not be in a bachelor household without any female guidance."

"I do not know if that is wise."

"I beg your pardon? Are you insulting me or Miss Lancaster?"

"My primary duty is to my sister. I honor you for protecting your goddaughter, but I must ensure no scandal attaches to my sister's name. Her own behavior will not allow for any such lenience."

"You are being ridiculous! Emma's name would not be soiled were it not for your brother's outlandish and unwanted attentions."

"She took to the stage long before any Knight brother had anything to do with her." Arguing was pointless, and his aunt was right. He ran his hand through his hair. "It is a devilish fix. I do not wish Miss Lancaster to come to any harm. She has been good to Eugenia and Eugenia adores her."

"Then help me help her. The *ton* would not defy both of us. It has been done before."

"Unless word got out, then life would be very, very bad for her here. If Society thinks it has been duped it will cut her faster than the blink of an eye."

"Who knows besides Heath? Society will see what they wish to, although she probably would not agree. I could never convince her to go to any events with me other than small dinner parties and salons."

"I can take care of Heath, but I am not certain it is a good idea. These things always have a way of been discovered."

"Hopefully not, but if we support her, do you not think the storm could be weathered?"

Rowley stood and walked over to the window, his hands crossed behind his back.

"I do not know. I wish I knew more of the details. Perhaps when Heath is stronger… why do we not take a little time to think on it? You speak with Miss Lancaster, and I will have a word with Heath."

"I feel I have failed her. I must do something to make this right," his aunt said, worrying her handkerchief.

"You bear no more responsibility than I, but I do not wish to see her back on the stage or on the streets."

"Her mother must be tossing in her grave! The whole purpose of a godmother is to prevent things like this!"

"I would argue that it was her father's responsibility. However, Heath was raised as a gentleman and no matter the female's station, he knows better than to take advantage. Please inform Miss Lancaster I wish to speak with her, not eat her." He walked back over to his aunt and kissed her on the cheek. "We will see her comfortably established somehow," he reassured her before taking his leave.

"EMMA? ARE YOU there?"

The servants' door to the morning room opened, and Emma came back in reluctantly and sat in the chair she had previously occupied. It still held the musky scent of the duke.

"I assume you heard every word?"

Emma nodded. "I cannot go into Society. I do not have any wish to be a part of it, even if my past remained hidden. Knowing the hypocrisy of the situation is too much for me. Society enjoys my talents and the gentlemen would be happy to sample my wares, yet they put on a separate mask when it comes to their wives."

"I know it is a double standard, Emma, but you belong among your own people. You are a lady and an innocent, still."

"I have not been innocent since mama died, but I still have my virtue," she said sarcastically.

"Will you not try a little for my sake?" Lady Hambridge begged.

"I will bring shame upon you. I cannot bear it. You are the best of souls," Emma argued.

"I am too old to give a fig for what others think of me. If people do not know me well enough, by my age, then they matter not to me. But you matter to me. I do not think it will be as bad as you fear."

Wallingford's head appeared around the door into the room. "Lord Edmund is here, my lady. Will you see him? He specifically inquired after Miss Lancaster."

Lady Hambridge looked at her questioningly.

"I will stay. Lord Edmund is a dear."

"Very good, miss."

Shortly, Lord Edmund was shown into the room and was bowing a greeting to them. "I am very relieved to find you here," he said to Emma. "I was very worried about you when I realized what had happened."

"Thank you for your concern, but as you can see, I am quite well."

"Is there any chance you would return once Heath is recovered? He can live somewhere else."

"I do not think that wise, my lord. I have no wish to displace him from his home."

Lord Edmund frowned, revealing the same lines between his brows as his brother. "What a pickle! There are many wrongs that need to be righted in this situation, and I am not certain what is best."

"Knighton said much the same thing," Lady Hambridge remarked.

"What is done is done," Emma said, growing impatient with everyone's need to meddle. "I must live with the consequences of my choices. It is not anyone else's problem. I will go into the country and find another position, if you will be so kind as to write me a reference, ma'am. Then no one will feel the need to do anything else for me. It was unlucky coincidence that I found a position with the one family I would have wished to avoid at all costs."

Edmund looked heartbroken at her words. "I only wished to help. Forgive me, Miss Lancaster. I truly only wish you well. You are very good for my sister and I had hoped you would be a positive influence where she is concerned."

"I did not mean to offend you, Lord Edmund. I appreciate your concern, but there is not a good solution here. I cannot go into Society without fear of someone exposing me at any moment, and I would wonder that you would want a former actress near your sister."

"I am the last person to judge your need to work when you are in a desperate situation. I do not know if you know of my life's work, trying to free women from brothels."

"I knew you helped women. Forgive me, I am a little defensive about the *ton's* hypocrisy."

"As you should be. And you suffered at my brother's hands."

"I did not realize, as a sheltered country girl, what becoming an actress would mean for my virtue."

Wallingford came into the room again with a look of bewilderment. "Lady Eugenia is here, my lady."

Eugenia did not wait to be shown in by the butler. She followed on his heels.

"Oh, thank goodness you are here!" She threw herself into Emma's arms and she laughed. It was surprising, the concern they were all showing for her well-being.

"What are you doing here alone?" Edmund asked.

"I came with my maid, but ensuring dear Emma is well takes priority. Whatever did Rowley say to make you leave? I will make him apologize and you can come home," she insisted.

"I am afraid it is not so simple. The duke did not say anything to force me to leave, I assure you."

Her brow wrinkled adorably, making her look much like her brothers. "Then you are coming back?"

"I am afraid I cannot. I meant to speak with you before I left, but circumstances made it impossible."

"If you are not coming back, may I come here? You are the only one who understands me," she whined.

"I am afraid I will not be staying here, either. I must find another position in the country."

"No! We can go back to the Grange. I do not need to be in London so much if you hate it here so."

"It would only prolong the inevitable. Besides, your brother will no longer approve of me, I am afraid."

Eugenia puffed out her chest, looking quite indignant.

Emma held up her hand. "Please do not. He is quite right, I must confess. After my mother died, I spent some time working as an actress. I did not realize at the time that actresses are considered to be of loose morals. I am guilty by association."

"No one who knows you would believe ill of you. It will not matter, Emma. Please!"

"I have told her the same thing, but she will not be swayed," Lady Hambridge added.

"There is more, Eugenia," Lord Edmund said softly. "Miss Lancaster is too much of a lady to tell you the whole. I do not know if Rowley would, but Heath accosted her and was not a gentleman. He tried to force her to be his mistress and when her brother defended her, he challenged him to a duel. Even though Mr. Lancaster refused, Heath ruined his business and ended a sordid episode by brawling with him, quite publicly, over Miss Lancaster."

"How dare he! Oh, what are we to do? How you must hate us! Why did you not say anything?"

"I could never hate you. I needed the position very badly, and I hoped I could stay safely in the country without being recognized."

"This is so very dreadful. I do not want you to leave me. I know I am very selfish!"

"No, I have enjoyed being with you. You have felt more like a sister than my charge. Your brother will find someone more worthy of you."

"But I do not want anyone else," she wailed, collapsing to her knees. Emma took a handkerchief and wiped away her tears and kissed her on the forehead.

Edmund lifted his sister up. She was still crying, into Emma's lap.

"Forgive me for deceiving you. One day soon you will understand why I must leave," Emma said tenderly.

Edmund looked at her while holding Eugenia tucked under his arm. "I am at Saint Michael's, should you ever need anything. I have a few connections if you cannot find a suitable place."

He smiled at her and led Eugenia away. Lady Hambridge was trying to hide her own tears and Emma could not hold back any longer. She went over to hug her godmother before running to her rooms to cower and cry.

Chapter Seventeen

"What can we do?" Edmund asked as he, Rowley, and Eugenia stood in the study quite angry with Heath, who was in a dressing gown sitting before the fire.

"I am not sure this will be appropriate for you to hear, Eugenia," Rowley stated.

"I am not leaving. I know you think me a child, but I know what Heath did." She glared at him. "We must do something for Emma."

"I agree," Edmund said, "but how can we restore her to her rightful place in Society after her being on stage? It has been done once or twice in recent history, but I do not think the ladies ever gained complete acceptance back into Society."

"I do not think anyone else would know her, for what it is worth," Heath said. "She was always well disguised. I was rather forceful in my attempts to persuade her," he admitted. "I only knew who she was because I had entered her dressing room uninvited. That was when things became ugly between Lancaster and myself, and you interfered." He looked to Rowley. That was an interesting piece of information. His aunt had proclaimed her innocence, could it be true? Could this whole situation be made right?

"Why did she not tell me?" Rowley asked out loud, though he expected no answer.

"To protect herself from recognition is my guess. She would have known who you were right away. You were there, after all," Heath reminded him.

"Aunt Violet said she did not wish to go into Society. I do not know if she would agree to any of your schemes." Edmund frowned.

"But she must! She is so beautiful and has been so wonderful to me. You have always said if we make something wrong we should make it right!" Eugenia threw up her hands.

His words would be thrown back in his face, Rowley wanted to groan aloud. He wanted all of this to go away and return to the Grange and his formally peaceful life. However, that was not possible for his own peace was cut to shreds by Eugenia's womanhood and now Miss Lancaster, who he could not rid his thoughts and dreams of.

"Heath was the one who made the wrong," Eugenia pointed out.

Heath could not have her, Rowley wanted to shout.

"If you are trying to make her respectable, I am the last person to do it," Heath drawled. "She did not want me then, I doubt she will want me now. But I will offer if you insist."

"You are not fit for Emma!" Eugenia snarled.

"I cannot argue with that. I do not fancy being leg shackled, myself. I think it would not give her the respectability you seek and might revive the memories of the *ton*, which is what you wish to avoid."

"Quite right," Edmund added.

"What can we do besides marry her to Heath?" Eugenia asked.

"I think you underestimate our family's name. Many sins are forgiven by the respectability of marriage."

Heath grunted his disapproval.

"I think Miss Lancaster deserves better than merely the title of marriage. She does not seem the type to care for Society's dictates," Edmund remarked.

"Yet, she hides from it," Rowley pointed out.

"And you do not?" Heath mocked.

"I do not hide, I avoid. Very different actions, I assure you."

"If we were to support her, would it not make a difference?" Eugenia asked. "We can be formidable altogether, I should think. And with Aunt Violet as well, I should think few would openly shun her."

"Most would accept her then," Rowley admitted, "but your own come out is soon and there might be some who would hold it against you."

"Why would I care for them if they are such snobs?"

"It is easy to dismiss cruelness until you are the object of it. It is why I did not wish to send you to school. Men may seem like brutes with their fists, but ladies' barbed tongues cut much deeper and leave permanent scars."

Eugenia was taken aback by his vehemence.

"All of this talk about our beloved Society has worn me out," Heath said as he stood gingerly, looking haggard with dark circles under his eyes. He walked slowly to the door, his breath somewhat labored. Edmund moved to help him, but Heath brushed his hand away. He turned back. "If Miss Lancaster requires the protection of my name, so be it. You know where to find me."

His siblings watched him leave, pitying looks on all of their faces. Rowley was stunned his brother had conceded to do the proper thing if needed without threat. Perhaps the brush with death had an effect after all.

"Perhaps a settlement so she can live somewhere quietly in the country?" Edmund suggested.

"I do not think she would be amenable to that, but that does remind me to send over her wages." He strode over to his desk and wrote out a bank draft.

"Can she not return to the Grange with me? I still have a need of a governess and no one there need know," Eugenia suggested.

Rowley frowned again. "I suppose that would be acceptable. I will try to speak with her again. She refused to see me when I called."

"I can try," Eugenia offered.

"I think it best if I do it. If she will not return, then I will try to help her best I can."

Eugenia accepted that and returned upstairs. Edmund took his leave as well, and Rowley was left feeling as though the problems of everyone were left for him to bear, as usual.

He sat at his desk feeling a little sorry for himself, which he never permitted himself to do. He had thought, for a brief moment, that he was developing a friendship with Miss Lancaster. He had enjoyed her company more than any other female of his acquaintance. He should know better and should stick to his previous resolution to avoid them. The one other time he had let down his guard, he had been naïve and thought the girl wanted him, but she had only wanted his title. Thankfully he had discovered her duplicity before the marriage was sealed by vows. Now he was faced with similar feelings of betrayal, and now he was forced to help her and let her go.

Debating writing a letter, he pulled out a piece of paper and dipped his pen and the standish. Instead of finding adequate words, he let the ink drip all over the page. He threw away the pen and wadded up the paper, tossing it into the fire. He picked up the bank draft and headed to the door and threw on the coat and hat that Quincy handed him.

"Will you be out long, Your Grace?"

"I do not know."

"Cook was planning on dinner before the theatre tonight, Your Grace," the butler murmured a reminder.

"Theatre?"

"I believe you had been persuaded to accompany Lady Eugenia and Miss Lancaster with Mr. Tinsley."

"Tinsley is in Town?" Rowley remembered none of this. He sighed.

"He came to call several times while Lord Heath was indisposed. I believe he took tea with the ladies and arranged for the play tonight."

The theatre was the last place he wished to go, and could he convince Miss Lancaster to go for Eugenia's sake? If she would not go into Society, would she go back to the place where she would almost certainly be recognized? He walked out into the blistering cold afternoon, and the wind slapped him brutally in the face and lifted his hat. Not even the weather wanted to be kind to him today, he thought caustically, as he headed to his aunt's house.

EMMA COULD HEAR the duke's voice from her chamber. She closed her eyes and tried to will away the pain that it caused. She did not want to see his face, and the disappointment it would show. That is, if he cared enough about her to even be disappointed. She had thought they were becoming friends, which was her mistake. She should not have allowed it to happen, but she had been weak and surprised by the person beneath the hard outer shell.

All day she had been contemplating her options, and she had about decided to leave Town. It would be for the best to go somewhere where no one knew of her or her past. Why was she so reluctant to leave? It was not fair to continue to live off of her godmother even though she knew she cared about her. Sometimes Emma thought she reciprocated more than her own children.

Emma might as well go down and speak with the duke. Unless she left Town, the meeting was unavoidable and she at least owed him an explanation if he wanted it.

"Good evening, Your Grace," she said, as she waved Wallingford away from announcing her. This was no time for formalities. She closed the door behind her. Lady Hambridge was upstairs resting, and goodness knew Emma had disturbed her peace enough for one day. The thought of a chaperone at this point was laughable anyway.

The duke was standing looking out the window with his hands clasped behind his back. That posture had become endearing to her, as had his scent, which filled the room.

He turned when he heard her approach. "Miss Lancaster."

She did not speak, for she did not know what to say. An apology seemed so inadequate.

The lines between his brow were there forming his familiar scowl, but the look in his eyes was not one of condemnation, just compassion.

"I have brought your wages," he said softly, and handed her a folded paper from his pocket.

"Of course, thank you," she said, for some reason feeling very hurt. He could have sent the money by a servant, so why was he here?

"You will be wondering why I am here. I have come to discover if you will return to the Grange with us. Now that Heath is recovering, there is no need for us to stay in Town. Eugenia wanted you to be reassured that she did not need to return to the metropolis for some time."

It was not what Emma had expected him to say. She furrowed her brow. "I do not understand, Your Grace. I would have thought you would wish me to be transported."

"My wishes are of no moment in this matter. Apparently Eugenia does not think she can live without you and believes my family owes you reparation."

'My wishes are of no moment.' He had no need to say more; his sentiments could not have been clearer if he had bellowed at her.

"Reparation?" she asked doubtfully.

"Need I elaborate on the treatment you received at the hands of my profligate brother?"

She turned away. "No, Your Grace. It is better forgotten. I think it would be for the best if I left altogether. You are being very gracious, when you consider my own lack of honesty to you in the matter."

"I will admit to being angry, but now I know the whole of the story, I find I cannot fault your actions."

"That is very civil of you." She tried to keep the sarcasm out of her tone.

"Where will you go?" he asked.

"I do not know."

"Will you at least allow me to help you, if you will not return to the Grange?"

"Why?" She turned and searched his gaze. His eyes, which she had once considered hard and evil, now reflected sadness and something else… could it possibly be longing?

He half-smiled in a self-deprecating manner. "For one, Eugenia insists that we make matters right for you. She says Heath wronged you. In theory, Heath should make it right and, to be fair, he did offer you the protection of his name, but we would not wish that upon you."

"Lord Heath offered to marry me?" Emma could not have been more surprised had her mother walked through the door, alive. She should be flattered, but she wanted to break down and cry. Clenching her fists behind the folds of her skirts, she adjured herself not to be a watering pot. He had given her no cause to hope, let alone harbor expectations.

"Perish the thought, I know, but you need not cry."

"I am not crying," she snapped.

"I hate to contradict a lady in the throes of distress, but I fear that is a wicked untruth." The gentle smile he gave her took the sting from his words and made her heart leap.

Slowly, he stepped closer. Emma tried to hold back the tears. Why must he be kind, *now*, when she least desired it—when she knew not what to think. He did not care for her, he had virtually said as much. He took another step toward her, his eyes on her face. Were they asking her forgiveness or was she imagining it?

"My dear Miss Lancaster, please do not cry."

Suddenly, he was inches away and his arms came around her in a comforting embrace.

Although mortified that she had broken down, Emma could not seem to pull herself away. The feel of his arms was too comforting. Then she made the mistake of looking again into his eyes, and wanted what she saw there… desire, yes, but so much more.

His lips brushed hers lightly, reverently. His hands cradled her face and his thumbs stroked her cheeks as though she was something delicate to be protected. He feathered kisses across her cheeks, her forehead and back to her lips. Emma was lost. A moment later, he pulled back and her heart at once protested.

"Forgive me. I am being as great a blackguard as my brother. I should not have done that to you when I am trying to convince you of my honor."

"Hardly," Emma whispered as she recalled the very different kisses Lord Heath had tried to impose upon her. But why had he ruined a sweet moment? Had he meant the kiss dishonorably? "Unless you mean to offer me a slip on the shoulder, I believe we should forget this happened. I do think it proves one thing, however, and that is I should not return to the Grange with you."

The look on his face was implacable. At her rebuff, he had turned back into the icy duke. "I can assure you it will not happen again, Miss Lancaster. I do not think Eugenia will ever forgive me if she knows why you will not come."

The problem was, Emma wanted to go. She had never felt so much peace as she had during those few weeks, but it could never be that way again.

"Will you do one final thing for me, Miss Lancaster?" he asked stiffly.

Emma looked at him with consternation.

"Apparently, my sister and Mr. Tinsley have arranged to go to the theatre tonight. Will you please accompany us?"

She turned away quickly. "I could not. Of all places, it is the most likely one where I would be recognized."

"Yet my brother says you were always well disguised. If that is the case, what do you have to fear? If you are recognized, you can always leave for the country as you are already planning to do."

Emma wavered. She did so love the theatre. What did it matter now if she was recognized? It was only one time.

"It would mean the world to Eugenia."

"I do not think it is a good idea."

He walked in front of her, reached out and took her hands in his. Warmth immediately spread all the way through her from his touch.

"If something happens, I will take care of you. I will not let you starve again."

It was so very tempting, and so very wrong.

She turned to look up into his face. "I hope you do not live to regret this."

"It is just the theatre. Everything will go well." Lifting her hand, he bowed over it, yet did not touch her again. The gesture made her heart squeeze. "We will pick you up at eight."

Emma would have to play a part one more time.

Chapter Eighteen

As he dressed for the theatre, Rowley found that he was feeling nervous—a fact which horrified him. He should not have kissed her. It had not been merely a friendly kiss, at least for him. He could have lost himself entirely on the altar of Emma Lancaster. They could never be more than friends, and yet he had invited her back to the Grange as Eugenia's companion, she had been harassed by his own brother, and he was betraying his own set of standards. It would never do.

Dressing for the evening in a black coat and breeches, he subconsciously chose a green waistcoat, the color of emeralds, when his valet held choices up for his inspection.

He wondered, *What would she wear?* and then cursed. He was behaving like an infatuated school boy.

For the sake of his sanity he needed her to leave, but he could not ask it of her. Eugenia was correct; his family bore some responsibility to help her. He would have to behave like a duke and put everyone else's needs before his own. It had been necessary since he was fifteen years of age, but why did it seem harder at thirty?

Rowley hardly said a word during dinner, but his introspection seemed to go unnoticed. Eugenia was so excited at attending her first play, she prattled on in a virtual monologue for the entire meal, while Edmund chirped merry replies in between her exclamations. Rowley brooded over his unfortunate fate at being born to a dukedom, which he knew made him no better than Heath moping about the house bemoaning his rotten luck. At least he now understood Heath's prior infatuation with Miss Lancaster. They were both doomed to failure where she was concerned. He would ignore her this evening, except as far as politeness dictated, and break himself of his infatuation if it killed him. He had survived them before.

Finally, dinner came to an end and they climbed into the carriage to collect his aunt and Miss Lancaster.

"I cannot believe you talked her into coming!" Eugenia exclaimed. "You are the best of eldest brothers!"

Edmund laughed. "Very diplomatic, Genie."

That was all the conversation they had time for, since his aunt's house was so close it was laughable. He alighted and went to the door himself.

"Good evening, Your Grace."

"Good evening Wallingford. Are the ladies ready?"

"Here we are," his aunt called, from the top of the stairs. She was dressed in a gaudy gown that looked from a previous era, with a turban boasting plumage enough for an entire ostrich. Poor bird.

Despite this outrageous vision, he had eyes only for Miss Lancaster. She was wearing the same green silk gown which she had at the assembly. Somehow he had known she would. Tonight, however, she had omitted the turban and he knew at once that all the fight had gone out of her. She was going to walk out of their lives and he would never see her again. It would have been easier if she had been belligerent.

He bowed to the ladies. "You look ravishing, Aunt Violet."

She rapped him with her fan as he gave her one of his arms and held the other out for Miss Lancaster.

"What has come over you, Knighton? It is not like you to flirt."

"Am I not allowed to be charming?"

She gave him a strange look. He turned to Miss Lancaster.

"You look beautiful," he said softly as they make their way to the carriage. He could feel her trembling underneath his arm. "Are you nervous?"

"I suppose I am." She had no adornment of jewels, yet he thought she was the most beautiful creature he had ever beheld. It made it quite difficult to breathe. He wanted to make the last evening they would have together memorable, yet he had to detach himself.

She climbed into the carriage ahead of him and sat on the seat between his aunt and his sister. He took the forward-facing seat with Edmund and looked out of the window so he would not be tempted to say something stupid to her.

He had already drawn up directions to his solicitor to bequeath her one of his small properties. That would provide her a home and an adequate income. She would be angry when she found out, of course, but when faced with no other prospects, perhaps she would be grateful for it one day. It was hers as long as she lived.

Eugenia was peppering Miss Lancaster with a thousand questions about her life as an actress. Rowley was curious to know himself, and listened attentively.

"What was your first part?"

"For several weeks I did little more than non-speaking roles, where a body was needed. I was fascinated by Sarah Siddons and would watch her rehearse and recite her lines. I memorized every single one," she recalled. Rowley noted her wistful tone.

"One day, Mrs. Siddons was ill and I was permitted to stand in for her. The understudy had not yet learned all of the lines, for shame. Her laziness was my gain. It happened that I performed for the remainder of the run of the play for two weeks."

"Was it wonderful?" Eugenia asked, appearing star struck.

"It was," Miss Lancaster said with a smile in her voice. "If it had only been that, I could have done it forever."

"Let us not return to that now," Lady Hambridge said, reaching across Miss Lancaster to pat Eugenia on the leg. "What is done is done. Let us enjoy the evening."

They pulled up to the portico at the front entrance of the Theatre Royal and the footman opened the door. There was a large crowd already gathered and Rowley knew their presence would cause a stir. For one, he could number on one hand how many times he had been to the theatre. For two, Miss Lancaster's beauty, and being an unknown, would draw all eyes and speculation. He assisted everyone from the carriage and took Eugenia's arm. Edmund escorted their aunt and Miss Lancaster. It was safest that way. Besides, it was Eugenia's first play and he wanted to enjoy it through her untarnished eyes.

The crowd parted to let them pass, and Eugenia was awed enough that she was quiet except for a few gasps of delight.

"Good evening, Knighton, Lady Eugenia," Mr. Tinsley said as he joined their party.

Rowley inclined his head to old acquaintances and did his best to smile more pleasantly than he felt. He saw the inquisitive gazes cast at Miss Lancaster, and he could only hope no one would make the association between her and her brother, who had once had a very public fight with Heath.

Rowley did his best to usher them quickly to the ducal box, but Lady Hambridge was busy introducing her goddaughter to all of her acquaintances as though she was the Queen herself. Miss Lancaster did not look pleased. Her eyes were averted and her cheeks were flushed with what he had come to recognize as annoyance. He fought back a chuckle.

"If you do not stop looking at her as if she is your favorite dessert, people are going to talk," Tinsley whispered in his ear.

Rowley felt as though he had been struck. He cursed under his breath and watched as Lord Emerson began to hover like a hawk circling his prey, or should he say vulture with his dark oiled hair, the beady eyes and beak of a nose.

He felt Tinsley's warning hand on his arm. "Ignore him. He will do nothing in such a public place. We can keep an eye on him."

Rowley nodded reluctantly. It was a good thing Tinsley was there to be his conscience. It would be disastrous if he were to confront Emerson so soon after his duel with Heath.

He saw Miss Lancaster visibly stiffen when Emerson drew close. She pulled Lady Hambridge away from him, back toward Rowley and Eugenia. Thank God.

What would a man of Emerson's reputation want with Miss Lancaster, though? Did he somehow recognize her?

"You are scowling at him like a rabid wolf," Tinsley said.

"I feel like one," he growled. "Get us to the box quickly."

EMMA HAD NEVER before seen this view. It felt much different to be a spectator. It had felt so large and grand from the stage with hundreds of eyes staring at her, but from here it felt intimate and cozy. They were in one of the luxurious boxes that surrounded the pit on the floor. Ornate cream and gilt trim outlined each box and the ceiling was painted similarly, with added carvings. Huge chandeliers glittered with what looked like a thousand candles. From an elaborately decorated arch, a heavy crimson curtain hung closed across the stage, just waiting to be drawn back. Men in their finest evening attire, the ladies bedecked with jewels around their necks and plumes dancing from their heads, greeted their acquaintances. The pit was full of raucous young bucks, harassing the orange sellers and heckling the young actresses who were the opening act. Emma was familiar with that, as well as the general hum of excitement which had always run through her veins before she set foot on the stage.

The ladies were seated at the front of the box and the gentleman sat behind. For Emma, this was an honor. She had been here hundreds of times, but never from this side. She was very conscious of the duke sitting behind her, but he seemed to have decided to ignore her, which was for the best. It would make leaving less painful.

It wasn't long before Emma realized people were staring and talking about them. She was determined not to pay it any mind, for it was more likely due to Lady Eugenia's presence—or the duke's for that matter—than her own, but they were definitely looking at this box. Even if no one was particularly looking at her, it was impossible to remain unseen. She had known this to be a bad idea, yet she had allowed herself to be persuaded because she had wanted to come. Hopefully, no long-term repercussions would come to the duke? Or her godmother. They could weather any storm, she was certain.

Once the curtain opened, Emma was lost to the performance of Sarah Siddons as Lady Macbeth. Emma had never aspired to be her equal, but performing had been magical for a time.

When the curtain fell on the first act, Emma felt a sense of loss. It was abrupt and she was not ready to face reality again so soon.

"You do love the theatre," a deep voice said from behind her. She did not turn around.

"I do. I never would have thought so before, but it does get in your blood, as they say."

She noticed, with some small horror, they were alone in the box. "Where has everyone gone?"

"They have all left. They went to obtain refreshments and promenade for a while. They invited you, but you were rather engrossed."

Her hand flew to her cheeks. "I ignored them?"

"Ignore would imply intent. You did not even hear them." He laughed.

Emma quailed as his laughter warmed her inside. She must not let herself weaken. She began to speak, but there was a knock at the entrance to the box. A group of gentlemen were standing there. Emma turned to face forward as the duke greeted them.

"Knighton, a rare thing it is to see you at the theatre," a familiar voice said. "May I take your presence to mean Lord Heath is recovering?"

"You may. He is moping about the house as we speak, I am sure."

The gentleman laughed.

"Will you introduce us to the lady?" another voice said. It must be the group of Lord Heath's friends that had come to call on him earlier in the week.

She could sense the duke's hesitation. He placed his hand on her shoulder and she had no choice but to turn around. "This is Lady Hambridge's goddaughter, Miss Emma Lancaster. May I present Lord Perth, Sir Martin Hardy and Mr. Petersham?"

"Cousin Emma? I did not know you were in Town," Lord Perth said.

As though he had ever cared. "I have been visiting my godmother. I will be leaving again for the country, soon."

"I am relieved to see you well. May I call on you before you leave?"

Emma did not miss the look of interest on the duke's face.

"Of course." What else could she say? The relationship between her mother's family and her father had always been strained, and they had done nothing to help after her mother's death.

"Is Lord Heath well enough for visitors?" Sir Martin inquired.

"I am certain he would appreciate anything to alleviate his burden," the duke replied. Shortly afterwards, the gentleman took their leave.

Emma watched the curtain close behind them and made the mistake of looking at the duke, who was still watching her.

"Your cousin? Was he not willing to help you in your desolation?"

She shook her head. "I do not wish to speak about it, Your Grace."

The others returned when the orchestra began to signal the second act would soon begin. Emma had neglected to attend to her own needs, and she needed to breathe. It was shockingly difficult all of a sudden.

"Pardon me," she said, as she stepped around the duke. "I need to visit the retiring room." That would at least allow her some privacy for a few moments. He inclined his head and she barely kept herself from running.

She did repair to the retiring room for ladies to compose herself. No one had openly exposed her or ridiculed her, but it was only a matter of time until people put two and two together. Where would she go? It was hard not to panic as she felt time running out and the walls closing in on her. She had her small competence and her salary from the duke, but it would not last long. It was not enough to buy a cottage in the smallest village in the remotest part of England. First, she must get through the remainder of the play. Her godmother would help her sort it out in the morning. She hated being such a burden to Lady Hambridge's conscience. Emma splashed some water on her face and dried it off with a cloth. She fussed with one of her curls that had come loose and then gave up. The room had cleared of all of the ladies and there was one attendant there who was cleaning and paying Emma no mind. Maybe she could return to the theatre in a less obvious capacity. She would never be Sarah Siddons, but she had been able to make a living. If only she could discover how to do so without being accosted by the privileged, entitled gentlemen of the *ton*! She walked back out into the open lobby and considered going to speak with the manager who had taken pity on her—no, saved her—that day that felt like so very long ago. She knew he would take her on again, he had said so at her parting.

Emma felt the hairs rise on the back of her neck. She had been lost in thought and forgotten to watch her surroundings. One would think she would be safe where she was, but no, predators came in pretty packages, too.

"My, my, my, the one that got away. I never thought to see

Gemma Hamilton again," Lord Emerson drawled.

Had he seen her before? Emma did not think so, but she knew who he was. The entire theatre company knew about him and tried to warn all of the girls away. She decided it would be best to feign ignorance and remained quiet.

"Has Lord Heath decided to make you respectable, then? He must have more talent than I gave him credit for. All these months, I thought he was losing his touch but he has had you secreted away."

The cur had come too close and she could smell his breath, ripe with spirits and cigars. He circled her and she felt his breath on her neck.

"What is his price? I will double it." He had hold of her wrist and was squeezing it.

She tried to withdraw it, but he held on tighter. "I am not for sale, my lord. I never have been, and I never will be," she spat.

"I love a woman with venom." He raised his brows in a disgusting look. "I am surprised, however, that Knighton would condescend to let you near his innocent sister. Or does he not know?" Emerson cackled maliciously.

"Let me go," she seethed. How dare he accost her so!

His eyes narrowed as he continued to hold her. "You had better watch yourself, Miss Hamilton."

He released her with a thrust and she almost fell back as he strode away. As she tried to still her breathing, any thoughts of remaining in London vanished.

Chapter Nineteen

Where was Miss Lancaster? Twenty minutes had passed. She had been gone longer than one would expect, but who was he to question a lady's time in the retiring room? He did not think she would miss the play unless something had happened. She had been engrossed in the first act.

Perhaps he should not have pressed her to come to the theater tonight. What was taking her so long?

He whispered to Edmund, "I am going to check on Miss Lancaster. She should be back by now."

Edmund, the dear soul, looked concerned. "Should I come with you?"

"Not yet. I do not want to draw more attention to the box."

Rowley hurried away and almost ran head-on into Emerson. Instead of apologizing, the man sneered at him and then cackled as he hurried away. What had possessed Heath to become involved with that man? He was well rid of him. Rowley turned a corner and Miss Lancaster was there, looking as pale as a ghost. She threw herself into his arms.

"What has happened? Miss Lancaster? Emma?" She was trembling like she had the day she had fallen in the river, except she was not cold. He held her and tried to whisper reassurances in her ear, but they would soon be discovered in the public hallway of a very crowded theatre, although the hall was blessedly deserted at the moment.

"Was it Emerson?" She stilled. "Did he recognize you?"

She nodded. "I must leave at once."

"I will call my carriage. Wait one moment while I tell Edmund or he will worry himself sick."

He was in and out of the box in a flash. He did not want to leave her alone. She was clearly terrified.

Rowley said not a word as he ushered Miss Lancaster to the carriage. She had the hood of her cape up over her head and was looking down. He could not blame her. He was bristling with anger that someone could make her so afraid. Suddenly he wished Heath had taken Emerson out in that duel. He still wished he knew what had been the underlying cause. He would be having words with his younger brother later.

For now, Rowley directed his driver to take them to Lady Hambridge's house. He thought Emma would be most comfortable at her godmother's, for Heath was still prowling about Knighton House. He would send the carriage back to the theatre for the others.

Once they were safely inside and Miss Lancaster was seated by the fire with a glass of brandy, he sat down across from her.

"Please tell me the whole or I will not be able to help you."

"I do not wish to involve you, your Grace."

"It is too late for that. Besides, Emerson has been associated with my brother, and was the other party in the duel that almost killed him. I need to know what he said to you. Did he threaten you?"

"It is of no consequence, Your Grace. It is all things I have heard before. I was simply caught off guard out in the foyer."

"I would hardly call your reaction earlier of no consequence."

"At least it is painfully obvious why I could never go back into Society," she said. "No man of honor would offer me anything other than what Lord Emerson did."

Rowley hit the arm of the chair in anger. "Did he offer to make you his mistress?"

If she was surprised by his outburst, she did not show it. "To be accurate, he offered to pay me double what Lord Heath did. However, I doubt what he intended was as respectable as being a mistress. His reputation is unsavory at best." He saw the repulsion in her face. At least she seemed to know what Emerson was capable of. Rowley was not even certain he understood the depths of that depravity himself.

"From what I understand, my brother threatened to expose some of his schemes. I believe that is why Emerson shot him. However, I will acknowledge I might be giving my brother too much credit, though I do know he was responsible for alerting Edmund about Miss Thatcher's circumstances."

Recognition dawned in her eyes. "That poor child!" Miss Lancaster exclaimed with tears in her eyes.

"Edmund's task is a thankless one."

Her eyes closed. "If Mr. Sheridan had not found me when he did, I very well could have fallen into Emerson's hands. I still could have if Lady Hambridge had not taken me in."

"Did Lord Emerson say anything else?"

She hesitated then looked him in the eye. "Only that I should watch myself," she whispered.

"You are safe now, Emma. I will not let him harm you," Rowley reassured her.

She nodded distractedly. "If you will forgive me, I think I will retire. I am not good company anyway."

"You have nothing to apologize for. I will wait here until my aunt returns."

He stood as she went to the door. She turned back and he felt a sinking pain in the pit of his stomach. There was look of despair he saw in her eyes that he knew he would move heaven and earth to take away. Emerson would pay.

WHY WAS DOING the right thing always so hard? It would be so much nicer to crawl into that warm bed and sleep away her troubles, but it would only be harder to leave the longer she waited. She took a piece of paper from the writing desk and penned a note to her godmother. At the very least, she owed her an explanation. She also wrote to Lady Eugenia, her brother Matthew, her sister Ruth, and penned a small note of thanks to the duke.

Emma had over a hundred pounds saved, thanks to the duke's generosity. It would be enough to get her to America and hopefully get by until she could find some employment. John had always told her she had a home with him if she ever wanted a change or needed to escape. It did not have to be forever, she kept telling herself. She could come back if she hated it there. But now she had little choice. She could not so impose on Ruth, who struggled to feed six little ones as it was. Besides, far north Scotland sounded very dreary in winter according to Ruth's letters.

Packing her trunk, she dressed in her warmest clothes of thick wool—also due to the duke's generosity. She dreaded being cold again, for when you were poor and all alone, everything felt colder. She already felt frozen inside.

Lugging her heavy trunk down the back stairs, she pushed it out the door and hailed a hackney cab. The less questions asked, the better. Everyone would know soon enough, but hopefully not before she had made it to the stage. She would lose her resolve otherwise.

Emma kept her head down while she waited for the stage to Liverpool at The Swan with Two Necks in Cheapside. She purchased a ticket and waited as far away from the raucous men in the taproom as possible. She huddled against a pillar outside and bent her head against the biting wind. She was feeling rather sorry for herself.

She was sure America was lovely, but she would be leaving her heart behind. At least she was healthy and whole, she reminded herself. It would be good to see John again. Did he have a child yet? What did his wife look like? She hoped he was happy. She had never gotten over the guilt of him leaving because he defended her honor. It seemed she was never to be rid of her past, however. She still could not fathom how Lord Emerson had known her identity unless he had spied or looked through peep holes. Based on his reputation, she would not put it past him.

"You were not thinking of leaving me, now, were you dear?" a deep menacing voice said from behind. So close behind she could feel Lord Emerson's body heat and smell the brandy and cigars again. Her stomach lurched.

How had he found her and what did he want with her? Why could she not be left alone? She had never asked for any of this attention! He was holding her arm so hard it would leave bruises, and he was a big brute of a man. There was no doubt at all he would break her if she fought. Her heart pounded and her palms were damp in her gloves, but outwardly she determined to not let her fear show.

"Now come without making any trouble and you will not get hurt."

Emma was frozen in shock, but she resisted. Where could she run to? Looking around, the courtyard was almost empty, save one or two ostlers about their tasks with horses. If she fought, he would only say she was his misbehaving wife. As she hesitated, he pulled out a blade. She could hear the scrape of the metal as the blade was pulled from its sheath.

"Now is the time to cooperate," he whispered in her ear. She stopped fighting, for now. Emma would never give in to Emerson. She would die fighting if she had to. It could not be worse than the alternative.

"That's a good girl. Now climb into my carriage." He practically shoved her and she stumbled in, to the seat.

He climbed in and took the seat opposite, she noted with relief. As she watched him across the carriage, she was surprised to realize how normal he looked. There were signs of dissipation of course—the yellowed eyes, the bulbous red nose and veins, the paunch, but half of the gentlemen of the nobility bore the look. Dressed in a well-tailored package with a fine carriage and four, his habits were likely never questioned.

"It was cleverly done, I will admit, to send you on the stagecoach. I applaud his trying to send you somewhere safe, but without a maid? Does he think I am that stupid?"

What was he talking about? Emma wanted to know, but she dare not ask. Emerson had been drinking, and the last thing she wished to do was anger him. Her father had never laid a hand on her, but his temper was not to be trifled with when he had drank too much.

She sat quietly in the corner trying to think of a means of escape.

"Now what should I do with you?" Emma could see a blank look in his eyes as they passed the occasional streetlamp.

"He owes me. And when he comes after you, I will get my revenge."

"He will not come after me."

"Oh, I think he will. You underestimate your charms. If he convinced Knighton to have you near his innocent sister, he will not let you go so easily."

He was still carrying on like he thought she was Lord Heath's mistress!

"All this time he had you hidden away. He thought my memory was so short or that I would not retaliate after the duel?" He shook his head and took a swig from his flask.

She would not try to argue with him. If he kept drinking, perhaps he would go to sleep and she could escape. Thankfully he had not bound her. The carriage was going faster than she thought possible in the city. Had they gone away from Town? She tried to look out the window, but dawn had not yet broken, and she could make little out. Panic was beginning to fester inside of her. "Where are we going?"

"Somewhere he will not think to look for you. I want him to suffer as he has made me suffer."

Like you made all the innocent young girls and boys suffer? She wanted to scream at him.

As the carriage continued to roll at a clipping pace, Emma knew they were no longer in London. And no one would even know to look for her. She had told them she was leaving for America. It would be easy to give in to fear right now, but she must keep her wits about her, for the farther away they got from London, the slimmer her chances of escape would be. Thankful she had placed her money in pockets about her person, a trick she had learned living in poverty, but she did mourn all of her belongings that were probably on their way to Liverpool.

All of her earthly possessions had been in that trunk. The portrait of her mother, her Bible, some letters she had saved. It was no use pining over what was lost. She would have to re-draw the portrait of her mother before she could no longer remember what she looked like. A tear escaped down Emma's cheek and she recalled with a start where she was. A snore or a hiccup escaped from Emerson and Emma prayed he would be out for some time. They were rolling along much too fast for her to jump, of course, but at least she could try to ascertain their whereabouts while he was none the wiser. If only she had ropes or a weapon. Did he mean to defile her? Bile rose in her throat just even thinking about him touching her anywhere.

CHAPTER TWENTY

ROWLEY WAS EMOTIONALLY drained as he finally set foot in his townhouse. A nice long sleep would make it easier to know what to do in the morning. At least Miss Lancaster would receive the deed to the cottage in the morning and she would have one less thing to worry about, he consoled himself as he stopped by his study to pour himself a nightcap.

"What the devil?" Heath, Perth, Sir Martin and Mr. Petersham were all lounging about on the sofas, quite comfortable as though they had spent hours enjoying several bottles of his finest spirits. No doubt they had.

"Row, come join uth," Heath said merrily.

At least he was pleasant when inebriated, Rowley thought sardonically.

"You look like you need a drink," Heath said with a furrowed brow, patting the seat next to him. "Do you need to talk about it?"

"No, thank you. I am in need of my bed."

"You always were a sober sides. I was just trying to help."

Rowley sighed. Heath always was irresistible after a few. "Oh, very well. One drink."

"That's the ticket," Heath slurred. "We were just discussing Miss Lancaster. Didn't know she was Perf's cousin. Did you?"

"I had not made the connection, no." Although, now that he

thought about it, his aunt had mentioned the connection.

"We tried to find her after her mother's death, but she had disappeared. No one at the school knew where she went," Perth remarked.

They did not look too hard, Rowley thought bitterly. Lancaster was in Town drinking himself to oblivion while Miss Lancaster almost starved to death.

"She must have been with Lady Hambridge the whole time," Perth said to no one in particular.

"Your cousin is dashed pretty," Sir Martin remarked as he stared, mesmerized by the flames. Rowley had thought he was asleep.

"Too good for the likes of me," Heath added. "Wouldn't have me." He belched.

Rowley sipped his brandy and listened warily. Did they all know the connection?

"You made her an offer?" Perth asked, perhaps not as intoxicated as Rowley wished at this moment.

He eyed Heath, who seemed to be realizing perhaps he should tread cautiously, but not sure why.

"Never got that far," he mumbled.

"Shaw Emerson at the theatre," Petersham said out of the blue. "Shlinking in the shadows."

"He must have heard you are recovering, Heath, if he dared show his face," Rowley said. "I wish I had seen him."

"I heard he still wants revenge on Heath," Sir Martin chimed in.

"A hole in my chest was not enough?" Heath asked, looking a bit more sober.

"Rumor is, he blames you for ruining his business."

"Dashed nasty business, if you call it that," Heath grumbled. "I am glad to hear he is ruined. I would do it again." He held out his glass to Sir Martin who promptly refilled it.

"What business is that?" Rowley asked, though he suspected he knew.

All three men looked up at him warily, apparently not willing to voice it out loud.

"The one where he abducts young children and uses them in his houses of ill repute," Perth answered.

"Not at all the thing," Petersham hiccoughed. "Tried to lure us in, he did. Deuced rotten fellow."

"But a bullet through me for my troubles," Heath commiserated.

"We must work together to see he is unable to re-establish his unfortunate abuse and profiteering of children. There has to be a way to help those poor sods."

"You might stop Emerson, but someone else will pick up where he left off. No one wants 'em."

Rowley knew that to be true. He had seen the evidence of it in the slums. Perhaps he and Edmund could come up with something more to help. Once he had sleep.

"I am for my bed," he announced and stood as he heard someone at the door. It was much too early for visitors. He went to answer it himself since it was much too late, or too early for the servants to be awake.

"Knighton!" his aunt said, hustling inside, looking as though she had seen as ghost and come straight from her bedroom. A scarf had been wrapped around her hair and she looked as though she had dressed herself.

"Whatever is the matter, Aunt?"

"It's Emma! She is running away! You must stop her." Her hand was shaking holding out a letter to him.

"Come inside where it is warm. I will start a fire for you."

Rowley turned to tour the drawing room. He could hardly take her into his study with four inebriated men.

"Rowley? Is someone at the door?" Heath was standing there trying to recover his breath from the effort. "I say, Aunt Violet, is that you at this hour?"

"Heath!" she exclaimed, running over to hug him. "I am very vexed with you!"

"Join the club," he said affectionately. "Come inside where it is warm. What is the matter?"

Heath could be so charming at times. Rowley despaired of him.

He opened the letter and read while he had a minute of privacy.

Dearest godmother,

Forgive me for stealing away in the night, but it is easier this way. I have taken the stage to Liverpool, where I will take passage to America. I will visit John for a while and see if I can make a home there. After being recognized at the theater tonight, I realize there is little hope for me in England without always having that dark shadow over me and those whom I love dearly. Please do not feel as though you failed me. There is little you could do in my situation, but I love you dearly for hoping. I will write to you when I arrive. I have written to Ruth, Matthew, Lady Eugenia and the duke. Please give them my eternal thanks for giving me a chance.

All my love, Emma

Good God! Emerson must have frightened her more than Rowley realized. The blackguard would be lucky if he lived when Rowley was through with him!

He hurried into his study. "Does anyone know what time the stage leaves for Liverpool?"

Five pairs of eyes looked at him blankly. He cursed. How useless the aristocracy was at times! He pulled the rope to summon a servant.

"Why would you want to go to Liverpool and on the stage, no less?" Sir Martin asked as though offended.

"I do not want to go at all. I want to stop somebody else from taking it."

"Oh. Why didn't you say so?"

Quincy came into the room looking fresh and immaculate. Rowley envied him. "Good morning, Your Grace."

"Do you know what time the stage leaves from Liverpool and where?"

"The closest leaves from The Swan with Two Heads in Cheapside. I believe it departs at six in the morning."

"Have my horse saddled at once."

"What is happening?" Lord Perth asked. "Do you need assistance?"

"Your cousin has decided to leave for America. She decided to take the common stage to Liverpool and I mean to stop her."

"But there are no passenger voyages to America right now with the war."

Lady Hambridge was sniveling into her handkerchief, Heath's arms around her providing comfort.

"Then we must try to stop her at once," Perth said.

"I will follow in my carriage," Lady Hambridge said. "She cannot be all alone."

"I will accompany you. She is my cousin after all," Perth was saying.

Rowley did not have time to argue. He just wanted to find her safe. The whole lot of them could follow for all he cared. Running up the stairs two at a time, he changed into warm riding gear as quickly as he could. By the time he returned downstairs, his horse was saddled and waiting for him. At this time of the morning, it was a quick ride to Cheapside, and he found the inn quickly. Rowley threw his reins to a groom, instructing him to hold him for now.

Finding the innkeeper, he strode up to him and was granted immediate attention.

"How long since the stage left for the north?"

"Over an hour before, your lordship."

"Can you tell me where the first few stops are? I need to overtake it. My wife was a passenger."

The innkeeper looked at him sympathetically. "I understand.

There was a pretty lady as bought a ticket, but her trunk is still here."

Did she have a change of heart? Raleigh wondered hopefully. "Did that lady direct the trunk be returned to her home?"

"Not to my knowledge, but I can ask my men. I did not see her after she purchased her ticket. She waited outside."

"If it is hers, I will arrange to have it delivered home."

"Excellent, your lordship. I put it in the parlor next to the fire-place."

Rowley went into the small room and saw the trunk. It was locked, of course, but he immediately knew it was hers. Her unique scent filled his nostrils with longing. He hoped she had come to her senses and was now safely tucked in a warm bed at Lady Hambridge's, but he must make certain.

He went outside to find some grooms and ostlers. No one paid any mind to the stage travelers, apparently. Rowley questioned every single person he could find, and no one had seen her.

Giving up, he decided she had boarded the stage without her trunk. He went back in to arrange for it to be returned to Lady Hambridge's home, when a young boy ran into the top room and tugged on his coat.

"Get out of here, urchin!" the innkeeper yelled.

"Mister! Mister!"

Rowley looked down at a street boy, who looked dirty and starved.

"Leave his lordship and my customers alone. Get on with you!" he snapped his cloth at him.

"Wait," Rowley commanded and bent down on his haunches to be face-to-face with the boy.

"What do you need to say?"

"I saw a fine lady waiting here this morning. She did not board the stage though. She left with a toff in a bang-up rattler."

Rowley's heart sank. Had Emerson gotten her?

"What is your name, son?" Rowley asked.

"Timmy."

"Thank you, Timmy. Did you see which way they went?"

He nodded and pointed. "That way." Away from Town.

"Do you have parents?"

The boy shook his head.

Rowley sighed. "Then you had best come with me." The boy took his hand trustingly and Rowley thought with disgust how easy it was for Emerson to recruit these helpless children. They would pass Saint Michaels on the way back to his home, and Edmund would know what to do with him. Rowley could not leave him on the streets, but he had to find Emma and soon.

THE COACH SLOWED much sooner than expected and Emma hoped if they were changing horses she would have an opportunity to jump. However, the carriage was only turning and took a southern road.

The curiosity must have shown on Emma's face, and Lord Emerson must have not been fully asleep.

"To my thinking, it will take them some time for them to realize you are not on the stage. They will assume you were headed home to Shropshire."

Emma said nothing. Why did he think she was returning to Shropshire? She wondered.

"That gives me several days' advantage. They will have been told we took the northern road, which we did for a while, if anyone remembers us by that time. Once we are satisfactorily settled, I will hide you in plain sight. Of course, they may not realize I have you, but if they do, they will start by searching my properties."

He was expecting them to come after her. Should she disillusion him? Would it help or hurt her? He had not heard her yet, but she was not certain what his intentions were other than to get revenge on Lord Heath.

"What if they do not come after me?"

"I have plenty of uses for you, I assure you," he answered, a little too quickly.

When hell freezes over, Emma seethed to herself, beginning to imagine the ways she would torture him to repay his like services.

"Plain sight means London, I gather. At your grandma's house?" she asked, hoping he would leak out some useful information.

"I considered it, but no one would even think to look for you where we are going. I use it often when I have need for discretion."

Emma wanted to be sick, but she would not let Emerson see her fear.

"You must think me valuable indeed if you think Lord Heath will rise from his sick bed to mount an expedition to find me. What do you imagine he can do? You almost killed him. He can hardly fight you."

"Is that the way of it, eh? I had only heard he lived, not the extent of his injuries."

"What did you duel about? I assume it was not over me."

He belched. "I had thought you long gone. It was a stroke of luck you turned up tonight."

At least the plan might not be well-formed, which could work to her advantage, she reasoned.

"How did you know me?"

"I know everything that goes on there. I am the funds of the theatre."

Of course. That was the connection. He probably did have peep holes among other secret hiding spots. Amazing to think his reputation preceded him. Did he mean to hide her there then? At least it was somewhere familiar.

They drove back into the city as the sun was beginning to dawn over the buildings. Emma was exhausted, but she must stay alert, for any hope she had of escaping was best when they were moving from place to place.

Instead of approaching the theatre district, the smell of the pungent river assailed her nostrils, along with the sounds of the docks.

"Ah, at last. Welcome to my special place."

Was he going to leave her in an abandoned warehouse?

"Do not try anything foolish here. Becoming lost at the docks is a worse fate than what I have planned, I assure you."

Emma's spine prickled with fear and revulsion and she was still in the carriage. What awaited her outside?

The other actors had whispered about Emerson. He ran brothels, yes, but he catered to eccentric tastes. Emma could not have told you what that meant until someone else had mentioned children were involved.

Emma had resolved not to give up without a fight, but whatever happened, she would never let them take her soul. It was separate from her body, and she would do what she must to survive.

She wondered with sadness how long it would take anyone to realize she was missing. They might not ever. John didn't know she was coming, and no one knew she had been taken by Emerson. Unless he decided to tell them. He would not have his revenge otherwise. Emma thought it was ironic that he believed Lord Heath would care. But Heath never cared about anyone but himself, as far as she could discern. The duke, however, he put his family above all else, she thought with the pang of envy. To be cared about by him… it did not bear thinking of. He had felt it his duty as a gentleman to help right a wrong, and that was all where she was concerned.

The carriage lurched to a stop along with Emma's stomach. Now was the time to be brave, not sick, she told herself.

"Here we are. Now, the less fuss you make, the less hurt you will be. This time of morning hardly anyone will be about to help anyway."

Less hurt?

He stepped down from the carriage and held out a hand to her. She begrudgingly took it and tried to keep her stiff legs from buckling. Falling into Emerson's arms was the last thing she wanted.

She was surprised by what she saw. A yacht was docked at the pier just before them.

"I told you it would be the last place they would look for you."

"Except your grandmama's." Why she was trying humor at a time like this, she could not fathom.

"Yes." He smiled, showing her his tobacco stained teeth. No more humor from her.

"I told you they will not be looking for me. I was leaving for America."

He stopped and jerked his head around. The sounds of waves lapping the shores and sides of the boats mixed with dirty river water seemed magnified as she wondered what he would do with her now.

"I am not Lord Heath's mistress. I never was. Surely you knew of the fight."

He eyed her suspiciously and she saw a moment of uncertainty in his beady, black gaze. "We cannot talk out here." He led her across a gangplank into the boat labeled the *Molly Jane* and down a narrow ladder into a cabin. It was large, and decorated luxuriously in dark wood panels. Bright crimson sofas, covered in velvet and silks, lined the edges. Emma did not want to know what took place there.

Another ruddy-faced man, dressed in dark wool from head to toe with a wool cap over grizzly, grey hair came forward and spoke to Emerson. Emma could only assume it was the ship's captain. She strained to overhear.

"An unexpected visitor. I must leave again. I have arrangements to make for her. Make her comfortable and leave her untouched for now. Understood?"

"Yes, my lord. Is she to be restrained?"

"I've no notion if she can swim, but would not trust her if she said no. She would freeze to death before she reached the pier. Keeping her locked in my cabin will be enough if you drop anchor deep offshore. I do not expect her to give you trouble, thus far she has been complacent. Do not let her near the others." The last was said in a loud whisper.

The captain narrowed his gaze and looked at Emma as though assessing her worth. She tried not to squirm or affect that she had heard a word they'd spoken.

"When will you return?"

"I cannot say. I will signal as usual. Not before dark."

"Yes, my lord."

Emerson left without a word or backward glance to Emma. She supposed she should be relieved as she heard the carriage roll away. The captain came toward her and told her to follow him. Emma hesitated. Should she make a run for it before they cast off? She might not get another chance. Calculating her odds, they were not good for her to outrun him in skirts. She needed a head start to get up the ladder. Looking around for something to use as a weapon, her eyes alighted on what she thought was called a spyglass. How very careless of him to have left that there.

While the captain was taking out a key to an adjoining cabin, Emma grabbed the spyglass and shoved it behind her skirts. As he opened the door, she lifted it and thrust it at his head as hard as she could, wincing as a sickening crack rent the air. And then she ran.

CHAPTER TWENTY-ONE

ROWLEY STOPPED LONG enough in front of the St. Michael's rectory for Timmy to slide down from the horse and run up to knock on the door. Thankfully, Edmund was home. Edmund looked curiously at the small boy, but then noticed his brother sitting atop the horse. He hurried out to him.

"This is Timmy. Can you bring him to the house? I did not want to leave him behind where I found him. Miss Lancaster has been kidnapped and I will need your help to find her. I must go at once to alert the others."

"Yes, of course. Timmy and I will be over directly."

Rowley had told Timmy what a kind man his brother was and that he could trust him. He also assured him that there would be a warm meal waiting for him when they arrived at his own house.

Having delivered his new charge, Rowley urged his horse forward to Knighton House, hoping he could catch the others. A groom caught his reins as he slid down and ran up the steps. Quincy held the door for him as Rowley stopped to catch his breath.

"Are my guests still here?"

"All except for Lady Hambridge, sir. She went to gather a few belongings, I believe, and was to return here before setting out north."

"Excellent." Rowley strode into his study, where the four men stopped talking and looked at him.

"No luck?" Heath asked.

"Yes and no. I need your help. Miss Lancaster's life may be in peril."

"Tell me what has happened." Lord Perth was instantly alert.

"To be succinct, Miss Lancaster bought a ticket to Liverpool, but her trunk was left behind. A little urchin saw a 'toff' take a lady of her description away in a fancy carriage."

"Who the devil would want to harm my cousin?"

"I believe it was Emerson. He accosted her at the theatre last night." Rowley cast a glance at Heath, who was looking very pale.

"It matters not why at this moment. We must discover where he has taken her. I understand you were his associates for some time."

"We have been doing our best to disassociate ourselves from him!" Petersham was instantly on the defensive.

"You must have some ideas. This is your chance to put some of it right."

"There is his club," Heath suggested.

"They were seen taking the northern road," Rowley added.

"If I know Emerson, it's a ruse," Sir Martin interjected. "He has always prided himself on outmaneuvering his opponent."

Rowley looked at him with interest.

Sir Martin shrugged. "I was at Harrow with him."

"What about his properties?" Perth suggested.

"Too obvious." Sir Martin dismissed that idea swiftly. "He would not want to sully his personal affairs with his business interests. I would think he would try somewhere in plain sight."

"What were his haunts in London?"

"I still think we need to ascertain why he would go to such lengths to abduct my cousin. It makes no sense." Perth paced across the room anxiously while Rowley looked out of the window, his hands clasped behind his back.

"He means to enact revenge upon me," Heath said softly.

"What is the connection?" Perth eyed him with confusion.

Heath hesitated. Rowley motioned for him to go ahead. "Your cousin was the actress Gemma Hamilton for a time." That sentence explained everything to Heath's closest pals.

Perth sat down with a jolt, looking as though he had been struck.

"Emerson saw her last night and recognized her. He made some kind of threat and she ran away this morning," Rowley said, finishing the explanation.

"She meant to go to her brother?" Perth asked.

"Yes. The one Heath challenged, then later fought in her dressing room."

"This is a disaster!" Perth clenched his hands.

"It need not be, if you give me your word as gentlemen to protect her honor."

"She is untouched by me," Heath confirmed.

"Since she left the stage, she has been living with her godmother. If you are satisfied, I suggest we split up and search. I have sent my most trusted groom to Emerson's stables."

"I will go to the club," Sir Martin suggested and left on the words.

"We will search near the theatre and his rooms." Perth and Petersham left to carry out their task.

Heath sat staring out of the window while Rowley penned a note to his aunt and had Quincy deliver it.

He sat back down and took a moment to let his head fall into his hands.

"You care about her," Heath said, barely above a whisper.

"Yes."

"I hope you find her."

"I have no idea where to look." He knew his voice held desperation. What would he do if Emerson harmed her?

"I am sorry, Rowley. I never meant to hurt her. I have no idea why he is taking out his revenge on her… and now I am helpless to do anything."

"He thinks to harm you through her. Help me think where he might be holding her," Rowley pleaded. "Is there anywhere else he took you?"

Heath closed his eyes and Rowley thought he must have gone to sleep. If anything happened to Emma, Rowley did not know if he could forgive his brother.

Edmund arrived with Timmy just as Rowley was about to go out and start searching. Even though he had no idea where to begin looking, it was better than waiting, doing nothing.

"Any word?" Edmund asked as he entered the room, holding Timmy's hand.

"Quincy, would you take Timmy to the kitchen and see that he gets a hot meal?" Rowley asked.

Timmy clung to Edmund's side. Rowley was not surprised in the least.

"On second thoughts, have something sent in here, will you?"

"Yes, Your Grace."

Edmund took the seat by the fire and Timmy tucked up next to him, surveying his surroundings with awe.

"Can you think of where Emerson could have taken Emma?"

Edmund shook his head. "I have been trying to think since you left us." They all fell silent, each lost in thought.

A few minutes later, Quincy entered with a tray for Timmy and the boy's eyes grew wide. He seemed shy to take any.

"It is for you," Edmund reassured him, and the boy tasted the sandwiches and fresh scones with wonder.

"I have heard there is somewhere secret he takes the peculiar clients." Edmund was clearly trying to convey the information carefully.

Heath opened his eyes. "Yes, that is true. I was never privy to it. It was, in a large part, what we argued about. I did not agree with his peculiar clients."

Edmund nodded his head. "Not that I approve of the trade at all, but there is a difference in adults performing a trade for compensation and children being stolen from the streets and forced into unforgivable acts!"

Rowley watched Timmy as Edmund spoke, but he was solely absorbed in the feast before him.

"Is there anyone Emerson did confide in, that you know of?"

Heath's face assumed a look of concentration. "No one who would speak with me. Occasionally, I saw an older, grizzled man at the club, but he kept to himself. Once or twice, Emerson mentioned a madam named Molly Jane. I never met her, though."

"Molly Jane is a boat," Timmy chimed in, with a mouth full of bread.

All three men turned simultaneously to look at him.

"Where did you see this boat?"

"In the Thames. All of the street boys know to stay far away from it. They do bad things to you there. Even if they do give you a warm cot an' food."

Rowley, Heath and Edmund exchanged glances. "Can you take me to the boat, Timmy?" Rowley asked.

The boy paused with another bite prepared to shovel in his mouth. He nodded. "Ain't far from the fireworks."

"Vauxhall?"

Timmy nodded.

"Do not worry. You will not be hungry again, and we will not let anyone take you to the Molly Jane."

"Heath, will you send for the constables? I do not know what we might be facing."

Rowley called for the carriage, and blankets and warm bricks, while he gathered several weapons and knives. He wanted to be prepared, whatever they found.

"I want to come with you." Heath was standing before him.

"No. You are not strong enough. If Emerson shot you again, it would finish you."

"This is my battle to fight. I should finish it."

"Perhaps you will have the chance, but first I must find Emma. You depart now and send the constables to help me and possibly the children."

Heath gave a reluctant nod. Whether or not his brother would stay, Rowley did not know, but he did trust that Heath would send for help first.

EMMA HITCHED UP her skirts, scrambled up the ladder and then ran for her life. She had no idea where she was, but she ran until her sides were screaming in pain. Not once did she look back. Of course, it had begun to drizzle, so she slid a few times on the slippery cobblestones and felt her boots becoming cold with damp, squelching with every step. She could not hear anyone giving chase, but the blood was pounding so hard in her ears that she probably would not have heard anyway.

When, finally, she thought herself far enough away, she stopped and hid in a doorway to catch her breath. Taking stock of her surroundings, it seemed she had run away from the river. It did not appear that anyone was chasing after her. For a moment, Emma wondered if she had killed the man, but if she had not hit him, she would now be locked away as a prisoner, with untenable acts awaiting her.

Hoof beats approached, and Emma ducked down into a ball inside the doorway in which she was seeking shelter. It was unlikely that Lord Emerson would be chasing her yet, for he had said he would not return until dark. Nevertheless, she could not be too careful. Alternating streets would help cover her tracks, but would she only become more lost? The sky was cloudy and spitting rain, so there was no help from that quarter.

What should she do now? She did have money, so if she could find a hackney cab, she could ride back to Lady Hambridge's house. She began walking carefully, keeping her gaze averted. Dock workers and shopkeepers were beginning to stir in their daily activities. Emma pulled her hood down low, but she knew there was no doubt she was a lady if anyone looked too closely.

The further she went, the more lost she felt. Why were there no hackneys available? Perhaps if she could find a main road, her chances would be better, although she was more likely to be spotted if anyone was giving chase. Her feet were going numb if the creeping deadening sensation were any indication, and she had walked past a dozen streets already. There had to be a main road soon. She was losing track of time; she had passed beyond warehouses to residential streets with five story buildings that were all the same shabby, dirty brown.

Everything was beginning to look the same. Was she walking in circles? The rain was coming down harder, and the thick layers of wool she wore were growing heavy, her hair hanging in strings and whipping against her cheeks.

She feared she was about to collapse with fatigue and hunger. Memories of the desperation she had felt before, on that day Mr. Sheridan had found her, flooded through her again. Living with her godmother and then at Knighton Grange seemed like a distant dream, as did that enchanted kiss she had received from the duke.

This was not the time to become delirious, she told herself fiercely. She tried to shake herself from her maudlin thoughts, but she was lost in a strange neighborhood and someone wanted to kidnap her.

All of a sudden, there seemed to be more people and she grew wary. Even though she was no longer near the docks, it did not appear safe. Another carriage approached and she turned away. It turned down the street in front of her, so she crossed over and went in the other direction. Was anything ever going to look familiar?

How long had it been since she ran away? Soon she sensed that she was being followed, but she refused to turn around and look. The footsteps gained on her, and she tried not to panic, but as they grew close, she set off running again. Everything began to appear as though she were in a tunnel, and she knew she could not go on like this much longer. The buildings and streets were distorted through the rain and she ached with fear and exertion. At last, a hackney cab drew up to the curb ahead! She tried to hail it as she crossed the street. Relief was in sight!

A cart came out from nowhere and she tried to stop herself in time, but tripped on her skirts and landed in a puddle of mud. A large pair of hands hauled her up and dragged her out of the way of the lumbering vehicle.

She began to fight, kicking and screaming. "Let me go!"

"Emma! Emma! Stop fighting! You are safe!"

Safe? Arms wrapped around her, trying to hold her still.

"Emma, it is Rowley. Stop fighting me!"

The voice of command broke through the fog and she stilled.

"Thank God," he said as he kissed her cheek. "My carriage is here. Come inside at once. You are drenched."

Emma looked up to see the duke's beautiful face in front of her, looking at her with concern.

She nodded and let him help her into the coach. Once he had joined her inside, he rapped on the ceiling and they pulled away.

Emma was still shaking with fear. Wordlessly, he covered her with blankets and began to chafe her hands. She looked up into his eyes, tears overflowing her own. Was it real? Was he here?

"Dear God, Emma! I thought I had lost you!"

"I have never been so happy to see anyone in my life!" She leaned her head into his chest and shook.

"Shh! I will never let anyone hurt you again." He wrapped his arms around her and rocked her as though she were an infant. Not in a very long time had she felt so protected.

"I was so afraid. I thought... he was going to lock me up... I might have killed a man..."

"Hush. I will deal with Emerson."

"I have never been so scared. If you had not saved me..."

"You saved yourself! We have been searching everywhere, and when you were not on the boat, I feared something else had happened. Thank God I found you, Emma."

"Yes. Thank God you found me," she whispered. "I was lost. I did not know where to go. I was so cold. And when I heard footsteps..." She began to shake again.

He pulled her into his lap, and in that moment it was the best place on earth.

"We need to stop meeting like this." He laughed. "Much though I enjoy having you in my arms, there has to be a more comfortable way than pulling you from cold rivers or muddy puddles."

She chuckled. "I had to get your attention somehow."

"You have it, Emma. All of it." He turned her head and looked into her eyes with enough love to warm her from the inside out. He brought his lips to hers and kissed away the trembling which was from more than just being cold. How could she have ever thought this man cold and unfeeling? He might be rather dictatorial, it was true, but when one considered all he had to manage, and starting at the tender age of fifteen, it was no surprise. She could feel his love in the tenderness of his touch and his gaze, and she tried to show him how she felt in the return of his embrace.

Some minutes later, they pulled back and once more gazed into each other's eyes. Emma knew the feelings she felt were mutual without either of them uttering a word. She nuzzled closer, tucking her head beneath his chin. He rested his cheek upon her head, and they remained so until the carriage pulled to a halt.

"We are home, Emma, and you will not run away from me again. I could not bear it."

Home.

After the carriage stopped, the next few minutes were a whirl of activity that Emma could hardly fathom. The duke insisted on carrying her to her chambers, where maids were waiting with warm water and blankets and a hot toddy. The servants bathed, clothed, and tucked her into a warm bed, almost without any effort on her part. She was so exhausted and relieved, she would have been pleased to sleep on the floor of the kitchen in her wet clothes. She was safe. The duke had saved her. He had said other things as well. She wished she could stay awake to think about them, but she knew deep inside that he cared for her. Her eyes closed; she could not keep them open any longer. Emerson had not hurt her and the duke had saved her. That was enough for now.

CHAPTER TWENTY-TWO

ONCE EMMA HAD been made comfortable, Rowley cleaned himself up and put on dry clothing. Emerson would have to be dealt with as quickly as possible and hopefully without any public scandal. Perth, Petersham, and Sir Martin would keep their mouths closed, but Emerson must be handled carefully and time was of the essence. Rowley went downstairs to find Heath. He knew more about Emerson's habits and might provide some insight into how to deal with him.

Sir Martin was in the study, but Heath was not.

"Knighton," Sir Martin said. "I heard you found Miss Lancaster."

"It was a near thing," Rowley admitted. "She is resting now. Were you able to discover anything at the club?"

"He has been about, but I was not able to run him down."

"At least he is still in Town. He must be dealt with today," Rowley said with quiet calm. He had moved into a mood where he would not stop until his task was complete.

"I saw Perth and Petersham. I left them to deal with Emerson's yacht. That is where he had taken Miss Lancaster."

"A yacht? That was clever. How did you discover it?"

"A street urchin. As it happens, he was the one who saw Emerson take her from the posting inn."

"I suppose he will no longer be an urchin," Sir Martin remarked with acuteness.

"Just so. He will have a home and whatever he desires for the rest of his life," Rowley replied with a smile.

He walked to the door. "Quincy, do you know where Lord Heath is? Is he resting?"

"I have not seen him for some time, your Grace. I will send someone to his apartments."

"Thank you, Quincy." A rap on the door signaled the return of Lord Perth and Mr. Petersham.

"Quincy, have Cook send up some food for everyone, will you? I know I am hungry."

"Yes, Your Grace." Rowley directed those present into the study and closed the door.

"Miss Lancaster is resting upstairs," he assured the men. "Have you been able to discover anything?"

"Thank God," Lord Perth said, sitting down with evident relief. Rowley still wanted to know why he had not helped Emma when she had been in need before, but much could be forgiven his willingness to help now.

"Quite a lot, in fact," Petersham was saying, "when we discovered Miss Lancaster was not on the boat, and had run away."

"That was when I left to search the streets for her," Rowley stated.

"We were able to convince the captain of the yacht to tell us the plan."

"At least Miss Lancaster did not kill him as she feared."

"No. She did give him a nasty blow," Perth said appreciatively. "The captain said he was told to lock her in a cabin and pull the yacht out into deep waters. Emerson was to return after dark and the captain would await his signal."

"So Emerson is to return there tonight. What did you do with the captain?"

"We locked him in the cabin," Petersham said with a cheeky grin.

"Excellent!" Rowley exclaimed. "That gives us a few hours to rest and come up with a plan."

Quincy entered with a tray of sandwiches and the men did not speak while they ate heartily. The butler came back into the room only a few minutes later.

"Lord Heath is not in his apartments, Your Grace. No one knows where he is."

Rowley frowned. "Did anyone see him leave?"

Quincy shook his head. "I have sent Thomas to the mews."

Rowley nodded, but was filled with foreboding. Had Heath set out after Emerson? He did not have the strength to do such a thing!

"I will need to find my brother, but I believe we should meet back at the yacht before dark and pull it out into the water so Emerson does not suspect anything. We will lie in wait for him there. Do you believe the captain can be made to cooperate?"

"Who knows how deep his loyalty to Emerson is? I would not trust it," Petersham said.

"I can steer the boat well enough that we should not need the captain," Lord Perth offered.

"Will we need more men? Do you think Emerson will come alone?" Petersham asked.

"His grievance is with Lord Heath. He will try to draw him there. I believe Miss Lancaster was to have been the bait," Sir Martin added. He knew Emerson best.

"I suspect you are correct, but where is my brother?" Rowley sighed. "Let us proceed regardless. I would prefer to keep this as discreet as possible. Bring your weapons and hopefully we can subdue him peacefully."

The men finished eating and prepared to leave.

"Did Lord Edmund return to his own home?" Rowley asked.

"That reminds me," Perth said. "We found four young boys hidden on the boat."

Rowley closed his eyes with disgust.

"Just so." Perth agreed with his sentiments. "Lord Edmund took them back to the rectory with the young urchin."

Rowley nodded. "At least they will not be caught in the middle of this evening's events."

"I, for one, hope Emerson tries to flee so we can rid the earth of the bastard!" Petersham exclaimed.

Rowley looked with keen interest at each of the gentlemen, who seemed in agreement. "That would be too easy for him, but it would certainly make disposing of him less messy if he were to fall into the Thames."

The gentlemen departed, agreeing to meet at the docks an hour before dusk.

Having snatched what rest he could in the circumstances, Rowley arrived at the docks a few hours later, but earlier than the appointed time. Heath had not returned home, and Rowley was afraid he would do something rash. He was not physically able to defend himself, and that led Rowley to believe he intended to shoot Emerson. Much though Emerson deserved it, Rowley could not condone cold-blooded murder. He intended to persuade Emerson he would be much more comfortable living abroad.

Rowley had gathered together several of the family's long-time retainers to stand guard in the area. They had devised signals with whistles and lamps to use once it was dark. He hoped it would be enough. Edmund would not come aboard the craft, for Rowley needed someone in his family to be able to protect Emma and Eugenia if something should go very wrong. Thankfully, Emma would be provided for even if she did not become his duchess. He prayed it would not come to that, but Heath had almost died and who knew what Emerson would have done to Emma had she not escaped?

Rowley smiled as he thought of little Timmy, who was the real hero in today's rescue efforts. Not only had he saved Emma, but several other little boys. He had no doubt they were being coddled and cuddled by Edmund's motherly housekeeper. Rowley settled into an empty warehouse across from the wharf where the *Molly Jane* was anchored. If Emerson returned during the day to see it still at the quay, they would not be able to carry out their plan as devised. Perth and Petersham had assured him that the captain was the only person left on board when they departed that morning.

He sat on the windowsill and settled down for a long wait. It was still raining and freezing. It would be nicer if it were just snow. Oh, how he longed for this to be over with and to be back at the Grange with Emma as his duchess! He knew she would resist, but in this, he was determined. He had always put everyone else's needs ahead of his own, but there was no other woman for him, of that he was certain.

The first person to arrive was Sir Martin. He was on foot, having been dropped off as Rowley was a few streets away. Perth, Petersham, and Edmund arrived not long after.

"Is everyone ready?" Rowley asked. "You need not stay if your conscience forbids it."

"My conscience would not let me stay away," Perth said with fierce gravity.

The others agreed.

"Very well. Edmund will stay here and alert the authorities if something goes wrong."

His brother nodded solemnly.

"We all know the signals? I have men stationed on every corner for several streets in each direction."

Again they all nodded. Rowley was thankful they were taking this with proper seriousness. He could never tell with Heath and his associates.

Rowley gave Edmund a quick hug as they departed.

"Did Heath return home?" Edmund asked.

Rowley shook his head. "Hopefully he knows what he is about."

He and Edmund exchanged glances of doubt before he patted his brother on the shoulder and followed the others to the boat.

Petersham and Sir Martin were checking through the boat to make sure there were no surprises, while Rowley helped Perth prepare to pull up the anchor and move the boat out into deeper water.

After they had moved, they would wait on Emerson's leisure.

Once they had withdrawn far enough away so that Emerson would probably be satisfied, one of the servants kept watch while the rest of them explored the yacht and tried to decide how best to deal with Emerson.

The more Rowley saw of the yacht, the more disgusted he became. Everything about the ship screamed depravity, and he began to have second thoughts about how best to deal with such a monster. If he was turned over to the authorities, he would be tried in the House of Lords. Peers would not like being forced to deal with such a matter, especially not involving one of their own members. There was also a strong chance that it would expose some of them, as well, not to mention the likelihood of Heath and Miss Lancaster being dragged into the ensuing scandal.

"You look deep in thought," Sir Martin remarked.

Rowley pointed to the small cabin where the boys had obviously been kept prisoner. He could not even verbalize his thoughts.

"Death is too good for him," Sir Martin said.

"But a public trial would be worse," Rowley said.

"What do you want to do, once we have him?"

"I suppose it depends on his reaction. Clearly the duel did not satisfy him, since he kidnapped Miss Lancaster. I expect he will fight."

Perth called down from the hatch. "I just saw a signal from the quay. I am ready to pull anchor."

"Get into place," Rowley said to Petersham and Sir Martin.

The two of them were to hide at either end of the large, open cabin. Perth and Rowley were going to wait on the deck, since Perth needed some assistance with ropes and other equipment. Rowley climbed up the ladder and helped Perth lift the anchor and then retreated behind a mast and the pump-well while the other man began to steer the vessel back to the dock.

It only took a few minutes and Rowley could feel his pulse quicken in anticipation and dread. There could be no good ending to this situation. A man so sunken to depravity had everything to lose by exposure and would not behave as a gentleman.

The boat heaved as the anchor dropped. Perth had dressed in similar garb to the captain, and was busy tying ropes and securing the yacht. Rowley was grateful he knew what to do, for it was imperative that Emerson not suspect anything yet. Perth kept his head down as he secured the boat, in order to allow Emerson to board. When Rowley caught his first glimpse of Emerson, his heart sank as he realized he had not come alone. Heath was with him.

Rowley cursed under his breath. Everything became much more complicated—doubly so.

Both of the men boarded and Emerson was speaking in a low voice to Heath.

Rowley had instructed Perth to pull the boat away immediately, to give them the advantage over Emerson. He had meant to distract him in the meantime, but that was no longer feasible. They still had the upper hand, however, since Miss Lancaster was gone and the captain was incapacitated. Heath was, of course, unaware that Emma was safe.

Rowley watched as Emerson led Heath to the hatch and he nodded to Perth to take the boat back out. He moved stealthily to the hatch to prevent Emerson coming back up.

"What the devil?" He heard Emerson yell as the boat pushed off again from the quay.

Emerson's head immediately appeared at the opening and Rowley saw his irate face glaring up at him. Emerson let out a string of invectives that would have scorched anyone's ears.

Rowley knew that Sir Martin and Petersham were hiding, their weapons pointed at Emerson. He only hoped Heath was wise enough to stay out of the crossfire if it came to that.

Emerson climbed the ladder and looked around. Rowley allowed it since he was still at an advantage, being higher on the deck.

"Return to the quay at once, Duncan!" Emerson commanded.

Perth ignored him, of course. The tide was in, and there was a slight breeze, so the ship would not be easy to maneuver in the other direction for some time.

"I demand to know what is going on and why you are on my boat!" Emerson boomed at Rowley.

He stood over the devil, preventing his coming fully up to the deck. "Certainly. Would you care to explain why you kidnapped Miss Lancaster?"

"Not to you," he spat. "My complaint is with Lord Heath, as you see." He inclined his head backwards.

"You will forgive me if I disagree. First, you try to kill my brother, and according to the gentlemanly code of honor, that should have settled your aggrievances. Not only did you not abide by this code, you dragged an innocent party into it."

Emerson chuckled. "How acute you are, Duke. If you have already established I am no gentleman, what do you hope to accomplish by trespassing now?"

"I had hoped there was a shred of decency left in your soul, but after seeing what you have done to those poor, innocent boys, I am well aware this will not be settled in a satisfactory manner."

Emerson put his hands on his hips haughtily, but Rowley suspected he was reaching for a weapon.

As Rowley put his hand on his own waist ready to draw, he heard a pistol cock behind Emerson. Heath was standing at the man's back with a gun inches from his head.

"You would never live it down if you shot me in the back, you coward," Emerson growled. "Besides, you need to get to your precious Miss Hamilton. My man has orders to kill her if I am not the one to release her."

"I am certain I can manage him once I dispose of you," Heath drawled.

"Miss Hamilton is no longer on board," Rowley informed him. "Neither are the young boys. All you will find on this ship are men who wish you harm."

"You are bluffing."

Rowley raised his brows in his most pretention-quelling manner. "Your man is no longer captaining the ship." He inclined his head toward Perth, who smirked and gave a little wave to Emerson.

Rowley recognized the moment Emerson decided to bolt. An instant later, he flung himself toward Rowley to knock him out of the way, but Rowley jumped from his path and Emerson landed face down on the hatch. He rolled over, and Heath, Petersham and Sir Martin surrounded him. They had come up the hatch on the other side of the boat.

"Get up, man!" Rowley commanded.

"Just shoot me and get it over with," Emerson begged.

"You deserve no such kindness. I believe we should let him explain before a jury of his peers what he has done," Rowley said to the present jury.

"You would not dare," Emerson snarled. "Your own precious family secrets would be nothing to sneeze at."

"Very well, we will put you on a ship to Botany Bay. There is a spot reserved for you in the hull with the other prisoners. I have it all arranged."

The six men stood around Emerson while he considered this. Rowley had no such thing arranged, but he did not flinch.

The sweat began to pour down Emerson's brow. Again, Rowley saw the moment the man panicked; scrambling to his feet, he made a dash for the railing. With deadly calm and precision, Heath fired and the weight of the blow assisted Emerson over into the water.

The men walked across to watch as the resulting splash slapped water on to the deck. No one made a move to help as they viewed the prone body floating away in the wake of the ship.

They were quite a way from the quay by this time, with the tide and the winds moving them swiftly. Rowley hoped the body would make its way out into the Channel.

"Do you think he is done for?" Petersham asked as they watched the distance between them grow. "I would hate to find that he, of all people, had survived, like one of those Gothic horror stories!"

"I planted him a facer. If that did not get him, the icy water soon will."

"He got off too easily," Sir Martin added with evident disgust.

"True, but he was not worth the trouble. And we can be sure he will not live to hurt another person."

Once the body was no longer visible, Rowley turned to look at his brother, who had done the right thing. Heath looked pale and haggard.

"Let us repair down below and rest. It will be a while until we can turn the ship back." Even now, Perth was trying to slow their momentum against the wind and tide.

"Are you putting me to bed, Row?" Heath managed to drawl. "I had to do it, y'know."

"I know. Now hush," Rowley said, as he laid him on a sofa without further arguments.

Chapter Twenty-Three

It was several hours before they were able to return the yacht to the quay. All the men returned home exhausted and somber, just before dawn. Rowley was anxious to see how Emma did, but he did not wish to wake her. Hopefully, she would be relieved that her secret was now safe. He could think of no other hindrance to their happiness, but it did not mean she would agree.

After a nap and a bath, Rowley went in search of her. He found her with Eugenia, cuddled up on Emma's bed, cups of chocolate in hand, having a coze. It was inappropriate for him to be in Emma's room, but with his sister being there, perhaps he could be excused. He watched with amusement as Emma related her harrowing tale to his sister.

"How dashing you are!" Eugenia exclaimed as Emma shook her head in denial.

Rowley pushed the door wide open, since they had not noticed his presence. "Yes, she was very dashing and brave."

Emma's cheeks took on a rosy hue as she eyed him over the rim of her cup.

"How are you, Your Grace? We were worried when none of you returned last evening."

Rowley sat in one of the chairs near the window. He crossed his legs and rested his elbows on the arms of the chair, steepling his fingers before him. Eugenia interrupted his thoughts as he debated how much to say.

"Something has happened. I can tell by that look on your face, Row!"

"Indeed, something very grave."

"Tell us!" she said impatiently.

"Emerson is dead." Whatever reaction he had expected from Emma, "Thank God" was not it. She sank back against the headboard with relief.

"I suppose it is very wrong of me to say that, but he was a vile man. If you knew what he did to innocent children…" She broke off, emotion choking her words. Eugenia hugged her close. "I thought he would do that to me, too."

"He can never harm you again," Rowley assured her, wishing his sister to perdition at the moment, so he could scoop Emma into his arms.

"How did it happen? Or is it too gruesome to tell?"

"It was not particularly gruesome, but I had rather not give all the details. We set a trap for him on the yacht where he intended to imprison you. He fought, and did not survive. He fell overboard and was washed out into the Channel." It was best to keep it simple, he reflected.

Eugenia looked shocked. Good.

"Do you think we could return to the Grange for the Christmas season, after all?" Eugenia asked sheepishly.

"That sounds delightful to me, but we must ask Edmund. He was the one who wanted us to spend Christmas here, if you recall."

"I will ask him."

A footman knocked on the door, which Rowley had left open, and looked surprised to find his master tête-à-tête with the ladies.

"Begging your pardon, Your Grace, Lord Perth has arrived and is asking to speak with Miss Lancaster."

She glanced at him as though she needed his approval to speak with her cousin. He gave her a questioning look and a nod.

"Tell him I will be down momentarily," she said to the footman.

Rowley stood up. "We will leave you, then," he said, holding his hand out to Eugenia, who left with him although clearly reluctant.

Rowley went on down to greet Perth. "Good morning," he said as he entered the drawing room. "I trust you got some rest?"

"A little," Perth admitted. "I came to see how my cousin fairs and to see if she wishes to join us in the country for the Christmas season."

"You will have to ask her, since I have no claim to her—yet."

Perth's head snapped up and he looked at Rowley suspiciously. "Yet?"

"I mean to ask her to be my duchess, if you have no objections?"

"How could I object? I may be the head of her family, but I have no right to reject such an offer on her behalf."

"Her brothers might not think it is such a good alliance, but I do believe I can make her happy," Rowley mused.

"I thought she would need my assistance," Perth laughed. "Yesterday's events make much more sense to me now, though I suspect you would have acted the same on your brother's behalf."

"I cannot venture to say," Rowley admitted. "However, it appears my brother was able to take care of himself, as was Miss Lancaster."

"I wish I had known of the dire straits she was in. She could have come to me, though I understand why she was reluctant."

"Your sentiments do you credit, Perth. Do not feel bad, for she did not go to her godmother at first, either, even though she was, and is, very willing to give her a home."

Emma entered then, looking more beautiful than ever in a simple lawn-colored muslin day dress. Her hair was tied back in a single ribbon and his throat tightened at what could have happened to her the previous day.

"I will leave the two of you to converse." He shook Perth's hand. "I am indebted to you."

He took himself off to his study, but paced the room anxiously as he waited for Emma to finish with her cousin. He had no more qualms about making her his duchess, but he was very nervous she would not agree.

"What has you in the fidgets?" Heath asked as he walked gingerly into the room and sat near the fire.

Rowley stopped and looked at his brother, assessing his demeanor. "If you must know, I mean to ask Miss Lancaster to be my duchess."

Heath stared into the fire; his only sign of irritation his clenched jaw.

"Does that anger you?"

"Why should it?" Heath asked, annoyed. "You may do as you wish."

"I should like your blessing, all the same," Rowley answered honestly.

"I asked her to be my mistress, Your Grace," Heath said in a low voice.

"She was in dire circumstances then and she refused. She is a virtuous lady."

"Then there you have it in a nutshell."

Rowley should have expected this reaction. Even though Heath had defended Emma's honor, it had not made it acceptable for her to be a duchess, or perhaps just not Rowley's. He would press no further.

"I would like to travel abroad for a while," Heath remarked, still looking mulish.

Rowley watched his brother struggling. He had always been so self-assured, but this had rattled him. Did Heath harbor hopes of something more with Emma? Had he had feelings deeper than Rowley had known? "Perhaps that would be for the best," he conceded, "because things cannot go on as they were."

"Do you think I look for trouble on purpose?"

"Sometimes it is hard to know."

"I did not mean her harm," Heath said softly.

"It is not me you need to apologize to, Heath, but things will have to change."

Heath looked at Rowley as though he were the one who had begun this. As though he had failed. Perhaps he had, but he had to do something now to try to save him.

"I had meant to delay this discussion until you were recovered, but if you feel well enough to travel then I will speak now."

Heath was still looking at him as though he were Lady Macbeth.

"When you return from your travels, I will give you six months to find a suitable bride."

"Or what?" Heath snapped. "I have my own fortune, in case you have forgotten."

"You have it because I say you do."

"And if I do not agree?"

"You will be obliged to find a profession like your brothers have."

Heath scowled. "What you really mean is I am not welcome because of her."

"I mean you cannot continue to carry on as though you are invincible. You almost died!"

They stared at each other, the tension thick.

Emma appeared on the threshold, and Heath bit back whatever he was about to say.

"Forgive me," she said. "Am I intruding?"

"Of course not. We were discussing Heath's future."

Her lips formed a small "O". "I can speak with you later. I intend to return to my godmother's."

"Heath has something he wishes to say to you," Rowley interjected with a pointed stare at his brother.

"Please do not leave on my account, Miss Lancaster. I will trouble you no further, in fact, I will be abroad for the near future. A warm climate suddenly appeals to my state as an invalid."

Emma frowned.

"May I humbly beg your forgiveness for the distress I have caused you? I truly meant no harm and had no notion what Lord Emerson would do to you."

Rowley watched as his brother made an attempt to right the wrongs he had committed. It was a start, but it would take more than that to heal all of the wounds Heath had caused with his selfishness. Rowley wondered if he himself was taking the right course. Heath's smooth tongue always got him out of the worst fixes, but not this time. Rowley hated being heavy-handed with him, but lesser methods had not worked.

"I appreciate that," Emma said, wiping away tears, "but you need not leave on my behalf."

"I think it would be for the best, considering." He cast a look toward Rowley before leaving the room.

Rowley felt like he was being torn in two—having to choose between two people he loved. He only hoped that being away would help Heath see he could have better for himself, and in time, they could heal the chasm between them.

EMMA WATCHED LORD Heath leave and knew she had no reason to stay any longer. She turned around to see the duke watching her with hooded eyes.

Her heart was confused, so she turned away so she would not have to look at him while she said what she must.

"I expect this is goodbye. I do not have adequate words to express my gratitude, sir. I do not know where I would be without your assistance." She fidgeted with the tassels on her gown, trying not to rip them off in her despair.

"I do not want your gratitude, Emma," he said softly in her ear, sending shivers down her spine and causing her no little trepidation. She had not noticed his approach, so lost she had been in her anguish of leaving him, but she knew she could not be near him and not want more.

"What do you want, then, Your Grace?"

"Can you not know by now?" He turned her around to face him, keeping his hands on her shoulders. "I want you, Emma. All of you."

She shook her head. "While I am certain you do me a great honor, and I have come to care for you very much, my conscience would not permit it."

He was looking at her with his icy façade in place again. Had she hurt him?

"I apologize. I had thought my attentions were welcome… reciprocated, even."

She closed her eyes and felt her chin begin to tremble.

"Dear God, Emma. Please do not cry! Anything but that. I will send for the carriage so you may be rid of me and my unwelcome attentions!"

"Forgive me. I did not mean to give you a false impression of my acquiescence." She brushed away the stubborn tears which insisted on streaming down her cheeks.

He watched her in that disarming manner of his as she dried her tears. "Is there nothing I can say to change your mind? It is an unusual situation, to be sure, but Heath will not bother you again. With Lord Emerson gone, there is no one else to bring up your past."

Emma nodded. That was true, but how could she explain to a duke that she wanted a respectable marriage—perhaps even children, one day? She had not thought it possible, even two days ago, but with Lord Emerson dead and now her cousin wanting to welcome her into the family, she had a chance of being respectable.

"Emma, would it be so terrible to be my wife?"

She spun about. "Your wife?"

"You thought I would ask you to be my mistress, after everything Heath put you through?" His jaw was practically hanging open as her cheeks burned with embarrassment. Then he surprised her by throwing his arms around her and laughing mightily.

"I am pleased to offer you amusement, Your Grace," she said tartly. "It has been my wish to make you smile. If I had known humiliating myself in such a manner was all it needed, I would have done it long ago!"

"Oh, you precious girl," he said, beginning to feather kisses over her ears, her eyes, her forehead and even her nose before reaching her lips. If she had thought their previous kiss was in danger of melting her bones, then there were no words to describe how this one turned every part of her insides to mush. When he decided to return her to her sensibilities, he placed his forehead to hers.

"Please, dearest Emma, say you will be my wife." His eyes bored into hers with such longing and desire, it muddled her senses even further.

"You are certain?" She could still not believe the haughty, cold duke she had once hated was this warm, romantic man who wanted her… respectfully.

"I have never been more certain in my life. I am doing something selfish for once. Why do you not do the same? Will you allow me to wed you, Emma?"

She could feel her reciprocating smile. "I believe I will."

He led her to the sofa and pulled her into his lap. "This is where I like you best," he said as she nestled against his chest. "Would you mind terribly if we were married at the Grange?"

"I think my sensibilities could make shift," she quipped.

"I wondered if you would prefer a grand London wedding at Saint George's, but I suspected you would prefer something quiet and small."

"I realize there are some formalities that must be observed for a duke to wed."

"That is true, but wedding in the winter, at the edge of nowhere, will prevent many a party from accepting the invitation."

"You are wise as well as handsome," she teased as she kissed his cheek.

"Remember that the next time you are cross with me. I recall the first time a green-eyed termagant dared to cross swords with me. I think that was when I first realized I must love you."

"You love me?" She pulled back to look him in the eye.

He sighed heavily. "You little minx, do you think I would have put myself through these tomfooleries for anything less?"

"I had no notion you felt anything more than desire for me."

"That I do—even in those dreadful caps."

She gurgled with laughter. "I enjoyed that very much."

"Of that I have no doubt," he said dryly.

"You must admit the turban was a stroke of genius."

"And when did you realize you loved me?" he asked with haughty impertinence.

"You are very certain of yourself, my lord duke."

He took the opportunity to kiss her senseless and show her how sure he was. He pulled her into him and slid his arms around her, circling her fully. She returned the pressure, making him struggle to keep his own mind from losing himself completely as she returned his kiss with equal fervor.

"Do you require more convincing?" he asked with a raised eyebrow and the scowl lines between his brows appearing.

She brushed them away with her finger. "I have long wanted to do that. Very well." She pretended to think as she tapped her index finger against her chin. "I believe I first knew when I awoke in your arms after you pulled me from the river."

"Only then?" He looked affronted.

"Oh, yes. I very much detested you before then. I was certain you had ruined my brother and sent him to America. I did not want to be attracted to you at all, but you won me over by degrees."

"I suppose that is better than not at all," he said begrudgingly.

"Are you pouting, Your Grace?"

"A little," he conceded. "And my name is Rowley, if you please. People only call me 'Your Grace' if they want something or mean to toady me."

"I will keep that in mind," she said with a devilish grin. "Your Grace?"

"Yes?" He looked at her with mock exasperation.

"Kiss me, please."

"Perhaps I like 'Your Grace' after all, Your Grace." His lips descended on hers again and this time they enjoyed a long, tender kiss.

"I am not Your Grace yet," she reminded him.

"We should remedy that rather quickly. Does a Christmas wedding trouble you?"

"As long as it is not Christmas Day. I should not like to take away from the birth of Christ."

"No indeed. In that case, I shall have Cummins arrange everything. Shall we tell the family?"

"I think I prefer to stay where I am. They will find us eventually," she whispered wantonly.

He looked at her with astonishment, but she caught the twinkle in his eye. "I am not a saint, my dear. Remain at your own peril."

She hastily scrambled to her feet, whereupon he threw back his head and laughed.

"What is going on in here?" Eugenia asked as she entered the room, her face full of curiosity. "Heath said he is leaving for Italy."

"The warmer climate will do him good," Rowley explained.

She cast herself ungracefully into one of the chairs, pouting. "I should like to go with him. I cannot come out yet anyway."

"One day you can," he replied flippantly.

She scowled at him. "I wish to go now!"

"But if you go now you shall miss our wedding."

"Your wedding?" Eugenia looked at Rowley and then at Emma. "You do not mean it?"

Emma smiled and nodded. "Someone has to keep him in order."

Eugenia jumped to her feet and threw her arms around Emma. "This means I get to keep you!"

"I am not marrying her for your sake, Genie," he said dryly.

"There is enough of me to share," Emma retorted with a wink at her betrothed.

Chapter Twenty-Four

Rowley hated being the center of attention, but he need not have worried. Once Emma arrived, all eyes were on her. While a few people remarked how handsome he looked, more still declared that he was a lucky devil. He knew it. As he looked around the chapel, full of those souls brave enough to come to the far end of England to be with them on their special day, he felt both a mixture of nerves and excitement.

Rowley had not been in the chapel at the Grange since his mother died, but it was time for new beginnings. Even in the winter, the gardeners had outdone themselves. The pews and altar were decorated with holly, garlands of greenery and ribbons, and inside the chapel smelled as fresh as the outdoors. Candles provided a warm glow on an otherwise cold, wintry day.

Heath was missing but no one remarked on it. Lady Hambridge had braved the long journey again, but this time she did not seem to mind.

When at last the doors opened, Lord Perth stood there with Emma on his arm. For a man who had disavowed the marital state, Rowley was, surprisingly, completely void of doubt. He was struck by how much he wanted this marriage—this woman—and everything that entailed. Perth led her down the aisle and handed her to him.

She was dressed in a simple ivory gown with a lace over-slip and a lace veil on her head. It was as if she read his mind, for she looked upward to the headpiece and smiled at him with a mischievous twinkle in her eye. He could not wait to take it off.

"Dearly beloved, we are gathered together here in the sight of God," Edmund began. Those words made it real. Rowley tried not to think of who was missing—two of his brothers and Emma's immediate family, not to mention their parents. Instead, he tried to think of who was there to bless them and their union.

As Edmund read the familiar lines, Rowley took each one to heart. In the past, he had endured countless weddings and had largely ignored or disdained most of the words.

"Signifying unto us the mystical union that is betwixt Christ and his Church; which holy estate Christ adorned and beautified with his presence..." Edmund was smiling as he spoke.

"...And therefore is not to be enterprised, nor taken in hand unadvisedly, lightly, or wantonly, to satisfy men's carnal lusts and appetites, like brute beasts that have no understanding; but reverently, discreetly, advisedly, soberly, and in the fear of God..." Rowley almost laughed aloud when he remembered that he had been called a beast. He tried to ignore the part about carnal lusts.

"One cause was the procreation of children, to be brought up in the fear and nurture of the Lord, and in the praise of God." Children did not sound quite as horrid when he thought of having them with Emma...

"Secondly, it was ordained for a remedy against sin, and to avoid fornication; that such persons as be married might live chastely in matrimony, and keep themselves undefiled members of Christ's body."

"Thirdly, for the mutual society, help, and comfort, that the one ought to have of the other, both in prosperity and adversity. Into the holy estate these two persons present come now to be joined. Therefore if any man can shew any just cause why they may not lawfully be joined together, let him now speak, or else hereafter for ever hold his peace."

That was the part that made Rowley nervous. He could see Emma felt the same, and he squeezed her hand in reassurance. He heard her sigh when no one spoke and Edmund continued.

"Now for the good part," Edmund whispered, smiling.

"Wilt thou have this woman to thy wedded wife, to live together after God's ordinance in the holy estate of Matrimony? Wilt thou love her, comfort her, honor, and keep her in sickness and in health; and, forsaking all other, keep thee only unto her, so long as you both shall live?"

"I will." Rowley spoke to Emma.

The thought of honoring this woman and protecting her made him want to weep with the gift he was being given. He had been responsible for hundreds, if not thousands, of people as a duke, but never before had the import struck him as it did with this one person.

"Wilt thou have this man to thy wedded husband, to live together after God's ordinance in the holy estate of Matrimony? Wilt thou obey him, and serve him, love, honor, and keep him in sickness and in health; and, forsaking all other, keep thee only unto him, so long as you both shall live?"

"I will," Emma said, looking into his eyes and he knew the words meant as much to her.

Time seemed to stand still for that moment. He had heard people say the ceremony was scarcely remembered, but personally, he knew he would recall every second.

"Now you may join hands," Edmund directed.

"I, Rowley Edward George Knight take thee *Emma Grace Lancaster* to be my wedded wife, to have and to hold from this day forward, for better for worse, for richer for poorer, in sickness and in health, to love and to cherish, till death us do part, according to God's holy ordinance: and thereto I plight thee my troth."

Emma repeated her vows, then Rowley took the gold wedding band and placed it on her finger.

"With this ring I thee wed: this gold and silver I thee give: with my body I thee worship: and with all my worldly goods I thee endow: in the Name of the Father, and of the Son, and of the Holy Ghost. Amen."

Edmund prayed, they took holy communion and signed the register. It was happening so fast.

"Those whom God hath joined together let no man put asunder. Forasmuch as *Rowley* and *Emma* have consented together in holy wedlock, and have witnessed the same here before God and this company, and thereto have given and pledged their troth either to other, and have declared the same by giving and receiving gold and silver, and by joining of hands: I pronounce that they be Man and Wife together. In the Name of the Father, and of the Son, and of the Holy Ghost. Amen."

They walked down the aisle hand-in-hand, duke and duchess, husband and wife, to be greeted by those who could not fit inside the small chapel. Shouts of congratulations and joy greeted them, as did a shower of flower petals and seed. An open landau was waiting to take them back to the manor house. It had been decorated in ribbons and bells that jingled merrily all the way.

A grand celebration had been planned at the Grange for all—not just for the esteemed wedding guests. A harvest ball was held there every summer, but it was rare to open the doors at this time of year.

The floors shone and the candelabras had been polished and filled with hundreds of new candles. Every available surface was covered in more garlands of green foliage, holly and red and white flowers. Sprigs of mistletoe hung from every doorway and the scents of wassail and mulled wine wafted through the air. A London chef had been brought in to help Cook with the feast and Rowley was pleased to share this occasion with all of his tenants. He and Emma greeted everyone and enjoyed watching them eat, laugh, and dance. He only hoped they would not be too scandalized when he waltzed with his wife.

Once everyone had filled their plates and settled down to eat, and glasses of champagne had been passed out to all, he took Emma by the arm, leading her to the front of the room where everyone could see them. The crowd grew quiet.

"My new duchess and I are delighted that you have joined us to celebrate our marriage day. Many of you know I had not thought to marry. God seemed to have other plans for me."

The crowd laughed.

"Now, I cannot imagine my life without you in it," he said to Emma, "and I look forward to growing old together. The best is yet to come. As Shakespeare said, 'Now join hands, and with your hands your hearts.'"

Emma wiped away a tear as he kissed her on the cheek, then raised his glass.

"We hope you will eat, drink, and dance your fill. Now, if you will forgive me, I have been waiting all day to dance with my wife."

The crowd raised their glasses. "Hear, hear!"

He nodded to the musicians, who began playing the waltz. He had never particularly enjoyed dancing before now. He had always felt somewhat ridiculous mincing about, truth be told, but there was something magical in the air when he drew his beloved into his arms and held her for all to see how much he loved her. He was quite sure he was fawning over his wife and for once he cared not how he appeared.

"You look happy," Emma murmured, smiling up into his face.

"I truly am, thank you."

"I should be the one thanking you," she said with a scrunch of her nose. He desperately wanted to kiss the little wrinkle away.

No one joined them on the dance floor; instead, they watched and clapped and smiled their appreciation as if it were a new show to watch. A few months ago, Rowley would have been appalled at being on display, but he had come close to losing Emma by being too proud.

"What are you thinking?"

"Besides how lucky I am to have you?"

"Mm," she agreed saucily.

"I was thinking, what if you had not spoken up for Eugenia that day."

"You would not have noticed me," she remarked with a wry smile.

He furrowed his brow in thought as he twirled her about the floor. "Perhaps not. It certainly caught my attention."

"That was never my intent, you know."

"I do know. You wanted nothing to do with me and you spoke up for your charge because you felt it was right. Yet I also had some uncanny sense that I knew you from somewhere, and that stirred my interest."

Her face sobered.

"What did I say?" He did not want to ruin the moment.

"I hope I will not become a permanent wedge between you and Lord Heath."

"It will not for me," Rowley said honestly. "However, he has to live with the consequences of his behaviors. I was not going to give up my future happiness because of it."

She smiled at him. "I still cannot believe I am your duchess."

He chuckled. "You had better believe it, my dear. All the people here are quite taken with you." He inclined his head toward the onlookers.

"I dare not look or I will fall on my face."

"You can trust me not to let you fall."

"You have already proven that."

THE SUN WAS rising over the Amalfi Coast, and a warm, gentle breeze wafted onto the terrace, bringing with it a fresh, tangy scent. They were having a light breakfast, al fresco, and enjoying the rich, creamy coffee the Italians were famous for, along with cheeses, sausages and fresh fruits.

"It is divine here, Rowley," Emma said, smiling at her husband.

"If you are happy, I am happy." He returned the smile with uncustomary outward affection.

"The sight of you billing and cooing is enough to make an old woman want to jump off the cliff," the dowager remarked.

"Are you wishing to go for a swim, Grandmama?" Eugenia asked, completely missing the sarcasm. "Because I think it would be safer to walk down to the water. Edmund and Timmy are already there."

"I do not swim, you silly girl!" the dowager barked. "Nevertheless," she added with evident appreciation as she rose from her chair slowly but without assistance, "my bones do not hurt so much here," she said appreciatively.

"Shall I buy you this villa, Grandmama?" Rowley asked.

"Why not? You're full of juice!"

Emma laughed at the old lady's use of stable talk.

"Who would stay here with you?" Eugenia asked.

"My maid, of course," she snapped. "And Heath, I suppose, if he insists on making a mull of things. I will not tolerate his chère amies in the house!" Emma bit on her lower lip to keep from laughing. Thankfully, Eugenia did not seem to know the meaning of the words.

"Would you not miss England?" Eugenia asked.

"Not a bit of it. Have you been outside?" She looked at her granddaughter as though she had more hair than wit.

"It is very beautiful here," the girl said, looking sad, "but *I* would miss you."

"You may visit, of course. Now I wish to rest," the dowager declared in a voice brooking no contradiction.

"I will see you to your room, then I think I will join Edmund and Timmy. Edmund said they found some caves yesterday and that they are going to explore them today!" Eugenia said in a giddy manner, causing the dowager to cast her eyes heavenward in exasperation as they left.

"I cannot believe you persuaded me to bring them to Italy. Who brings their sister and grandmother on their wedding trip?" Rowley asked Emma. There was a twinkle of good humor in his eyes.

"It was a stroke of genius to bring your grandmother along to chaperone Eugenia. She may spit like a cat, but she is quite diverted, I assure you! Can you truly say you have been neglected?"

"No, but it is the principle of the thing. If this gets out, I shall be laughed out of my clubs. If I were a man who cared for such fustian, I fear I should be forced to rusticate."

"Then it is fortunate you are not such a man or Eugenia would not enjoy a come out. Of course, I should not have married you if you were," she teased, kissing him on the cheek. "Besides, just look out of the window and you will not care who is here."

So saying, Emma walked over to the balustrade. Overlooking the sea, it commanded a glorious vista. She was still in awe of the crystal-clear waters and the array of blues she saw there, ranging from aquamarine to turquoise to cerulean to midnight. It was one of the most beautiful images she had ever seen. "There are no words to describe the beauty here."

"I agree wholeheartedly," he said, coming up behind her and putting his arms around her. He rested his chin on her shoulder with a sigh of contentment.

"Thank you for bringing me here, even if I insisted on bringing Eugenia and your grandmother. The warm weather has done her a great deal of good."

"And Edmund and Timmy," he added sardonically.

"I am still surprised we were able to convince Edmund to take a holiday."

"He would never heed me. I blame you completely."

"You were both worried about Heath."

"I am not certain Heath was pleased to see us, but we can leave knowing he is recovering well."

"How long do you think he will stay?"

"Probably as long as he thinks he can. I gave him an ultimatum before he left."

"Did you?" She turned her head to look at him. "Do you think that was wise? It seems to me he will turn mulish when someone threatens him."

"He does. I cannot say if it was the right course to take or not. He has always been perplexing. You think he will do the right thing and then he plays some fool trick that almost gets him killed. This was not his first foray into idiocy."

"He did redeem himself as far as I am concerned."

"That he did, and I am grateful. It would have been untenable to choose between the two of you, and I am glad I did not have to."

"I cannot imagine having to make such a decision. I miss my brothers and sister very much."

"Then we shall make a point of visiting them. I was thinking of stopping in Portugal to discover if it is safe to visit Felix and Matthew."

She turned in his arms and wrapped hers around his neck.

"Do you mean it? Do not get my hopes up and then dash them!"

"I will do my best. We will take the ship to Lisbon and inquire of the British contingent there."

"You are very good to me, Rowley."

"I do my very best," he said. Leaning forward, he took wicked advantage of her lips being in front of his. "Since Edmund, Eugenia, and Timmy are gone down to the beach to play in the waves and even explore a nearby cave, I think we should make the most of this opportunity while we are alone."

"Do you think so?" she retorted with a mischievous grin. "I may take some convincing, you know." Perhaps that falsehood had been a mistake, she thought, with a tremor of anticipation. He began to torment her with slow, burning kisses which sent shivers of pleasure straight to her toes. "I surrender, Your Grace!"

"So I should hope, madam," he murmured in her ear as he picked her up and carried her to the bed. "I will do my very best to ensure it is worth Your Grace's while."

The End

About the Author

Like many writers, Elizabeth Johns was first an avid reader, though she was a reluctant convert. It was Jane Austen's clever wit and unique turn of phrase that hooked Johns when she was "forced" to read Pride and Prejudice for a school assignment. She began writing when she ran out of her favorite author's books and decided to try her hand at crafting a Regency romance novel. Her journey into publishing began with the release of Surrender the Past, book one of the Loring-Abbott Series. Johns makes no pretensions to Austen's wit but hopes readers will perhaps laugh and find some enjoyment in her writing.

Johns attributes much of her inspiration to her mother, a former English teacher. During their last summer together, Johns would sit on the porch swing and read her stories to her mother, who encouraged her to continue writing. Busy with multiple careers, including a professional job in the medical field, author and mother of two children, Johns squeezes in time for reading whenever possible.

Made in the USA
Monee, IL
11 May 2021

68342483R00134